LIQUIDATING
Larry

Books by Pamela Burford

Jane Delaney Mysteries
Undertaking Irene
Uprooting Ernie
Perforating Pierre
Icing Allison
Preserving Peaches
Simmering Stu
Liquidating Larry
Scrapping Scarlett
Jane Delaney Humorous Mystery Series: Books 1-3 Box Set

Romantic Suspense
Snatched
Going Commando
Storming Meg
A Case of You
Twice Burned (Double Dare book 2)

Contemporary Romance
Rags to Bitches
In the Dark
Snowed
Too Darn Hot
The Boss's Runaway Bride (a novella)

The Wedding Ring matchmaking series:
Love's Funny That Way
I Do, But Here's the Catch
One Eager Bride To Go
Fiancé for Hire
The Wedding Ring Matchmaker Series: Complete Four-Book Romantic Comedy Box Set

LIQUIDATING
Larry

A Jane Delaney Mystery
Book 7

Pamela Burford

RADICAL POODLE
PRESS

Paperback edition published 2022 by Radical Poodle Press
Copyright © 2022 by Pamela Burford

ISBN 978-1-944922-00-9
Ebook ISBN 978-1-944922-75-7

Interior design by BB eBooks
Cover design copyright © 2022 Patricia Ryan
Author photograph copyright © Jeff Loeser

www.pamelaburford.com

to the memory of my mother, Sue,
and my mother-in-law, Lore,
with love and gratitude for all they taught me

1

Good Luck, Suckers!

"*BEANS?* ARE MY old ears givin' out on me, Jane? You expect me to contaminate my fine Texas chili with *beans?*" Eighty-six-year-old Dawn Ann Hammond harpooned me with a look that was half disgust, half pity, and one hundred percent pure Texas outrage. "For your information, missy, it's called chili *con carne*, not chili *con frijoles*."

Sexy Beast, scouring the grass at my feet for dropped yummies, grumbled something in Poodle that sounded an awful lot like, *If anyone asks, I don't know you.*

"Don't shoot her, Dawn," Larry chuckled. "Poor little Yankee doesn't know any better."

I hadn't noticed him ambling over to join me under Dawn's display canopy. No surprise there considering Crystal Harbor's Fifteenth Annual Chili Cook-Off was well under way. Between the crowds milling about and sampling the various chilies, the children and dogs chasing one another around the grounds, and the Texas swing band belting out "Corrine Corrina" a short distance away, it was enough of a challenge just to hold a conversation.

You could be forgiven for assuming this cook-off was taking place somewhere in the Lone Star State, but let me assure you the town of Crystal Harbor is situated well north of the Mason-Dixon Line, specifically the North Shore of Long Island, New York. A large section of Nevins Park had been transformed for today's event, with canopies and tables for the contestants, a stage and awning for the band, a portable dance floor, and hay bales for seating.

"What's wrong with beans in chili?" I stirred the little sample bowl Dawn had handed me, still hunting for a fugitive legume. "I always thought they were pretty much standard. Like creamed spinach on sweet potatoes."

Dawn turned to Larry. "Can I shoot her now?"

"I didn't say *I* eat creamed spinach on sweet potatoes," I mumbled, feeling my face heat. "As if I would ever. It was just, you know, the first thing that popped into my head." I met Sexy Beast's accusatory stare. The two of us had shared more than a few I Yam What I Yams. *Yeah, I told a fib, SB. So sue me.* Who knew seven-pound apricot poodles could be so judgmental?

"And who are you to call me a poor little Yankee?" I asked Larry, as I decorated my chili with some of the savory toppings Dawn had set out: shredded cheddar cheese, sliced avocados, sour cream, and chopped tomatoes. "I happen to know you were born and raised in this town."

"Nevertheless…" He tapped the badge clipped to his Hawaiian shirt, which identified him as an official judge of the cook-off.

In fact, as Crystal Harbor's most renowned celebrity, Larry was an official judge every year, along with local caterer Maia Armstrong and Mayor Sophie Halperin, who just happened to be my best pal. So yeah, I guess he did know a little something about chili after helping to judge this cook-off for the past fifteen years.

With his signature jovial chortle, he said, "Most Texans will tell you that beans have no place in real, authentic chili con carne. The rest of the world is a little more flexible. As am I when I'm wearing this badge."

Dawn took a swig of bourbon. The transplanted Austinite, who owned a local piano saloon called Dawn's Depot, looked as out of place in this town as she sounded. Today, as always, the skinny old woman wore a Western pearl-snap shirt, jeans, fancy cowboy boots, and enough turquoise jewelry to double her weight. Her carroty hair was pulled back into a neat French twist, while my own strawberry-blonde mane kept springing loose from its claw clip. I'd decided to wear my hair up today in deference to the late August heat, but as always, it had other plans.

In case you're wondering about me, my name is Jane Delaney, but most people in town know me as the Death Diva.

Really? You think that's a scary nickname? Gee, I never heard that before. Listen, I didn't choose the creepy moniker, but I'm stuck with it. And trust me, there's nothing creepy about the services I provide.

Let me amend that. There's nothing creepy *to me* about the services I provide. All of which happen to involve dead people. Looking for someone to deliver less-than-loving last messages to your friends and family after you're gone? Done that. How about arranging for your cremated remains to be incorporated into a unique (read X-rated) example of ceramic art? You guessed it, I've done that, too. Want someone to break into the morgue and photograph the treasure map tattooed onto your great-uncle Oliver's back?

Lose my number. The jobs I do are strictly legal. Well, sometimes legal*ish*. And yes, someone actually tried to hire me to do that last one. As you can imagine, I turn down a lot of assignments.

"Eat, Jane." Dawn gestured at the bowl I still held. "You're lettin' good Texas chili get cold."

This statement was overheard by Norman Butterwick, a dapper gentleman well into his nineties who was strolling nearby with the aid of one of his elaborate antique walking sticks. "Sounds like it's time to turn up the heat! Is it time to turn up the heat, Larry?"

Larry responded with his usual bonhomie, offering a wave and a jolly, "It sure is, Norman. It's definitely time to turn up the heat."

"Sorry, Dawn," I said, "I've been too busy taking abuse from you two to actually taste the chili. I have to say, it smells amazing. Real smoky."

Sexy Beast licked his lips and sidled closer.

"Sorry, SB, but spicy chili is *not for puppy*." I delivered the last three words in a singsong tone I knew he'd correctly interpret as *Better luck next time*.

Did I mention? Sexy Beast wore a tiny cowboy hat, with a stylish little red bandana tied around his neck. It was all the costume he'd tolerate, and alas, not nearly creative enough to win today's Chili Dog contest, for best-dressed pooch.

Dawn filled another small bowl, heaped toppings onto it, and held it out to Larry. "I suppose you're gonna want some, too," she groused.

"Unless you intend to forfeit your place in the competition," he said, before leaning over the bowl and inhaling with a dreamy look on his face.

Larry and I took our first spoonfuls at the same moment, and groaned in unison. It was the most addictive chili I'd ever tasted, with a complex flavor profile that stood up to both the delicious smokiness and the spicy heat. I didn't miss the beans one little bit.

Larry made fast work of his sample before tossing the empty bowl and spoon into a nearby bin. Mine soon followed. He withdrew a notepad and pen from his baggy cargo shorts and jotted a few lines.

I greeted several of my friends and neighbors as they drifted over to sample Dawn's chili, as well as the Mexican street corn she'd prepared as a side dish. Attendees of the cook-off paid an admission fee, which entitled them to free samples from all the contestants' booths, all the water, soda, and iced tea they could drink (plus beer for a measly buck), and a ticket for a chance to take home the door prize: a Tex-Mex – themed gift basket. Proceeds from the event benefited Crystal Harbor's no-kill animal shelter.

Maxine Baumgartner, the pugnacious owner of Murray's Pub, a historic local drinking establishment, called out, "Larry! It's time to turn up the heat!"

She and Larry exchanged warm grins and a thumbs-up. He said, "You got that one right, Max. It sure is time to turn up the heat."

Dawn kept one eye on Larry as she ladled samples from the big iron kettle sitting on a portable propane burner. "So? How's my fine, *authentic* chili stack up against the pitiful competition?"

He shoved the notepad and pen back into his pocket. "You know I can't comment, Dawn. Not while judging's still going on. What kind of meat did you use?"

"Pork and bison. Along with hickory-smoked bacon, chipotle peppers in adobo, smoked paprika—" She cut herself off, her suspicious gaze raking everyone within earshot. "That's all I'm gonna say. There are spies everywhere, lookin' to steal my secrets. *Good luck, suckers!*"

He said, "Before I move on, Dawn, I've love it if you'd—"

"I'm warnin' you, Larry, if I hear the words 'turn up the heat,' I'm gonna box your ears." She took another healthy gulp of bourbon.

"Me, she threatens to shoot," I told Larry. "You just get your ears boxed."

He shrugged and tapped his judge's badge again. "What can I tell you, Jane? The privileges of power. I was just trying to say, my dear, delightful Dawn, that I would love it if you'd set me up with a little of that Mexican street corn."

"Comin' right up."

In the few seconds it took Dawn to dish it up, I noticed Larry absently rubbing his midsection. He'd been a hefty, barrel-shaped guy as long as I'd known him, with a healthy appetite. I'd never seen him turn down food. And today was no exception, though I couldn't deny he was looking a tad peaked under his summer tan.

He accepted an extra-large helping of Mexican street corn from Dawn before wishing her luck and moving on, with Sexy Beast and me at his side. I couldn't help noticing that Larry seemed a little unsteady on his feet. Also, his pupils appeared dilated, despite the intense sunshine. I'd never suspected him of abusing drugs. Perhaps it was a side effect of some prescription medication.

I lightly touched his arm, keeping my voice low to thwart eavesdroppers. "How are you doing, Larry?"

"Oh, I'm doing great, Jane. Having a swell time. I love this cook-off. Look forward to it every year."

"I know you do," I said. "I just thought you might be experiencing a little indigestion. I mean, there's a lot of highly seasoned food here today. I know you have to sample all the chilies, but maybe a bite or two of each one will suffice, and take a pass on the rest of it." I stared pointedly at the bowl of creamy, spicy corn he was digging into.

"Don't worry about me." He patted his stomach, a vigorous thump this time. "Pure cast-iron." His chuckle sounded forced.

Though Larry took care not to show his age (think dye job and aggressive comb-over), I happened to know his "cast-iron stomach" was seventy-four years old, and probably more sensitive to rich, spicy foods than it once was.

I also knew that even if he felt sick, he wasn't about to admit it. Appearances were important to Larry Kool, who'd been a professional actor his entire life, starting in early childhood when he'd played an apple-cheeked toddler on a television sitcom.

Yes, his last name was Kool, and no, it wasn't a stage name he chose for himself, though there's no denying it was, well, cool. Kool is a solid Dutch name, meaning either "cabbage" or "coal," depending on what your ancestors did for a living. Larry's cabbage-growing or coal-mining Dutch ancestors helped to settle New Amsterdam four centuries ago, before the English decided that what the place needed was a New York state of mind.

I know you're wondering about that "turn up the heat" business. Larry used to star in a detective TV show called *Chase & Knabbe*. He played a wisecracking homicide detective named Eddie Knabbe (you guessed it, the *K* is silent). His partner was Samson Chase. The show ran for just three seasons forty years ago, but gained immortality through constant reruns and streaming, earning an inexplicable cult status among younger viewers. I myself have seen all seventy-nine episodes multiple times, despite the fact that the show was canceled the year I was born.

Detective Eddie Knabbe had a catchphrase he deployed at opportune moments in the show. Which is why "It's time to turn up the heat!" followed Larry wherever he went, even now, four decades after *Chase & Knabbe* ceased production.

Not that he minded one little bit. Larry was the most gregarious "people person" I'd ever met. He loved nothing more than being the center of attention, and the residents of Crystal Harbor were more than happy to oblige. Even on normal days, his status as the town's most famous home-grown celebrity, combined with his naturally outgoing personality, pretty much guaranteed a steady stream of adoring hugs, fist-bumps, and smooches galore, wherever he went.

"Hey, Frank, how are you doing today?" Larry had proceeded to the next booth, where contestant Frank Martinez was dishing out samples. His chili wasn't the same rich, dark color as Dawn's masterpiece, and I spotted plenty of kidney beans. I was no longer sure how I felt about those. Still, it looked and smelled appetizing, and there was nothing wrong with the sample I tried. Less spicy and flavorful than Dawn's, but still, comparable to good restaurant chilies I'd enjoyed.

His side dish was Southern-style corn sticks: corncob-shaped sticks of cornbread baked in specially shaped cast-iron pans. They were crunchy and flavorful—a perfect accompaniment to chili.

Frank was the administrator of Whispering Willows Cemetery, the local graveyard, so he and I were well acquainted. Our paths frequently crossed when my Death Diva assignments took me to his place of employment.

He was in his late thirties, with brown eyes, a swarthy complexion, and longish, dark hair that he'd corralled today with a navy-blue bandanna, do-rag style. He appeared to be carrying an extra fifteen or so pounds on his frame, possibly from overindulging in his own chili and corn sticks.

Larry was his usual extroverted self as he sampled the chili—thumping Frank's shoulder, asking about his family, joking with him. Or trying to. Frank never once cracked a smile during the few minutes we spent with him, and offered only dour, monosyllabic responses to Larry's friendly overtures. Not exactly how I'd choose to ingratiate myself to one of the judges, but to each his own.

Just as we were about to depart, Frank finally strung a few words together. "So are you going to be fair this year?"

Larry sighed. "Frank, we've been over this. You know we aim to be fair in our judging every year."

Frank leaned his fists on his table and treated Larry to a blistering glare. I resisted the urge to back up. Clearly this man harbored more than a little suppressed rage.

So much for hugs and kisses following Larry wherever he went.

"I've entered this cook-off every year for the past four years," Frank said.

"I know you have," Larry said, "and you make a damn fine chili, no doubt about it."

"Then why haven't I ever won?"

"It's not just me doing the judging. You know that, Frank. This kind of thing is totally subjective."

"All those other people who won," Frank said, "their

chilies couldn't hold a candle to mine. I never use ground meat, it's all chopped by hand, and I use premium dry-aged beef."

"And it shows," Larry said. "No one ever said your chili is inferior. For heaven's sake, Frank, we had the same conversation yesterday. What good does it do to rehash—"

"I know the other judges love my chili. It's *you*, Larry." Frank jabbed a finger at the other man's chest. To his credit, Larry never retreated or lost his temper. His expression remained pleasant, though he looked even paler than before and his face was sheened with perspiration. It was warm, but it wasn't *that* warm. Clearly he wasn't feeling well, but I'd brought it up once. There was no point in doing so again.

"You've got something against me," Frank said. "You always have. You've been convincing Maia and Sophie to vote down my chili, and you're going to do the same this year. You think you're so special, but you're just a washed-up old has-been, cashing in on your former glory, *Detective Knabbe*."

Larry raised his hands. "Okay, I'm sorry you feel that way, Frank, but it looks like we're going to have to agree to disagree. I wish you luck. I mean that sincerely."

Frank flipped him off as we walked away. Once we were far enough from the booth, Larry said, "For crying out loud, the point of all this is for families to come out and have some fun, and to make a few bucks for the animal shelter."

"He does seem to be taking it a little too seriously," I said.

"I know everyone wants to win this thing," he said, "I get that. But most folks have the sense to at least pretend to be adults about it."

"Did I hear you say you and Frank talked about this yesterday?"

"Yeah, he showed up—" Larry cut himself off with a resigned groan as a couple approached us.

The woman appeared to be in her late fifties, though, like Larry, she made a conspicuous effort to appear more youthful. Her makeup was a touch too heavy, her acid-yellow sundress a couple of inches too short. Her jewelry was impossible to ignore: sparkly shoulder-duster earrings, bangle bracelets on both wrists, and flashy cocktail rings on almost every finger. Gray roots marred an otherwise pretty head of long, dark blonde hair.

She appeared more excited to see Larry than he was to see her, racing up to him to bestow a bone-crushing hug and a loud smack on the cheek. "I wanted to surprise you. Did it work?"

"Liddy," he said, without his usual smile, "if I live to be a hundred and fifty, you'll never stop surprising me."

You would have thought this was the most hilarious witticism, judging by her manic laughter. She yanked her companion to her side and latched on to him. "I wanted you to meet Wes. My friend Bexley—you remember Bex, don't you? the artist who works in peanut butter and jelly?—well, Bex introduced me and Wes at this thing out in the Hamptons last week and we've been *inseparable* ever since."

Wes was a good-looking man with wavy, auburn hair. He was also, at around forty-five years of age, more than a decade Liddy's junior. He extended his hand, and Larry shook it.

Wes said, "When Liddy told me her big brother is Larry Kool, I thought she was putting me on. Great to meet you, man. I'm a huge fan."

"Thanks," Larry said. "This is my friend Jane Delaney. Jane, I don't think you ever met my sister, Liddy."

Handshakes all around as we said the polite things. Liddy squatted down to make friends with Sexy Beast, pitching her voice up several ear-ringing octaves. "What a *cutie!* Oh, just look at that little *outfit!* You're a little cowboy doggie, yes, you are! Where's your little *horsie*, you little cutie? Are you a good boy? I bet you are, I bet you're just the bestest boy in the whole wide *world*, yes I do." SB, though clearly startled by her enthusiasm, nevertheless accepted the adoration as his due.

Okay, I'll be the first to agree that my dog is indeed a little cutie, but I can tell when someone's laying it on too thick. Call me cynical, but I found myself wondering what this woman's game was.

She straightened and grabbed hold of Larry's arm, clinging like a lamprey. "Most people who see us together think Larry's my dad," she laughed. "I always have to explain he's my half brother. My mom was Daddy's second wife. I'm a lot younger than Larry. Like, *a lot*."

A gap of fifteen to eighteen years would be my guess. True, there was a family resemblance, but I would never mistake these two for father and daughter.

"Liddy, we'll have to catch up later," Larry said. "I'm real busy today."

"Sure, sure," she said, "I know you are, but I texted you, like, a million times, Larry, and I left a bunch of voicemails. I was just hoping I could have a couple of minutes—"

"Not today," he said, and strode quickly away.

The last thing I wanted to do was stand around schmoozing with Larry's half sister and the boyfriend du jour. The way Liddy was looking at me, I just knew she was angling for a way to suck me into whatever drama she had brewing.

I tugged on Sexy Beast's leash. "Sorry, guys, but I'd better walk this little fella before he decides to lift his leg on a hay bale. Nice to meet you," I called over my shoulder as I scampered away.

I made a point of losing myself in the crowd, happy to swap greetings with my friends and neighbors on this gorgeous, sun-washed day. One of them was my physician, Louise Holliday, who had a thriving family-medicine practice in town. I knew she was Larry's doctor, too.

Louise was a petite, dark-skinned Black woman in her early fifties. Today her thick, gray cornrows were mostly hidden under a bright pink ball cap featuring the logo of a local craft brewery. Unsurprisingly, she held a plastic cup of beer.

She was accompanied by her Jack Russell terrier, Luci, who wore a little white lab coat with her name embroidered on it in script: *Luci Holliday, MD*. A toy stethoscope was tucked into the pocket.

Luci and Sexy Beast, already well acquainted, exchanged a few perfunctory sniffs as they checked out each other's costumes. I just know SB was thinking, *These humans have got some serious issues.*

Two young boys about eight years old sprinted past with a German shepherd wearing a homemade spider costume, complete with long, furry legs that stuck out everywhere. One of the kids called out, "Hey, it's Doc Holliday!"

"Look," the other boy said, "she's drinking *beer*. I'm gonna tell your mom on you, Doc," he added, giggling.

"Oh no," Louise deadpanned, "don't do that. The news might make Mama spill her Scotch."

The boys didn't hear that last part, which was just as well. Their dog had spied a comely Italian greyhound dressed in a crocheted pink bikini swimsuit (which included multiple tops to cover each row of nipples because this was, after all, a family event), and it was all they could do to keep up as he bolted after her, creepy spider legs flopping.

And yes, Louise Holliday, MD, was generally referred to, by young and old alike, as Doc Holliday, a name historically associated with one John Henry Holliday, Wyatt Earp's bestie. Louise was so tickled by the moniker, I half suspected she'd gone to medical school just so she could share the name.

I knelt to give Luci scritches. "I'm glad I ran into you, Louise."

"Something wrong? You feeling okay?" Louise peered closely at me through clear-framed eyeglasses.

"It's not me, it's Larry," I said, rising. "Have you seen him today?"

She rolled her eyes. "Stubborn man. Yeah, I pulled him aside for a little chat. He swears he's feeling fine, but I know him too well."

"You think it could simply be his age?" I asked. "Like maybe he's overdoing it today with all this rich food?"

"Could be. Or it could be he ate some undercooked chicken or a bad clam. The good news is, he doesn't have a fever, for what it's worth. I was able to feel his forehead before he could stop me, but he wouldn't let me check his pulse."

"Well, you know Larry," I said. "He'll die before he disappoints an audience. The show must go on and all that."

Louise laid a reassuring hand on my shoulder. "I'll keep an eye on him, Jane. The instant he's done awarding the trophy, I'll make him go home and get into bed."

"Good luck with that," I said. "I know his wife is around here somewhere. Maybe we can find Madison and enlist her assistance."

"Sure. Let's do that." Louise glanced around to avoid being overheard. "I'll look in the sandbox. You check the teeter-totter."

I chewed back a grin. "She's not *that* young."

"Don't tell that to the guy I saw carding her at the beer booth," she said. Which was a joke since we both knew Madison avoided both carbs and alcohol. "What would make a man end seven decades of bachelorhood to marry a vapid little twentysomething?"

"You're kidding, right?" We shared a knowing eye-roll at the folly of men in the throes of midlife crisis. Or in the case of Larry Kool, post-midlife crisis. "What he told me? She was his seventieth birthday present to himself."

"That was four years ago," Louise said, "and they're still together. I was kidding about that 'vapid' business, by the way. I really don't know Madison that well. She's not my patient, she goes to some alternative-medicine quack, I mean healer."

"I've met her a few times," I said. "She seems all right."

"Well, I hope it lasts and that Madison makes him happy," she said. "That hardheaded old so-and-so has brought a lot of joy to a lot of people during his long career, and he deserves to be happy."

"Amen to that."

2

Free Smooches

MY NEXT STOP was Maria Echevarría's booth, where about a dozen people had congregated to sample her chili. Maria, who happened to be Sophie's housekeeper, was locally famous for her delicious guacamole. She was an outstanding cook all around, so I wasn't surprised to see her at the cook-off, competing for top honors. And she was from Mexico, after all, having immigrated decades ago in her youth.

I happened to know there was some disagreement as to where chili con carne originated. Some said northern Mexico. Others insisted it was born in Texas. Dawn Hammond was adamant that her Lone Star chili was the real deal, but I could see how this plump, middle-aged lady from Hermosillo might legitimately claim that distinction.

Maria and I exchanged cheek kisses and *What have you been up to*s as she dished up a sample of her chili, studded with black beans, thank you very much. She topped it with slivers of pickled red onion, crushed homemade tortilla chips, and of course, a dollop of her ambrosial guacamole.

I tried a spoonful. "Maria, holy cow, this is unbelievably good."

Okay, now it was a horse race. *Watch out, Dawn.*

Maria wore a proud grin as she offered a tortilla chip to Sexy Beast. "You never had my chili before, Jane? All those years I was working for Mrs. M?"

"Trust me," I said, over a mouthful of heaven. "This, I would've remembered."

Maria used to be Irene McAuliffe's housekeeper, before Irene died under mysterious circumstances a year and a half earlier. It was Irene, in fact, who gave me my start in the Death Diva biz. It began with me pet-sitting for her poodles back when I was in high school, which led in due time to delivering flowers to the Best Friend Pet Cemetery, and eventually doing the same at its human counterpart, Whispering Willows Cemetery. Irene and her many well-heeled pals kept me busy and helped put me through college. Other, more interesting and innovative (a polite way of saying icky and ghoulish) assignments followed, and the rest is Death Diva history.

Irene and I became so close over the years that she named me in her will as Sexy Beast's guardian. And get this, she left her elegant McMansion to SB (yeah, you read that right). I am to live there with him until he is no longer with us, at which time ownership will revert to me. Oh, and she left a pile of money to maintain the house and her precious poodle.

I know, it's nuts, but that was Irene. She had her own way of doing things.

Word must have spread about Maria's chili. More folks swarmed her booth, jostling for position, no doubt worried that her chili would run out before they'd had a chance to taste it.

"Let me give you a hand dishing out samples," I said.

"Thanks, Jane, but Cesar just ran to get some more chips from the truck. He should be back any minute. Oh, there he is now."

I turned and waved at Maria's husband as he jogged toward us with an enormous plastic tub filled with his wife's homemade tortilla chips.

The local animal shelter, the beneficiary of this event, had taken over a small area of the park for an adopt-a-pet event. That was my ultimate destination—not that I was looking for another dog or cat at the moment, but one of the volunteers at the booth was of particular interest to me.

So distracted was I as I made my way there that I failed to notice Kyle Kenneally waving vigorously from under his display canopy, until he called out, "Jane! Jane!"

Automatically I glanced his way, then mentally kicked myself as he beckoned me over.

"I only have a minute, Kyle," I said, as I joined him in his booth. "I have to, um, be somewhere."

Kyle was in his late twenties, with short red hair and a gigantic beard that had at one time been kept reasonably trim, but was now officially out of control. It was superlong, divided into two scraggly sections, and unencumbered by anything as unmanly as a hairnet as he leaned over the chili he was stirring in a big, steel pot.

Which settled the matter. I would not be sampling the offerings at this booth, thank you.

He leaned in for a kiss, clearly aiming for my mouth, prompting me to quickly bend down to adjust SB's little cowboy hat. Last summer Kyle had hired me for a Death Diva assignment—one that involved a very old, very dead giant tortoise—and since then, he seemed to think we were friends. Specifically the kind with benefits.

Kyle owned The Harbor Room, a local restaurant dating from the 1840s. He'd bought the place dirt cheap from a recent widow who hadn't been in the appropriate frame of mind to negotiate a fair price for the historic landmark. But that was Kyle Kenneally, always working the angles.

Speaking of working the angles, Kyle might be a restaurateur (strictly an investment decision), but he was no cook. I had little doubt he'd forced The Harbor Room's chef to make the chili he was palming off as his own concoction.

The reason this mattered? The cook-off didn't have many rules, but there was one biggie. All contestants were required to personally make their own chilies. Taking credit for someone else's culinary creativity was a major no-no, one that could get you banned for life from the cook-off.

Kyle was gaming the system. Otherwise known as cheating. The judges were no dummies. They knew this self-important lout couldn't boil an egg, much less whip up a few gallons of chili con carne. I did not see this ending well for him.

He openly leered at my chest, which was modestly clothed in an embroidered white peasant blouse. I picked up Sexy Beast as a kind of shield.

"What do you want, Kyle?" I snapped.

He glanced around and lowered his voice. "I saw you and Larry earlier. You guys seem pretty tight."

"What's your point?" I asked, but of course, I knew.

"I want you to put in a good word for me. For my chili, I mean."

"*Your* chili?" I said. "Seriously? Kyle, no one believes you made—"

"There's a C-note in it for you," he said, "if I win this cook-off."

"A hundred bucks? American?" I asked. "Gee, I dunno…"

"Two hundred."

"It would take a lot of convincing," I said. "Have you tasted Dawn's chili? Or Maria's?"

He waved away my words. "Chili con carne is a man's game, Jane. Now, don't pout, it's just biology. Three hundred. Final offer."

For the record, I wasn't pouting. Jane Delaney does not pout. "A thousand bucks," I said. "*My* final offer."

"What?" He reared back. "Are you crazy?"

"How badly do you want that trophy, Kyle? I can make it happen, trust me."

Kyle's ruddy complexion became ruddier as he pictured Larry Kool announcing the winner, pictured himself grinning with pride as he held aloft the trophy for Best Chili Con Carne.

He gave a brisk nod. "It's a deal. I don't have that much on me right now. If I win, I'll, uh, pay you tomorrow."

SB looked at Kyle as if to say, *Even* I'm *not naïve enough to buy that one, and I'm a pampered little lap dog.*

"Oh, sure, no probs, Kyle. Tomorrow, then." Looking around, I spied Larry chatting with Nina Wallace under her canopy. Ugh, I'd been hoping to avoid her. I gave Kyle a conspiratorial wink and went to join Larry.

I make no secret of the fact that Kyle Kenneally was one of my least favorite Crystal Harbor neighbors. However, when it came to deviousness, cheating acumen, and just plain meanness, he couldn't hold a candle to Nina.

To give you an idea of what this woman was capable of, she'd managed to steal the mayoral election this past March through dirty tricks that included ballot tampering and buying votes. Fortunately, the Town Council got wind of it and reinstated Sophie for another three-year term.

Larry was dutifully sampling Nina's chili, which appeared strangely pallid in comparison to the other contestants' chilies. The toppings were chopped cilantro (um, okay), toasted pumpkin seeds (what?), and sliced radishes *(what kind of sick joke is this?)*. After one bite, he set down his bowl and scribbled something in his notepad.

"So? Do you love it?" Nina's grin appeared both confident and, unless my eyes deceived me, coquettish. Pretty and petite, she had silver-gray eyes and dark hair worn in a short, feathery style. "You love it, don't you?"

He offered a strained smile. "Very tasty, Nina."

You'd think a professional actor could do a better job of faking sincerity. It might have had something to do with his being under the weather. I noticed he'd lost even more color and seemed a bit wobbly.

Nina's kittenish smile transformed into something closer to a scowl. "I hope you're not taking points off for originality, Larry. Red-meat chilies are a dime a dozen. Everyone *adores* my chicken and white bean chili."

Was this the same "everyone" who was staying away from her booth in droves? Larry and I were the only ones there.

"Nothing wrong with originality," he said. "We encourage contestants to push the envelope."

She dished out some of her anemic-looking chili and shoved it into my free hand before I could stop her. It didn't even smell that good, more sour than spicy. I was still holding Sexy Beast. His little nose twitched once before he pointedly averted his gaze from the bowl. I set it down next to Larry's.

"I'm sure it's divine, Nina," I said, "but I'm so full right now, I couldn't eat another bite."

She crossed her arms and glared at Larry. "You're not even going to give me a chance, are you?"

Something about the way she said that made me wonder if we were still talking about chili.

Larry was clearly uncomfortable, and not just from whatever ailment he was fighting. He started to back away. "Good luck in the contest, Nina."

Furious color flooded her face as she stomped up to him. "Don't give me that crap, Larry. You've been avoiding—" Her gaze shot to me and she clamped her lips shut.

Grabbing hold of Larry's arm, I chirped, "Bye, Nina. Good luck and all that," before steering him to a quiet spot in the park away from the hubbub of the cook-off. I settled us on a wooden bench under a shade tree and let SB wander on his leash.

I started to speak, but Larry stopped me with a raised hand. "I'll be fine, Jane. Just give me a couple of minutes."

I gave a frustrated little growl. He wasn't going to make this easy. "All right then, just tell me this. Have you tasted all the chilies yet?"

Wearily he nodded.

"That's great," I said. "You can compare notes with Maia and Sophie, then go home and let them present the trophy. No one will think any less of you."

"It's my job, presenting the trophy. It's always been my job. People expect it." Before I could counter this, he deftly changed the subject. "So how much did he offer?"

I barked out a laugh. "I got him up to a thousand bucks. He'll 'pay me tomorrow,' after he receives the trophy."

"All Kyle Kenneally can expect to receive is a sternly worded letter from the cook-off committee disinviting him from any future competitions."

"I figured." That's when my inherent nosiness got the better of me. Yeah, it's been known to happen. "So, um, Nina seemed pretty worked up back there."

"You know that woman," he said. "Always has to have her way."

"And not just about the cook-off, unless I'm totally misreading things." I let that hang there.

One look at my face told Larry I'd picked up on Nina's not-so-subtle subtext. "Jane, I was raised to believe a gentleman never besmirches a lady's reputation."

"Wasted effort in Nina's case," I said. "She prefers to do the besmirching herself."

We both knew I wasn't referring only to the crooked election. It was no secret that Nina Wallace's youngest child, a baby girl named Laura, had been fathered, not by her husband, but by a notorious individual from Crystal Harbor's recent past. And yes, Nina and Mal were still married because Mal was a stand-up guy who was determined to be a good, full-time father to all his daughters, including the one who'd sprung from another man's loins.

"For the record," Larry said, "I'm a happily married man who has zero intention of straying. Too old for that nonsense anyway. Ah. Right on cue."

I followed his gaze and saw his wife racing toward us. Madison Kool was a true beauty, not yet thirty years old, with pale-green eyes, flawless skin, and curly, black hair that fell to her shoulder blades. She wore a flowy batik sundress in shades of blue and lavender, and little jewelry aside from her wedding and engagement rings.

She bent over her husband and felt his forehead, her brow

wrinkled in concern. "Why didn't you tell me you're feeling lousy?"

"Louise should mind her own business," he grumbled.

I said, "She's your doctor, Larry. This *is* her business."

Madison sat on his other side, letting the strap of her fringed hobo purse slide off her suntanned shoulder. "I suppose it'll do me no good to insist you go home. Let Maia and Mayor Sophie pick up the slack." Taking note of her husband's mulish expression, she sighed. "I didn't think so."

"It's either food poisoning," Larry said, "or one of those twenty-four-hour bugs. Either way, no big deal, Mad."

"So you've been throwing up?" she asked.

He shook his head and pushed back the hair behind an ear to show her a small round sticker. "A scopolamine patch left over from our cruise. You think I want to toss my cookies in front of the whole town?"

Now that his wife was there, I figured my continued presence was not only unnecessary but quite possibly unwelcome. I stood and shortened SB's leash. "Can I bring you anything, Larry? Something to settle your stomach? A little ginger ale?"

Madison rummaged through her purse. "I have some candied ginger. It might help—"

"Nah, I'll be fine." He wagged his hand at us. "Don't worry about me. Cast-iron, remember?" He thumped his belly again, though with less vigor than before.

As I turned to go, Madison caught my eye and mouthed, *Thanks.*

I finally made it to the animal shelter's fenced-in adopt-a-pet area, which appeared to be doing a booming business, judging by all the young families actively making new four-legged friends, of both the canine and feline persuasions. Several staff members were on hand to facilitate adoptions. They'd been joined by a handful of volunteers, including Martin McAuliffe.

My man.

Ridiculously, I still felt a giddy rush every time I set eyes on him, even though it had been almost three months since he'd officially become *my man*.

Martin was supervising the kissing booth, a painted plywood structure decorated with red kissy lips, multicolored paw prints, and a cloth banner that read, *Free Smooches.*

Three dogs were on duty inside the booth, standing behind placards identifying them by name: Baxter (a senior wire-haired dachshund), Ticker (a gray pit bull puppy), and Layla (a large, black mixed-breed dog).

Children giggled with delight as they sought slobbery kisses from the trio, who were more than happy to oblige. I suspected that even some folks who'd stopped out of curiosity, with no intention of taking home a cat or dog, would find themselves with a new family member before the day was through.

I unhooked Sexy Beast's leash so he could socialize with the other dogs, but kept a close eye on him in case someone decided he looked eminently adoptable.

Martin was looking especially hunky in worn jeans and a snug red T-shirt advertising the animal shelter. He had his hands full trying to get the big black dog, Layla, to remain in the kissing booth. Every time he got her settled, she leapt out of the enclosure and ran to him, tail wagging. All she seemed to want out of life was to glue herself to Martin and gaze adoringly into his pale-blue eyes. And I mean, really, who could blame her?

"I see I have competition," I said, as I gave Martin a quick kiss and scratched Layla behind her floppy ears. "A younger woman. Should I be worried?"

"She's been like that all day. Haven't you, girl?" He gave her a few brisk pats, causing her to roll onto her back and beg for belly rubs. The big, smooth-coated dog was black all over, except for white toes and a white patch on her chest that looked like an angel wearing a fedora.

As Martin bent down to comply with the needy dog's demands, I was treated to a pleasing view of what my friend Georgia liked to call his killer booty. During the year and a half I'd known this man, it had not escaped my attention that he was a particularly fit, athletic specimen of manhood. However, it was only recently, once we'd taken our relationship to the next level, so to speak (yeah, you know what I'm talking about), that I learned just how fit and athletic he is.

And that's all I'm going to say about that because, as we all know, I am a lady.

Okay, I did nothing to deserve that snort of derision, so I will thank you to control your snide outbursts.

Before Martin could disengage himself from Layla, she managed to give his hair a thorough licking.

"Looks like you have a new stylist, Padre." I reached up to finger-comb the short, sandy strands, now thoroughly bedewed with dog spit. I was looking around for something to wipe my hand on when Martin took hold of it and slowly stroked it over his T-shirt. That cheap feel would have to tide me over until I could get him alone.

If you're wondering why I call Martin "Padre," it goes back to our first meeting, when I thought he was a priest because, you guessed it, he was impersonating a priest. Yeah, well, don't ask what *I* was doing at the time.

Pint-size Sexy Beast and jumbo-size Layla were just getting acquainted when a deep male bellow made all heads turn. "Looks like this is where the action is!"

The voice seemed vaguely familiar, as did the handsome face attached to it, though the fellow's identity eluded me. He was an older gentleman, fit-looking and on the tall side, maybe six two or three, with curly, salt-and-pepper hair and dark brown eyes. He wore a cream-colored polo shirt left untucked over slate-gray shorts.

His companion was a geriatric pug wearing dark goggles with red frames, and a little motorcycle helmet.

Was this man a neighbor? A friend of a friend? A former client? It wouldn't do to act like I'd never met him if I, you know, kinda sorta knew him.

Martin was less worried about embarrassing himself. He said, "I know I know you from somewhere, man, but I can't put my finger on it."

"I get that a lot," he chuckled, transferring the cup of soda he held to his left hand so he could shake. "Rex Noble."

"That's why you look familiar," the padre said. "You're Samson Chase."

"Not for the past forty years, except in reruns."

Mystery solved. Rex Noble had starred with Larry Kool in their long-defunct detective show, *Chase & Knabbe*. Rex had played Larry's—or rather, Detective Eddie Knabbe's—partner, Detective Samson Chase.

"And this fine specimen—" Rex indicated his dog, who'd flopped down in the grass for a rest "—is Piglet. Those goggles actually serve a purpose. Bright sunlight bothers the old fella's eyes."

Martin and I introduced ourselves and gave Piglet a little love. I said, "What've you been up to lately, Rex?"

"Well, I'll tell you, I've been looking at some interesting projects. I don't want to jinx anything by talking about it, but one of them looks very exciting." He gave us that big, toothy Samson Chase grin. "*Very* exciting."

Rex scanned the crowded adopt-a-pet area, still grinning. If he hoped to be recognized, he was in for a disappointment. Meanwhile I tried to recall what roles I'd seen him in, aside from old *Chase & Knabbe* reruns. I drew a blank.

"Well," Martin said, as he tried to coax Layla back into the kissing booth, "that sounds really cool."

"Speaking of cool," Rex said, looking around, "I understand Larry Kool is supposed to make an appearance. Have you seen him?"

Something about the way he said it made me suspect Liddy's calls weren't the only ones Larry had been dodging.

I said, "He's here, but he's pretty busy at the moment."

"I realize that, I just wanted to—"

"*Larry!*" One of the shelter volunteers, a young Latina wearing chili-pepper earrings, cupped her mouth and hollered toward the judges' dais, a small raised stage some distance away. "*It's time to turn up the heat, Larry!*"

The dogs all seconded this with a howling chorus, while the cats looked on with disdain.

Peering past the crowd, I spied Larry conferring with his fellow judges. He offered the girl a jocular wave before returning his attention to Sophie and Maia.

"Martin, Jane, it was nice meeting you." Very gently, Rex lifted Piglet and kissed his grizzled little face, while thwarting the dog's attempt to lick the plastic soda cup. "Let's go, champ.

Daddy has to say hi to someone, then we'll find a nice shady spot where you can have some water and treats." That last word brought the old boy's head up.

I watched Rex make his way through the throng to the raised judges' dais. Unfortunately, the men were too far away for me to overhear their conversation, but if body language was any indication, Larry was less than thrilled to see his old television costar.

And okay, I might've been doing a little amateur lip reading, too. Don't judge me!

Larry's hands came up in the universal *Not now* gesture, which didn't appear to deter Rex, who never stopped grinning and laughing, slapping Larry on the back, and trying to engage him in conversation.

Squinting, I managed to make out a few words. *Did you get my… I thought you were going to… All I'm asking for…*

Martin had noticed the direction of my gaze. "How about that, huh? The two stars of *Chase & Knabbe* together again, right here in our humble hamlet."

Which wasn't exactly the way I would have described Crystal Harbor. The town might have qualified as humble back in the seventeenth century when the first Europeans settled here, but humility had little to do with its current incarnation. An hour and a half from Manhattan, with an average household income nudging the stratosphere, Crystal Harbor could best be described as an affluent bedroom community.

That said, there'd always been a solid middle-class enclave here, as well, which seemed to be spreading as some of the snootier residents fled the town's growing economic and racial diversity. And recently, artsy types had been moving in and shaking things up a bit.

I considered the changes to be all for the good, but as you might expect, not everyone concurred, particularly those whose families had lived in Crystal Harbor for multiple generations.

The lead singer of the Texas swing band informed the crowd that the winner of the cook-off was about to be announced. Wanting to get as close to the action as possible, I gave the padre another kiss, and Layla a few more scritches, before scooping up SB and elbowing my way to the front of the crowd, close to the raised dais. The contestants all seemed to have the same idea, no doubt to facilitate a quick leap onto the stage when their name was called as the winner.

Larry shared the stage with his two fellow judges and pub owner Maxine Baumgartner, who'd just won the door prize. Max hooted in triumph as Maia Armstrong handed her an enormous, cellophane-wrapped basket overflowing with Texas-themed snacks, sweets, and sauces, as well as a generous gift certificate to a local Tex-Mex restaurant.

Maia was a pretty Black woman in her mid-thirties, with dark, catlike eyes and a profusion of natural curls that just brushed her shoulders. The two of us routinely collaborated on large funeral receptions, jobs that required the services of both an experienced caterer and a Death Diva with mad event-planning skills.

Sophie Halperin was up next to announce the winner of the Chili Dog contest. Sophie was a spunky, well-padded woman in her mid-fifties, with chin-length gray hair and a fondness for good cigars. We'd been friends for years but had grown particularly close over the past year or two.

"As the mayor of this damn burg," Sophie hollered, "I hereby decree that every dog here is an outstanding specimen of costumed canine cuteness. Not to mention a very good boy or girl. But there can be only one winner of the Chili Dog contest, and that winner is… Drum roll, please." The band's drummer was happy to oblige. "The winner is *Betty,* the one-dog Tex-Mex restaurant. Come on up, Betty!"

Betty, a golden retriever, appeared oblivious to the small tabletop strapped to her back, covered with a red-and-white checked cloth. A bowl of chili, some tortilla chips, a fork and napkin, and a bottle of lemonade were balanced (screwed and glued in place, I assumed) on the table. Clearly Betty had no idea why everyone was cheering and clapping for her, but judging by her wagging tail and happy barks, she reveled in the attention.

Betty's human, Susanne Travert, owned Patisserie Susanne, a French bakery and café on the ground floor of the Town Hall. Sophie presented Susanne with a gift certificate redeemable for a professional portrait of Betty by a renowned local pet photographer. Of more immediate interest, to Betty at least, was the bone-shaped doggie treat Sophie offered her, a handmade creation from Crystal Harbor Pet Boutique.

At last it was the moment everyone had been waiting for. I wondered if anyone else noticed Larry's pallor as he stepped front and center to announce the day's big winner. His exuberant grin never faltered as he prepared to hand off the gold-plated trophy, crafted in the shape of a kettle.

I had to hand it to the guy: He was one heck of an actor. If I didn't know he was feeling poorly, I never would have guessed it from his performance in front of the crowd.

Larry's voice was strong as he called out, "I've been judging this cook-off for fifteen years, and every year I tell myself the same thing. 'Larry,' I say, 'these chilies beat anything you've ever put in your mouth. It can't possibly get any better than this.'"

Enthusiastic applause and hoots of glee punctuated his words. Did he just teeter, ever so slightly?

"Yet somehow," he continued, "my talented friends and neighbors here in Crystal Harbor manage to outdo themselves year after year. Today's cook-off is no exception. I wish I could—" He broke off with a wince, causing a ripple of unease in his audience, but recovered immediately, patting his sternum with a wry chuckle. "I love chili, but it doesn't always love me. I tried to pace myself, but how are you supposed to do that when the best cooks in the world are offering you the most amazing chilies this side of Texas?"

The crowd responded with wild cheers amid calls of "Yeah!" and "We love you, Larry!" and "It's time to turn up the heat, Larry!"

"If I could, I'd present one of these to every single contestant," he said, while lifting the trophy, "because they all went above and beyond. In the end, it came down to a choice between two stunners. I think my fellow judges will agree with me that this year's decision was the toughest yet."

As if everyone in attendance couldn't guess the identity of the two "stunners." Everyone except Kyle Kenneally, that is, whose smug expression told me he was in for a rude shock.

"It is my honor and privilege," Larry announced, "to award this trophy to Maria Echevarría, the official winner of the Fifteenth Annual Crystal Harbor Chili Cook-off!"

This was met with raucous applause, whoops, and whistles as Maria accepted hugs from Cesar and their three grown kids. The couple's grandchildren jumped up and down, squealing with joy.

Kyle's face, always florid, turned into a pomegranate as he absorbed the fact that he'd failed to cheat his way to victory.

Frank Martinez muttered something it was just as well I couldn't make out, then turned and stomped away.

Nina didn't look any happier. She glared at the man onstage, whether because she'd failed to win the trophy or failed to win *him*, I couldn't say. Perhaps the two were inextricably linked somehow.

As Maria made her way to the dais, Maxine called out, "Don't shoot her, Dawn!"

Dawn Hammond's leathery features creased into a scowl as she barked, "Why's everyone always sayin' that? I tell you what." She moved like a rattlesnake, locking her bony fingers around Maria's arm before she could step onto the stage. The crowd gasped. "If it was any of you other phonies that beat me outta that trophy, we'd have some words about it. Y'all know I'm not real big on losin', but there ain't no shame in losin' to the best." Whereupon she wrapped Maria in a smothering bear hug. "*Felicidades,* darlin'. You deserve it."

When Maria finally joined Larry onstage, he was sweating profusely. And was it my imagination or was he having trouble taking a full breath? I looked around for Louise and saw her shove her way through the crowd, her unhappy gaze locked on her stubborn patient.

Despite his obvious discomfort, he soldiered on, grinning broadly and congratulating Maria. Still holding the trophy, he raised her arm in a triumphant gesture.

In the next instant Larry crumpled, dropping the trophy and clutching his chest. A roar of dismay rose from the crowd. I shoved SB into Cesar's arms and leapt onto the stage, followed closely by Louise. Madison frantically screamed his name as she battled her way through the crowd. I heard multiple voices talking to 911 operators.

Larry lay on his back, seemingly unresponsive as Louise checked his vital signs. "There's an AED in the rec center," she hollered. "A defibrillator. Someone go get it—*stat!*"

The shelter volunteer with the chili-pepper earrings ran off toward the recreation center, located on the opposite side of the sprawling park. The girl covered ground like a cheetah—a high-school track-and-field star, I guessed—but was she fast enough? Several people raced toward the parking lot, but I knew the runner would make better time fetching the lifesaving device, considering the circuitous nature of the park's roads. I willed that building to magically move closer.

Madison and I knelt by Larry, ready to give Louise any help we could, while Sophie, Maia, and Maria linked arms to push back the throng of people threatening to swarm the stage. "Back off, folks," Sophie bellowed. "You'll just be in the way. Give the doc some room to work."

Liddy tried to force her way past the human blockade. "I'm his *sister*," she screeched. "Let me through. Who do you bossy bitches think you are? I have a right to be with my brother."

Sophie caught my eye. I gave the tiniest shake of my head. *No.* It was an automatic impulse, based mainly on Liddy's agitated state and Larry's earlier displeasure at running into her. The last thing we needed while trying to tend to him was this shrieking woman making it all about herself.

Meanwhile, Rex Noble cradled Piglet and stared grim-faced at the proceedings.

Larry's eyes were slitted, his face gray. His comb-over, which had no doubt been meticulously shellacked into submission that morning, had flopped to one side, revealing a shiny bald spot. Louise ripped open his Hawaiian shirt, and my immediate thought was, *Is he wearing Spanx?*

The only one who seemed unsurprised by the girdlelike garment squeezing Larry's hefty torso was his wife, Madison, who unceremoniously yanked the undergarment down to provide unimpeded access to his chest. Louise started CPR immediately, interrupting the rapid chest compressions every twenty seconds or so to deliver two mouth-to-mouth rescue breaths.

Madison, meanwhile, spoke to her unconscious husband in an unending litany of encouragement, telling him how much she loved and needed him, how strong he was, how he had to fight, had to stay with her.

Sophie allowed Martin to join us. As he knelt next to us, he said, "Jane and I know CPR, Louise. We can spell you."

She nodded to acknowledge the offer. The situation seemed more than a little surreal, in part because just three months earlier, the padre and I had found ourselves working together to save someone else's life in just this way. We'd been successful then, but I had little hope of a repeat performance.

I see a lot of dead folks in my line of work, and my gut told me Larry Kool was already gone.

3

In Which Larry Is Liquidated

THE CRIME-SCENE technician stops photographing the corpse sprawled on the carpet long enough to give Detective Eddie Knabbe's cigar a dirty look. "Hope you're not plannin' to fire that thing up in here, Eddie."

Eddie plucks the unlit stogie from his mouth and gestures toward the heavy crystal ashtray lying next to the poor sap with the fatal head wound. "Whaddaya know, the docs weren't kidding," he snickers. "Smoking really is bad for your health."

Sophie sighed as she stared at the television. "God, how young Larry looks there. And so slim."

It was true. Larry Kool would have been in his early to mid thirties when this episode of *Chase & Knabbe* was shot. He'd never been matinee-idol handsome, but what he lacked in looks, he more than made up for in talent and an engaging sense of humor. His character, Detective Eddie Knabbe, was a jaded, unkempt cop with a bottomless trove of witty one-liners.

By contrast, Eddie's partner, Samson Chase, played by Rex Noble, was the dapper heartthrob responsible for turning millions of female TV viewers into ardent fans of the series.

It was Monday evening, two days after Larry's heart had given out on him during the cook-off. It was over so fast. The chili-pepper girl made astonishing time fetching the defibrillator, and the ambulance was right behind her, but they were too late. I suspect Larry was dead before he hit the stage.

The legitimate media outlets had, for the most part, treated the actor's sudden demise with the respect he was due as a hardworking, prolific, well-loved entertainer. The two sensationalist evening "news" programs that aired live Monday through Friday on competing channels, however, were another matter. *The Romano Files* and *Ramrod News* were less concerned with truth and accuracy than boosting viewership and driving each other off the air by any means necessary.

Sophie had invited Martin and me over to watch *The Romano Files* with her, to see what kind of spin the host, Leonora Romano, would give the story. Sophie was probably worried that if she watched it alone, there'd be no one around to stop her from hurling a bottle of twenty-year-old single-malt Scotch through her brand-new gigundo TV screen.

Which is how I found myself seated between the padre and the mayor on the massive leather sofa in her inviting den. The sofa itself was barely visible under an avalanche of crocheted afghans and needlepoint pillows (the work of Sophie's industrious late mom). The room was made all the more inviting by the fully stocked wet bar behind us.

Sophie had already handed me a small ceramic sake cup that held, not sake, but my favorite brand of fine sipping tequila. She'd served Martin Irish whiskey on the rocks, and poured a splash of the aforementioned single-malt for herself. We nibbled from a bowl of popcorn on the coffee table.

Leonora Romano had chosen to commence her tribute to the late Larry Kool with a clip from an episode of *Chase &* *Knabbe*, one I'd watched several times over the years. In this scene, a business executive has been found murdered—bludgeoned with a heavy ashtray in his fancy corner office. Which kind of dates the series, right? I mean, how many ashtrays would you find in the average office nowadays?

Something on the carpet snags Eddie's attention. As he squats to examine it, we see what he sees: a cigarette butt, which presumably fell out of the murder weapon when it made contact with the victim's cranium.

"Bag that up," Eddie tells the tech.

"Why bother?" he asks. "What's a lousy cigarette butt got to do with anything?"

Eddie points to a crimson lipstick stain on the filter. "Something tells me that ain't the vic's shade."

Cut to an austere interrogation room at the police station, where Eddie and his partner, Samson Chase, are interviewing the victim's pretty young secretary, her shapely figure displayed to advantage in a short skirt, tight sweater, and lethal-looking stiletto heels. She appears perfectly at ease, giggling as Samson chats her up. This, as every fan of the series knows, is Samson's interrogation style: utilizing his potent charm to lower a suspect's defenses.

As Eddie's gaze narrows, we read his mind. This gal doesn't look too broken up about coming back from her lunch break to find her boss with a caved-in cranium. Ah, but she has an alibi. The waitress at the nearby luncheonette swears she was there for a full hour, reading a fashion rag and choking down the Diet Delite special: cottage cheese and a canned pineapple ring on a bed of iceberg lettuce, topped with a maraschino cherry.

Eddie gesticulates with his still-unlit cigar. He's been trying to quit the habit for two and a half seasons. "Say, miss, that's a nice shade of lipstick you're wearing."

Now her eyes narrow. She's confident in her ability to disarm the big, handsome one, but his partner might be more trouble. "Um, thanks, Detective."

"Think I'd like to buy some of that lipstick for the wife," he says. "What do they call that color?"

"'Revenge.' I got it at Woolworth's."

Samson's flirtatious smile never wavers as he wraps up the interview. "You're free to go, Miss Schmidt."

"Oh, you." She gives his shoulder a playful smack. "It's Wanda. I told you."

"If you think of anything else, Wanda, I'd really appreciate your giving me a call." Samson hands her his card, inadvertently (yeah, right) caressing her fingers as he does so. "And do me a favor, will ya? Don't leave town for the time being. You never know, I just might need to get in touch," he adds, with a wink.

She bites back a coy smile and fans herself with the card. "I'll be waiting for your call, Samson."

Eddie watches her sashay out of the room before saying, "You know what time it is, Sam?"

"I think I can guess," his partner responds with a smirk.

Close-up of Eddie's wily grin. "It's time to turn up the heat."

Leonora Romano's nipped-and-tucked features suddenly filled the screen. "Sadly," she said, "Larry Kool has turned up the heat for the last time. The beloved actor, best known for his role as Detective Eddie Knabbe on the television series *Chase & Knabbe*, succumbed to a massive heart attack on Saturday."

Sophie turned to me. "I heard it wasn't actually a heart attack."

"Sudden cardiac arrest," I said. "That's how Louise Holliday put it. Heart attacks are caused by coronary blockages, but she said Larry's arteries were in pretty good shape. His heart's electrical system just went haywire."

Martin asked, "Does she know why?"

I shook my head. "I mean, he was somewhat overweight, sure, but that alone shouldn't have been enough to trigger cardiac arrest."

"But he was sick before he collapsed, right?" the padre said.

"With some kind of stomach bug," I said. "Who knows? Maybe that was masking a more serious problem. But you know Larry. He was determined to tough it out."

Onscreen, Leonora was introducing her guests. "For all you longtime fans of *Chase & Knabbe*, the man sitting to my left needs no introduction. Rex Noble, I must say, you're as handsome as ever. What's your secret?"

He gave her a jaunty wink. "Clean living, Leonora."

"*Borrr*-ing!" she cried. "Clean living might make you live longer, but is it worth it?"

He rewarded this stale gag with a chuckle. "You've got me there."

"I'll bet you're a gym rat," she said. "Are you a gym rat, Rex?"

"Not my favorite description, but I can't deny I like to keep in shape."

"Well, keep doing whatever you're doing, 'cause it's working," Leonora said. "The lady to my right is Liddy Kool, Larry's sister."

"*Half* sister," Liddy corrected. She wore a black, shoulder-baring cocktail dress, black onyx choker and dangling earrings, and fingerless, black lace elbow gloves, as befitted a woman in mourning. "Obviously I'm a lot younger than Larry. Everyone thought he was my *dad*."

"Then they're blind," said Leonora, with her usual tact.

"You're not *that* much younger." Then, possibly in response to a signal from her director, she offered a wooden, "Sorry for your loss."

"Thank you, Leonora." Liddy produced a handkerchief (yeah, it was black, too) and dabbed a dry eye. "It was just such a *shock*. And those nasty bitches—can I say that word on TV?—those awful women wouldn't let me anywhere near my own brother while he was lying there *dying*. And that's not even the worst of it. *They chopped Larry up into little pieces!*"

Sophie gave me a dubious look. "Does she mean what I think she means?"

I nodded. "Liddy objected strenuously to the autopsy. Which had to be done, under the circumstances."

"Did it?" Martin asked. "Even though his doctor was present, and she certified the cause of death?"

"It's standard in cases like this, though Madison might've prevailed if she'd chosen to fight it," I said. "But she had no problem with an autopsy, and as next of kin, it was her call. Liddy tried to prevent it, but legally she had no say in the matter."

"Which isn't stopping her from going on TV," Sophie said, "and raising a ruckus. I can tell you, if my loved one unexpectedly collapsed and died, I'd damn well want Magda to tell me why."

Dr. Magda Temple was the medical examiner and thus the person responsible for determining manner of death: as in natural, suicide, homicide, accident, or in some cases, *darned if I know.*

Leonora Romano lost no time shutting down the grieving sister's outburst. "It's done now," she snapped, "so move on. Rex, you were there when Larry collapsed. What was going through your mind at that moment?"

Rex adopted a sober expression and shook his head. "At first you can't believe it's happening—not to Larry Kool. The man was an institution. More than that, he's been an inspiration to young actors for decades. And when I realized he was gone… well, what can I say? Larry was more than a former costar. I lost a dear friend that day."

"And I lost a *brother*!" Liddy interjected.

Leonora didn't spare her so much as a glance. "Larry certainly was loved by millions, Rex. What would you say is the key to his enduring popularity?"

Rex thought for a moment. "Well, you certainly can't discount his outgoing personality. Larry loved his fans, and they sensed that love and responded to it. Three years ago when he published his autobiography, I was at one of his signings, and the line of customers was out the store and down the block. In the *rain*. He was scheduled to be there for an hour and a half. Do you know, Larry refused to leave until he'd signed every single book. It took him more than five hours. He said—" Rex cleared his throat, struggling for composure. "He said, 'These people came out to see me and buy my book. I'm not about to disappoint them.' That was Larry Kool in a nutshell."

"I was at that signing, too," Liddy said. "I didn't have to stand in the rain, though, 'cause I'm *family*."

"A winning personality is all well and good," Leonora said, "but that alone can't account for close to a half century of success in a ruthless industry. Face it, Larry had a genius for adapting to the times, for remaining relevant in a constantly changing entertainment market."

When Rex realized she was waiting for him to comment,

he said, "I imagine he did."

Her meticulously shaped eyebrows jerked up toward her honey-blonde hairline. "You *imagine* he did?"

"Uh-oh," Sophie said, "Leonora smells blood."

The padre said, "This is going to get ugly."

"Run away!" I shouted to the television. "You're in the path of Hurricane Leonora. Run for your lives!"

Rex and Liddy sat calmly, clearly oblivious to the impending storm. Had they never watched *The Romano Files*? Did they think they were on a normal news talk show?

Liddy spoke up. "Can I just say—?"

"No." Leonora's attention remained on Rex. "You were the big shot on *Chase & Knabbe*, weren't you? The one who got all the attention, onscreen and off."

He gave an embarrassed half laugh. "That was a long time ago, Leonora. I'm sure Larry had his female fans, too," he said, without conviction.

"I'm not just talking about sex appeal," she said, "though that's part of it. You never made trouble on the set, you were easy on the eyes, and *Chase & Knabbe* turned you into a household name. Everyone expected you to be the next Robert Redford. Then it's like you fell off the planet. What happened, Rex? Where've you been for the last forty years?"

He flinched. Leonora's predatory smile widened. Finally he said, "I, uh, decided to hone my craft on the stage. I appeared in several plays—"

"Broadway?"

"I felt regional theater offered the most innovative material and intense challenges—"

"Sure you did." Leonora let her dubious expression say what she thought of her guest's high-minded and entirely voluntary decision to eschew the bright lights of Broadway for the relative obscurity of small, semiprofessional theater companies. "After *Chase & Knabbe* ended, you thought you were hot stuff, didn't you, Rex? You turned down the leads in a bunch of movies that went on to earn gazillions and win Oscars. Want me to name them?"

He took a deep breath and pasted on a smile, but it never reached his panicky eyes. "Not unless you want to see me slit my wrists on live TV heh heh."

"Be my guest," she said. "It's all about the ratings. And then you turned down starring roles in a couple of major TV shows."

"It was—it was a different era," he stammered. "The small screen didn't have the respect it does now. Right now we're in the, well, they call it the New Golden Age of Television. Back then it was all about feature films."

"None of which you were a part of," she said, "because you were so full of yourself that you thought Spielberg and Tarantino and Scorsese would keep sending you scripts, no matter how many you thumbed your nose at. You lost three agents that way."

"There's nothing wrong with being discriminating," Rex bleated.

Liddy said, "Aren't we supposed to be talking about Larry?"

Leonora wheeled on her. "I'll get to you."

Any normal person would take that as her cue to hightail it out of there before Leonora got to her. Liddy simply rolled her eyes and folded her arms, waiting her turn for the full Romano treatment.

Leonora turned back to Rex. "So you were just being

'discriminating' when you self-sabotaged what could have been a phenomenal acting career. With the result that decades later, you're scraping by on your pitiful royalties from *Chase & Knabbe* and trying to drum up acting gigs wherever and however you can."

Rex jerked upright. "'Scraping by' is right. Larry made a lot more from that old show than I ever did. A *lot* more. Someone ought to look into that."

"Yeah, we'll get right on it," she said, deadpan. "So you're basically admitting you're finished as an actor."

Rex pulled himself up. "There are some interesting projects I'm looking at."

"Such as…?" The shark smile got more toothy.

"I'm not at liberty to say, Leonora. It's too early in the process." Rex's confident grin was at odds with the flop sweat sheening his brow. "I don't want to jinx anything by talking about it."

Martin said, "This is painful to watch."

"And what did your good pal Larry do after your show ended?" Leonora asked.

"I'll tell you what he did," Rex said. "He jumped at anything he was offered. All those goofy walk-ons in B movies and sitcoms. The tacky commercials. Game-show host. Competing on that dancing show. Spokesperson for KrunchWorks snack foods, of all things. I was embarrassed for him."

Liddy nearly leapt out of her seat. "*You* were embarrassed for *him*? That's a laugh. If I'd known what a loser you are, I never would've slept with you."

Now she had Leonora's attention. "When was this?"

"What the hell, Liddy!" Rex blurted.

"It was right after *Chase & Knabbe* was canceled," she said, "when Rex was still a hot property. I was eighteen and he was, like, forty. He took advantage of my innocence."

Spittle sprayed as Rex aimed a finger at Liddy. "I was thirty-five and *she* seduced *me*. And trust me, there was nothing innocent about her."

Liddy said, "I was a budding actress back then, and Rex told me he'd help my career if I was, you know, nice to him."

"Liar!" he cried. "You know damn well there was never anything transactional about our affair. It was hormones, pure and simple."

Sophie lifted the bowl of popcorn and passed it around. "Wonder what the real story is there."

Martin said, "Or how Larry felt about his former costar banging his little sister." He tossed back a handful of popcorn and followed it with a swig of whiskey.

"And then," Liddy said, "when I broke it off between us, Rex retaliated by spreading false rumors about me. He got me *blacklisted* in the industry."

Rex tossed up his hands. "You didn't get any parts because you had no talent, Liddy. You refused to take classes or do anything to learn the craft. You have no one to blame but yourself."

"And then he did the same thing to my country music career," she said.

Rex wore an insultingly baffled expression. "As if I have any pull in Nashville."

Leonora said, "What other careers did you have, Liddy?"

"Let's see. I was a clothing designer for a while."

"How did you learn to do that?"

"Oh, I've always loved clothes and fashion. Most people

have to take courses and, I don't know, apprentice and stuff, but I just have a natural gift for it." Liddy's expression hardened. "But it turned out I was *too* good. The other designers got jealous and turned everyone against me."

Martin said, "I'm beginning to detect a theme here."

"So then I became a personal shopper," Liddy went on, "but that didn't last too long. My rivals paid customers to complain about me."

Sophie said, "That's her story and she's stickin' to it."

"So what do you do now?" Leonora asked.

"I have a storefront on eBay. I sell designer fashion items like handbags and shoes and stuff." She grinned into the camera. "All at deep discounts."

And all cheap counterfeits if my guess was right.

Leonora apparently had the same thought. "You can support yourself selling crap on eBay?"

Liddy scowled. "It isn't crap, it's good stuff. Both new and vintage. And yeah, I get by."

"Uh-huh. From what I hear, you 'get by' with a little help from your friends."

Liddy frowned. "What's that supposed to mean?"

"What are you going to do," Leonora asked, "now that your meal ticket's gone? It's no secret you used to hit up your brother for cash every chance you got."

I'd guessed that her tracking Larry down at the cook-off had something to do with filthy lucre, and it would seem I was right.

"A lot you know," Liddy spat. "Larry was a very generous brother. He used to practically *force* me to take his money. He wanted me to have nice things."

"At one time, maybe," Leonora said, "but then he got

married a few years ago and the gravy train came to a screeching halt, am I right?"

Liddy's thick layer of makeup was no match for the mottled flush that stained her cheeks. "Madison was jealous of our close sibling relationship. Once that stingy bitch got her claws into Larry, I could've starved to death and no one would care. Plus I hardly ever saw him, *and he was all the family I had!*" Cue the black hanky.

Sophie picked up the remote control. "Sorry, guys, that's all I can stomach of Leonora Romano and her very dignified guests. Know I'll regret it, but let's see what Miranda's up to." She switched from *The Romano Files* to *Ramrod News*, hosted by the even more loathsome Miranda Daniels.

Miranda's familiar face and heavily lacquered helmet of platinum-blond hair dominated the huge TV screen. "Larry Kool is now Larry *Cold!*" she crowed, with more glee than was seemly. "And get this, folks. They dissolved his body in *acid!* Have you ever heard of anything so *revolting?*"

Click. The TV went dark. Sophie tossed the remote onto the coffee table and got up to pour herself more Scotch.

Martin leaned back and draped his arm over my shoulders. And stared at me.

I stared back. "What?"

"What was that business about dissolving his body in acid?" he asked. "If anyone knows, it's got to be you."

"Oh, that," I said. "Yes, he was dissolved, but it had nothing to do with acid—just the opposite, if you think back to ninth-grade chemistry. It's called alkaline hydrolysis, or aquamation, and it's the latest thing."

Sophie resumed her seat. "Think I read about that. It's considered a kind of cremation, but there's no fire involved."

"Right," I said. "Traditional cremation requires a lot of energy and creates pollution. Aquamation is a greener choice. They immerse the body in a solution of water and potassium hydroxide—otherwise known as lye—and subject it to heat and very high pressure. You're left with clean bone fragments, which get ground up and returned to the family, same as with regular cremation."

"How do you know Miranda was referring to aquamation?" Martin wore a teasing smile. "For all we know, Larry might've been a secret mafioso and they really did dissolve his body in acid."

Sophie swirled the amber liquid in her glass. "Nothing like a lot of gooey body-dissolving talk to make you appreciate a good Scotch."

I said, "Aquamation was Miranda's idea—she's all about healthy lifestyle choices, responsible stewardship of the earth, and all that—but Larry was fine with it. He said he didn't care what happened to his body after he was gone, and if this newfangled thing made his wife happy, then it made him happy. We talked about it last year because aquamation isn't legal everywhere yet, or widely available where it is legal, so they asked for my help making prearrangements."

"So it's been done already?" Martin asked. "Larry's been, uh, liquidated?"

I nodded. "Earlier today."

"Let me guess," Sophie said. "Liddy objected to that, too."

"No, which is a little surprising. I mean, here she goes ballistic over the autopsy, but when it comes to dissolving her brother's body in lye?" I shrugged. "Hey, sure, why not?"

"Strange woman." Sophie set the popcorn bowl on her lap.

Martin reached across me to grab a handful. Of popcorn,

not me, though you will be less than shocked to learn I would not have objected. "Your basic attention hog," he said.

"As well as self-delusional," I added, "to think she could make it as an actress, a clothing designer, or whatever, with no discernible skills or training."

"Apparently," the padre said, "she was able to rely on her brother for financial support for years. It's easy to be a dilettante when someone's throwing money at you."

I set my empty cup on the coffee table. "You know, Rex says he and Larry were real close, but from what I saw at the cook-off, his old costar wasn't all that happy to see him. You were standing pretty close to them, Sophie—you know, right before the awards, when he was talking to Larry. Did they seem like good buddies to you?"

"Nope, but you never can tell about people."

"Did you hear any of their conversation?" I asked.

"Just a little. The band was pretty loud. Sounded like Rex was asking Larry for a favor. Wheedling, really. Something to do with a guy named Sawyer? Then he gave him his drink and left."

"What, Rex gave Larry his drink?" I recalled the soda cup he'd been holding.

She nodded. "Up close, anyone could see Larry was a little green around the gills, so Rex says, here, a little Coke'll settle your stomach."

Martin said, "I hate to agree with Leonora Romano about anything, but she was right when she said Larry adapted to the times, that he managed to remain relevant for all those years after *Chase & Knabbe* was canceled."

Sophie propped her feet on a needlepoint footstool—more of Mother Halperin's handiwork. "Guess he knew his days as a big star had come and gone. Good for him for being a realist."

"Well, I for one," I said, "always enjoyed Larry's 'goofy walk-ons,' as Rex called them. And it was obvious Larry enjoyed doing them. His sense of humor was his strength. He never took himself too seriously."

"As opposed to Rex," Martin said, "who apparently assumed superstardom would just fall into his lap."

I raised my glass, and my companions followed suit. "Good-bye, my friend. I wish you hadn't left us so soon."

4

Planting Jelly Beans

FRIDAY DAWNED GRAY and misty—appropriate weather, some might argue, for the day's planned activities, namely a funeral for one of my clients, followed by the interment at Whispering Willows Cemetery, followed by a lavish reception at the home of the deceased, one Josephine Evangelista.

Josie herself had hired me to prearrange the whole shebang. Sometimes when folks ask me to help plan their own funerals, it's because they've received a dire prognosis and want to spare their survivors an unpleasant burden. You might be surprised, however, to learn that scenario is not the norm. More often than not they're in fine health but have inflexible ideas about the kind of sendoff they want in the not-so-foreseeable future and don't trust their nearest and dearest to abide by their final instructions when the time comes.

And let's face it, those final instructions are almost guaranteed to be somewhat, shall we say, unconventional or they wouldn't have felt the need to hire an outsider to make sure the dang thing got done properly. Or *im*properly as the case may be.

Which brings us to Josie Evangelista, age fifty. She loved her husband, Phil, to distraction, and while the feeling was mutual, there were limits to what Phil would agree to, even for her. Josie was a free spirit, to put it kindly. Her hobbies were competitive vodka oyster shots and naked karaoke. If she indulged in enough of the first hobby, the second was sure to follow, to the startlement of her fellow bar patrons. Her oblivious husband, meanwhile, would be ensconced in his comfy recliner at home, binge-reading apocalyptic science fiction.

Josie's three and a half years of gainful employment had been spent as a pet sitter, specializing in lizards. Apparently, if you're planning on taking a trip and leaving your Chinese water dragon or blue-tongued skink bereft of human companionship for a few days, it's not enough to toss your neighbor's kid a few bucks and a box of live crickets. And believe it or not, your average run-of-the-mill pet sitter might not be either qualified or enthusiastic.

That's where Josie came in. She felt warmly about the coldblooded among us, and actually gained a reputation during her short career as the go-to lizard whisperer. Then she won forty million smackers in the lottery and turned her back on the glamorous world of exotic reptiles—or as Dawn Hammond prefers to think of them, larval cowboy boots.

Josie was already married to Phil when her windfall came in, so no one can say he married her for her money. She opted to receive her winnings as a lump sum and might have burned through the cash within months (you had to have known her) if not for the guiding hand of her levelheaded husband.

Whoever coined the expression "opposites attract" clearly had Phil and Josie Evangelista in mind. Phil was an actuary. Go ahead, look it up. I'll wait. He was just sensible and practical and (yeah, I'll say it) boring enough to engage a financial advisor who knew how to let his wife have fun with all that dough while at the same time ensuring it wouldn't run out during her lifetime—which her loving husband, having soberly consulted his actuarial tables, had determined would last well into a dystopian near future of coal-powered flying cars, 6,284,875 flavors of Oreos, and sentient robot overlords with a taste for pumpkin-spice everything.

Oh, and in case you're wondering, Josie Evangelista had been in perfect health when she'd engaged my services three years earlier at the unripe age of forty-seven, and just as healthy last week while vacationing in Alaska with some gal pals. It seems she and her companions had been observing grizzly bears scooping salmon from a river, taking pix and videos from a respectful distance, when Josie decided she just *had* to snap a selfie with an adorable cub that was being taught the ropes by its watchful mom. You can guess the rest.

The sky had cleared by the time the groundskeepers closed Josie's grave and moved on to other duties. I'd lingered until I was certain I was alone in that section of the boneyard before extracting a couple of items from my large shoulder bag and kneeling on her grave, which was freshly mounded with dirt.

Okay, I didn't actually *kneel*, not wanting to begrime my gray skirt suit or two-inch black pumps, which, along with a crisp white blouse and faux pearls, constituted my go-to work uniform. The look was Death Diva chic: conservative, inoffensive, unmemorable. In lieu of kneeling, I adopted a sort of awkward squat and went to work with my yellow toy shovel, swiftly digging a hole just large enough to accommodate the other object I'd brought along, a pale-lilac cardboard box that had once housed a pair of hideously expensive Jimmy Choos.

Well, of *course* the Jimmy Choos weren't mine. How can

you even ask? As if I'd shell out that kind of bread for fancy-schmancy, toe-pinching footwear.

My thighs were burning by the time I finished burying the box and patting down the dirt with the little shovel. Rising, I examined my handiwork with a critical eye and decided no one would be able to tell the grave had been disturbed. As I shook clods of dirt off the little shovel, I glanced around to ensure I'd remained unobserved—and froze.

In the three minutes it had taken me to accomplish my clandestine task, a worker had begun trimming the yew hedge that partially concealed the old wrought-iron picket fence at the back of the cemetery, about forty yards away. He seemed not to have noticed me. Unfortunately, he wasn't alone.

Frank Martinez, cemetery administrator and cook-off sore loser, was staring right at me.

Dang!

I forced a smile and gave a little finger wave as I hotfooted it back toward the entrance gate.

"Jane!" he called.

I picked up my pace and played dumb.

Very funny. I'll bet it comes naturally to you, too.

"Knock it off, Jane, I know you can hear me!" Frank's voice sounded closer. I heard him huffing as he ran toward me. The man was not a natural athlete.

Cursing under my breath, I halted, and aimed for a pleasantly neutral expression as I turned to face him. "Hey, Frank. Can't stay and chat. I have to get to Josie's funeral reception."

"What were you up to over there?" He jerked his head back toward my client's final resting place.

"What do you mean?" Yeah, still playing dumb. Hey, I'm

good at it, and sometimes it actually works.

Not that day, though.

Frank crossed his arms over his beige suit jacket. His work attire, which included a pale-blue dress shirt, subtly patterned burgundy necktie, and complementary pocket square, was a far cry from the chili-stained T-shirt and do-rag I'd last seen him in. "You were messing around with her grave, Jane. You know the rules. It's not like we haven't been through this umpteen times."

His words brought to mind the set-to I'd witnessed during the cook-off. Only, in that case it had been Larry who'd said, *Frank, we've been over this... We had the same conversation yesterday.*

Why had Frank been so insistent that Larry was turning the other two judges against him? He seemed to think the town's most prominent celebrity had it in for him. And that Larry had the ability to unduly influence both Sophie and Maia, neither of whom could be described as a pushover.

As for his accusation that I was "messing around" with Josie's grave (okay, I might not put it that way, but yeah, a fair description), the fact was, he couldn't have seen what I was actually up to, considering the distance that had separated us, not to mention all the headstones and plantings that were in the way.

I emulated his stance, crossing my arms. "Listen, Frank, I don't know what you think you saw, but I was doing nothing untoward just now."

"That's what you said after I caught you burying Monica McNair in a jumbo picnic cooler."

I shrugged. "What can I tell you? The lady loved her tailgate parties."

"And how about that time you poured an entire box of wine on Dorothy Wentworth's grave?"

"How did you find out—?" I clamped my lips shut.

"I have a buddy on the force, Jane."

"Oh." After quenching dead Dorothy's prodigious thirst (having been hired by her son to do so), I'd discovered Ernie Waterfield's skeleton, complete with bashed-in skull, hence the police involvement. While poor Ernie had indeed been deposited in this very cemetery, he had not, I'm sad to report, been interred in an actual grave.

"What's your point?" I said. "Is there some rule about watering a grave with, you know, something besides water?"

"Here's a rule I know you're aware of because we've talked about it so often," he said. "No dogs on the cemetery grounds."

I made a show of looking around. "I don't see any dogs here, Frank. Do you see any dogs?"

"Seems like every time I turn around, you have that little poodle of yours here," he said.

"On a leash."

"Makes no difference, you know that," he said. "Dogs are not permitted."

I gave him a knowing smile. "You like Sexy Beast. Don't deny it." Frank often chewed me out for bringing SB with me, usually while giving the little guy scritches and hugs.

He adopted a stern expression. "That has nothing to do with it. It's still—"

"I know, it's still against the rules."

Speaking of rules, I found myself wondering whether Frank was aware of the gap in the old iron picket fence at the back of the cemetery. The gap that was nicely concealed by the yew hedge one of his groundskeepers was in the process of trimming. The gap that was just wide enough for a certain determined Death Diva to squeeze through when an assignment required a bit of "messing around" in, say, the middle of the night.

"All the nonsense you pull," he said, "it gives Whispering Willows a bad name. Plus other people probably figure, hey, if the Death Diva can get away with it, so can I."

"You really need to lighten up, Frank, you know that? You should be thanking me for all the business I bring here."

"Oh, so now you're claiming credit for every death in Crystal Harbor?" he said, with a heavy dose of sarcasm. "Excuse me while I call nine-one-one."

"You know what I mean," I said. "Whispering Willows isn't the only cemetery in town. Well, okay, it actually is the only cemetery in town, but people have options. There's no shortage of graveyards on Long Island, and most of them are a lot less rigid and rule-happy than this one."

"It's my job to make sure this place runs smoothly," he said, "and that can't happen if—"

"Yeah, yeah." I rolled my eyes. "I make you look good, helping you sell plots and maintenance plans and what all. Did it ever occur to you to recommend my services in return? You know, I scratch your back, you scratch mine?"

It was a rhetorical question. I knew Frank had no intention of steering customers my way. But to be fair, his only response when I violated all those cemetery rules was a little tedious nagging. He'd never tried to bar me from the premises or demand under-the-table payments to look the other way, so I figured I had no right to complain. Which didn't stop me from, you know, complaining, but I just thought you should know that while the guy might be an officious company man, he wasn't corrupt.

"Speaking of options for final disposition," Frank said, "how did you convince Larry to choose alkaline hydrolysis?"

"I didn't convince anyone of anything," I said. "Madison learned about aquamation, thought it seemed like a swell idea, and got Larry on board. They contacted me last year and asked me to facilitate it."

He scowled. "So much for you steering business to Whispering Willows."

"He had his mind made up," I said. "What would you have had me do, Frank?"

"It never occurred to you to use a little gentle persuasion?" he said. "Larry Kool lived his entire life in Crystal Harbor. I'm sure most folks assumed he'd be interred in the local cemetery."

"I'm sure most folks never gave it a thought. And for the record, I don't 'steer' people once they've decided what they want. Who told you it was my idea?"

"Madison mentioned you were handling the arrangements," he said.

"And you just assumed I put some kind of Death Diva hex on them." I accompanied this with arm movements that were intended to appear spooky but on retrospect made me look like a drunk attempting some intricate folk dance.

He frowned in concern. "You all right, Jane?"

"There was a bee." I made an unconvincing swatting motion. "Okay, it's gone. So how did you and Madison end up discussing Larry's prearrangements?"

"She was here recently," he said, "so naturally I mentioned it might be time for her and Larry to purchase side-by-side plots—in the historical section, of course. It would've been negligent of me not to bring it up, considering his age."

Not to mention Frank's desire to get credit for planting the town's biggest celeb in the most elite, and expensive, precinct of the boneyard he managed. I said, "Sorry that didn't work out for you."

Something in my tone made him cross his arms again. "So what *were* you doing on Josephine Evangelista's grave?" he asked.

"Praying," I said. "I was down on my knees praying for Josie's departed soul."

"And how does your little yellow shovel figure in to all that praying?" he asked.

I was all wide-eyed innocence. "Shovel?"

His gaze flicked to my shoulder bag. "The toy shovel you put in your purse when you were finished 'praying.'"

"Oh. That. I was just, you know, neatening up the dirt." I made a patting gesture. "Smoothing it out. It's all part of the Death Diva Deluxe Funeral Package."

"That's all right, I'll just go grab a real shovel and find out for myself." He turned to walk away.

"Okay, okay." I groaned in defeat and grabbed his sleeve. "Good grief. Josie had something she wanted done once she was, you know, in the ground."

"So I gather." He made a *let's have it* gesture.

"She wanted me to bury Jelly Beans with her."

Frank grimaced in confusion. "You put candy in her grave?"

I shook my head. "Jelly Beans was her bearded dragon."

"Bearded…?" His eyes widened. "Isn't that a kind of lizard?"

"Yep. He died two years ago. The two of them were very,

um, close, and she decided she wanted to spend eternity with him."

His raised palm said, *Just want to make sure I'm hearing this right.* "You're telling me Josie had an emotional attachment to a reptile."

"That would be correct. So she put him in her freezer until the two of them could be buried in the same plot."

"Jane," Frank said, "I know you know that we don't allow pets to be interred on the premises."

"Which only shows how behind the times Whispering Willows is," I said. "It's legal in New York now unless the cemetery specifically forbids it. Before the law changed, I had a few clients who actually chose to be buried in pet cemeteries with their nonhuman companions rather than be separated in death. This is another of your stuffy rules that's driving people away."

"It's not my rule," he said, "but I am obligated to enforce it."

"Please don't do that in this case, Frank," I pleaded. And yeah, I clamped my palms together imploringly. "Jelly Beans is in a cardboard box, completely biodegradable. Before long there'll be nothing left but a little lizard skeleton."

He looked dubious. "How little?"

"Um…"

He raised an eyebrow. "You know I can find out easily enough."

"Okay, about two feet from nose to tail."

"Jeez, Jane—"

"But Josie managed to fold him into a shoe box," I said. "Very compact. Go take a look at the grave. If you can even tell it's been disturbed, I'll, I'll, I'll *eat* Jelly Beans!"

I saw him struggle to maintain his stern glower. With a snort of laughter, he said, "As much as I would enjoy watching you make good on that promise, the fact is, we can't leave Jelly Beans where he is."

"Frank—"

"I take it you've never seen the assortment of wildlife that wanders through here in the middle of the night."

His raised eyebrow made me think, *Gee, maybe he* does *know about that gap in the back fence.* "Um…"

He said, "How long do you think it'll take a determined critter to dig up old Jelly Beans?"

I huffed out a frustrated sigh. "I thought of that. I guess I was just hoping it wouldn't be an issue since he's been dead awhile."

"No hungry fox or raccoon will turn up his nose at freshly defrosted carrion," he said. "I even saw a coyote once, over in the north section."

"So that's it, then? I won't be able to fulfill Josie's last wish?"

"From what I heard," he said, "that's not her only last wish. Or even her most bizarre one."

"Yeah, I have to get over to her house and make sure that other thing goes okay."

"This shouldn't take long. Come on." He began striding swiftly away.

"Wait." I had to practically jog to keep up with him. "Where are we going?"

"To the maintenance building for a shovel. We need to hustle. The grounds are pretty deserted at the moment, but that won't last."

"Why on earth do we need a full-size shovel?" I asked. "I

buried Jelly Beans with my toy shovel. I can exhume him the same way."

"We're not exhuming him, Jane. We're going to dig a hole deep enough to keep him from becoming a midnight snack. Course, if you prefer, I can just toss Josie's lizard in the dumpster. It's your call."

5

She Looks So Natural

"WHERE HAVE YOU BEEN?" Maia Armstrong looked me up and down as she arranged fragrant ham-and-cheddar croquettes on a platter in the Evangelistas' humongous, sun-washed kitchen. "And why do you look like you've been digging a grave?"

"Because I've been digging a grave. Don't ask." I tore a paper towel from the roll and began brushing cemetery dirt from my gray skirt.

Frank had been right when he'd said our chore wouldn't take long. He made short work of the digging while I stood lookout, then I quickly helped him refill the hole. We'd shed our jackets before starting, but you can imagine what his pants and shirt looked like by the time we tamped down the dirt over Josie and Jelly Beans. My duds weren't much better. Fortunately for Frank, he kept a change of clothes in his office closet.

Note to self: Keep a change of clothes in your car.

Unless I was mistaken, Frank Martinez appeared to get an illicit thrill from flouting the Whispering Willows rule book. Might this be the start of a new, more tolerant working relationship between the two of us? Only time would tell.

"Anyway, sorry I'm late," I said. "I'll tell you all about it later." And I would. Maia was a good pal and enjoyed hearing about the Death Diva's assorted adventures. More to the point, she knew when to keep her mouth shut. I didn't need the whole town buzzing about Jelly Beans's final resting place and daring one another to grab a shovel and find out whether it was true.

The caterer wore a yellow chef's apron over a sleeveless, cream-colored linen dress. Her Afro curls were concealed under a colorful Kente wrap. "Here. You're tracking dirt." She tossed me a damp paper towel as a rent-a-waiter swept in to exchange an empty platter for a full one.

"I polished these just last night," I groused, while scrubbing caked soil off my black pumps. "How many people are in there? Sounds like a full house."

"Guests started arriving twenty minutes ago," she said, while sliding four more pans of hors d'oeuvres into the twin ovens. "There must be fifty or sixty already."

"We're expecting over a hundred." I'd entered the mansion through a side door, not wanting Josie's friends and family to witness me showing up at her funeral reception looking like a, well, like a gravedigger.

I washed my hands, then extracted a small mirror from my purse to check my hair and corral a few errant strands. I turned to Maia, arms spread. "Will the grieving masses flee in disgust?"

She twirled her finger. Obediently I turned around.

"Did you *sit* in the dirt?" she asked.

"Oops. Forgot about that. Fell on my keister." I managed to stand still while Maia gave said keister several stinging swats with a cleaning rag. "Ow. Thanks. I think."

"Georgia's been asking for you," she said. "She wants you to see her while she's still in one piece."

"How does she look?" I asked on my way out of the kitchen.

Maia offered a wry smile. "Awesomely realistic."

"I was afraid of that."

I exchanged greetings with Josie's many friends and relatives as I made my way through the first floor of her ultramodern mansion. A gleaming showcase of glass, marble, and concrete, the place had more angles than a crooked politician.

I grabbed a couple of coconut shrimp and a smoked-trout blini from one of the wait staff who were circulating with drinks and fancy nibbles. I don't normally eat while working a reception, but I was famished. I'd planned to make a quick detour to the Burger King drive-through on my way over, but the unanticipated relocation of Jelly Beans had left no time for that.

I popped my head into the dining room, where Maia's three assistants were busy setting up the gut-busting luncheon buffet. We're talking herbed prime rib on one end of the eighteen-foot-long table, creamy lobster risotto on the other, and all manner of mouthwatering deliciousness in between. The mingled aromas prompted my empty stomach to imitate Martin's Harley when it's idling.

From there I headed for the foyer at the front of the house, a jaw-dropping entryway with glass walls, crystal spiral chandelier, double staircase with glass railings, and marble inlay floor in a multihued abstract pattern. The place was packed, and no wonder. Guests entering through the front door stopped dead in their tracks when they spied what was laid out in the center of the room.

I will remind you that Josie was already in the ground at this point, lest my use of the term *laid out* beget the wrong mental image. This was no old-school wake with the body present. Well, not the flesh-and-blood kind of body, anyway.

"Doesn't she look good?" an elderly matron asked.

Her friend nodded. "So natural."

Okay, let's get this over with. Josie's other final wish, aside from spending eternity with Jelly Beans, was to attend her own funeral reception in the form of a life-size cake crafted in her image. And I have to tell you, this thing looked exactly like Josephine Evangelista, right down to the skintight fuchsia catsuit, big red hair, glittery Jimmy Choos (well, duh), and colorful lizard tattoos.

And speaking of lizards, Josie wasn't the only deceased individual who'd been resurrected as dessert. Jelly Beans lay snuggled up with her in cakey repose, looking as he presumably had in life: a long, scaly reptile executed in several colors, with yellow and tan frosting predominating. He was positioned with head lifted, mouth gaping, spiny beard puffed up.

The perimeter of the cake was decorated with—oh, come on, do I really have to say it?—*jelly beans!*

As I took in this bizarre tableau rendered in cake, frosting, and a multitude of decorative candies, my stomach growled again—which seemed kind of wrong somehow. I mean, I know I told Frank I was prepared to chow down on Josie's defrosted lizard (well, *of course* I had my fingers crossed behind my back when I said it!), but this five-foot-seven-inch cake was just too freakily realistic. And I'm not referring only to the reptilian portion. Josie's mischievous grin was too on point, the whole thing too darn Josie-like. The thought of eating a slice of her was… well, it felt downright cannibalistic.

As guests elbowed their way past me to get a better look and snap pictures, their reactions ran the gamut from stunned silence to gasps of outrage to hearty guffaws.

"So whaddaya think, Jane?" It was Georgia Chen, the pastry chef I'd hired to bake this thing. Georgia was a tall Chinese-American woman about my age with a thick New York accent and shoulder-length hair dyed eggplant-purple. She gave me a big bear hug.

"This is an incredible achievement, Georgia," I said, and meant it. "I hope you took plenty of photos for your portfolio."

"Oh my Gawd, I practically wore out my camera. Though, I mean, come on," she said, laughing, "what are the chances of my getting another assignment like this?"

"You don't think some of the folks here are already making plans to one-up Josie?"

"You got a point there." Georgia laughed again. She liked laughing. "Send 'em my way."

I said, "It's so noisy in here," and steered her into the nearby music room, which was deserted just then and blessedly quiet.

"Just so you know," she said, "Henry was a huge help with that cake. I mean, my *Gawd*. The lizard's scales? The Jimmy Choos? I can't tell you how many times I nearly chucked the whole thing onto the lawn for the squirrels."

"I knew I could count on your talented man to give you a hand," I said.

She grinned. "To keep me sane, you mean."

Georgia's husband, Henry Noyer, was also a pastry chef. The two of them had recently remarried after a divorce that never should have happened. I was happy to offer her this assignment, and the hefty fee that went with it, paid from the funds Josie had placed in escrow for this purpose. Georgia and Henry had experienced their share of hardship and could certainly use the money.

"I haven't seen Phil yet," I said, "but he must be around here somewhere."

"Yeah, he's been trying to avoid…" Georgia jerked her head toward the foyer and its attention-getting centerpiece.

"How's he taking it?" I asked. Josie's husband had tried to talk her out of the cake idea, which is why she'd hired me to make sure it got done. At the time, of course, we all assumed she'd have three or four decades to change her mind. No one could have foreseen how soon her quirky wish would become a reality.

"He's not happy, but it coulda been worse," Georgia said. "He coulda refused to let me bring it into the house, but he didn't. What I think? I think Phil loved his wife so much, with all her eccentricities, that he couldn't bear to deny her this one last, crazy thing. I mean, how romantic is that?"

Pretty darn romantic, I agreed. "Well, I guess I'd better go make the rounds."

"Yeah, I need to get back in there and keep an eye on Josie and Jelly Beans before someone decides to start carving them up ahead of schedule."

As I moved through the mansion, which was getting more crowded by the minute, I checked to make sure there were no disasters in the making and that the hired help were being, well, helpful.

I was passing through the great room when I heard a familiar voice call my name. My ex-husband, Dominic Faso, was just entering from the veranda. He handed his empty wineglass to a busser and kissed me on the cheek. We found a quiet corner to chat.

"I didn't realize you knew Josie," I said.

"I didn't. Phil's one of my poker buddies. I kind of expected I'd run into you here."

"Why?" I asked. "Oh. The cake."

"The cake," he said. "That thing just screams 'Death Diva.'"

"I'm not sure how to take that."

Dom broke into a grin, which only served to ramp up his handsomeness quotient. "It's a compliment, Janey. You're one of a kind."

As you can probably tell, my ex and I were still on excellent terms eighteen years after the divorce. Not that I hadn't spent most of those eighteen years wishing I could turn back the clock and undo our breakup, but that was all in the past. I was completely over Dom, now that I had a new man in my life in the very agreeable form of one Martin McAuliffe.

Dom owned Janey's Place, a wildly successful chain of vegetarian cafés. And if you guessed that he chose the name of his business back when we were still together, you would be right. Tall and fit, with dark, wavy hair and espresso-colored eyes—and did I mention the bespoke Italian suit that looked like it had been sewn right on him?—Dom was the epitome of the eligible bachelor: rich *and* sexy.

Alas, I'd never shared in those riches, having divorced him early on when Janey's Place was in its infancy and firmly in the red. And as I mentioned, I was no longer in thrall to his sexy self. I'd been Mrs. Faso Number One all those years ago and had no intention of taking another turn as Mrs. Faso Number Four.

Yeah, that's right. He had two more wives after me, followed by two more amicable divorces.

He said, "I heard you were also handling Larry's arrangements."

I shook my head. "I don't know anything about the funeral plans. I just helped with the disposition." I explained aquamation, which Dom had never heard of but was open-minded enough not to dismiss as bizarre or disgusting.

"Such a shock," he said, with a sad headshake, "Larry just dropping dead like that. He was a good guy, always looking for ways to give back to his community."

"Not everyone felt that way, unfortunately," I said.

"Like who?"

I glanced around and lowered my voice, having spied Nina Wallace chatting nearby with some friends. Few people enjoyed fueling the Crystal Harbor rumor mill as much as Nina. "Just between us? Frank Martinez. He's really steamed that he never won the chili cook-off. And he blames Larry."

Dom was nodding even before I finished speaking. "I know. I overheard him griping to Maxine Baumgartner about it at the cook-off."

"Really?" I said. "What did he say?"

"Oh, you know, it was all about how the contest was rigged against him, how Larry bossed around the other judges and how unfair the whole thing was."

"Yeah," I said, "that's basically what I heard him tell Larry."

"Then he said something like, 'Larry won't get away with it again.'"

I frowned. "He said that? What did Max say?"

He smiled. "You know Max. She told him to grow up.

Told him that if he spent half as much energy working on his chili recipe as he did bellyaching about Larry, he'd have a shot at taking home the trophy."

"Yep, that sounds like Max."

"Well, hey, you two." It was Nina, acting all chipper while horning in on our conversation. That woman had an unerring nose for gossip. "What are we chatting about?"

I started to tell her that what *we* were chatting about was none of *her* dang business, but was preempted by my ex-husband, who happened to be the nicest guy in the world. He sent me a quelling look and pecked her on the cheek. "Good to see you, Nina, but what terrible circumstances. Poor Josie. Were you two close?"

"Oh yes," she said, a little too quickly. Had they even known each other? "I was just beside myself when I heard the news. By the way, I brought some cookies. Nothing much, just some shortbreads, three kinds of biscotti, Linzers, snowballs, and almond lace. Oh, and five different kinds of macarons. I gave them to Maia, but I notice she hasn't put them out yet."

Nina was an avid home baker. I would have been surprised if she *hadn't* brought homemade treats. She never went anywhere without an assortment. It was her only redeeming quality if you didn't count mudslinging, gossipmongering, stealing elections, and violating her marriage vows.

Glad to see you were paying attention. You're right, that baking thing was, in fact, her only redeeming quality.

"She'll probably bring out your cookies when they cut the cake," I said.

Nina's eyes lit up. "That *cake*! Did you ever *see* such a thing?"

I couldn't tell whether she was appalled by the vulgarity of the display or thrilled by the, well, by the vulgarity of the display.

All I could say was, "It's what Josie wanted."

She gave a knowing nod. "I figured you had something to do with it."

"Why is everyone saying that?" I asked. "I mean, yeah, I helped her fulfill her vision, but not every assignment I take on is so, um…"

"Macabre?" Nina offered. "Shocking? Grotesque?"

"I was going to say 'unorthodox.'" I like *unorthodox*. It gets the job done without reminding folks that the assignments I take on are often macabre, shocking, or grotesque.

"Do you have something like that planned for Larry, too?" she asked. "Something, you know, *unorthodox*?"

I wasn't about to explain aquamation to this unrepentant blabbermouth.

When I chose not to respond, Dom did it for me. "Janey doesn't happen to be involved in his funeral plans, Nina. You'll have to ask Madison."

"Like I would ever," she said. "She'd probably spit in my face."

"Oh, I'm sure that's not true," he said. "What makes you think that?"

"You try being the 'other woman.'" Air quotes here. "It's a thankless role."

Okay, first of all? Call me old-fashioned, but it would never occur to me to thank a homewrecker for sleeping with someone else's husband. More to the point, Nina *hadn't* been sleeping with Larry. He'd denied it and I believed him. Clearly she'd tried to interest him, but the interest just wasn't there. Either she was in denial about that or she was lying in a bid for attention—and with no regard for how it would affect others.

Dom looked at me. I looked at him. My ex-husband had always been able to read my thoughts, and I saw him get the message now. Nina was full of you-know-what.

The room was jam-packed with guests, and Nina didn't seem to care who heard her. I was about to ask her to lower her voice when she said, "Larry *loved* the little goodies I baked just for him. His favorite was café brûlot chiffon squares. My own recipe. I had to sneak them to him, though, because that wife of his was the sugar police." She rolled her eyes. "It wasn't just sugar. Anything with butter, anything that tasted good, it was all off-limits."

"To be fair," Dom said, "Madison got Larry eating more healthfully and going to the gym. He lost a few pounds and was no longer prediabetic. He credited her with prolonging his life."

"Well, look who I'm talking to," she said, "Mr. Health Food Nut himself. Of course *you'd* approve of her heavy-handed tactics."

I couldn't remain silent. "So it's heavy-handed to look after your spouse's health?"

"For your information, that Madison is no saint," Nina said. "She had affairs. Everyone knows. Larry knew."

The din of chatter in the room abruptly dwindled. I turned and saw a cluster of guests part to let someone through. My gut clenched even before I saw Madison Kool rise gracefully from a nearby sofa and approach us.

6

Love at First Sight

MADISON GREETED DOM and me with double air kisses before turning to the self-styled "other woman." She didn't smile as she offered a polite, "Nina."

I'd known Nina long enough to discern a hint of alarm beneath her confident façade. "I was hoping to run into you, Madison. I wanted to tell you how sorry I am about Larry."

"So sorry that you feel compelled to spread lies about us?" Madison spoke calmly, never breaking eye contact with the woman who'd aspired to be her husband's mistress.

Larry's young widow was as beautiful as ever, her outfit subdued yet still elegant: a sleeveless raw silk tunic and flowing cropped pants in shades of taupe and oatmeal, with a gauzy wrap draped over her shoulders.

Nina's jittery gaze took in the assembled throng, none of whom even pretended to ignore the juicy scene unfolding before them. "I, um, didn't mean for you to find out this way, about me and Larry—"

"I don't know who you think you're fooling, or why you feel compelled to tell such wicked and hurtful lies." Madison still had not raised her voice, forcing the other guests to shuffle closer. "My husband told me what you were up to back in June when you first tried to seduce him. I know in my heart that he never cheated on me, and for the record, that fidelity went both ways. I never looked at another man after I—" her words caught in her throat "—after I fell in love with Larry."

Nina's voice was reedy, her face scalded a nice, even magenta. "Well, I know the truth, Madison. I feel sorry for you if you can't face it."

The ladies Nina had been chatting with earlier openly snickered and rolled their eyes. A part of me pitied her, but no one could say she hadn't brought it on herself.

She tilted her chin up, mumbled, "Excuse me," and scurried out of the room.

Dom put his arm around Madison and gently turned her away from the gawking crowd. Quietly he said, "Can I get you something, Madison? A cup of tea? Some wine?"

"That's so considerate of you, Dom." She took a shaky breath. "A glass of cabernet or merlot would be lovely right now. I don't often allow myself a drink, but I think today I earned it."

I told him, "We'll be outside," and ushered her through the sleek steel-and-glass double doors onto the long, covered veranda, outfitted with modernistic chandeliers, abstract sculptures, and plush upholstered seating areas. Most of these were occupied, but I spied an empty pair of stuffed chairs at one end of the porch, and led Madison to them. We were far enough from our nearest neighbors to ensure a private conversation.

As Madison sat, she said, "I don't know Dom very well, but he seems so sweet. Forgive me for prying, but I can't help but wonder why you two got divorced."

"It's no state secret." I settled myself on the other chair, the two of us facing each other across a minimalist, and no doubt outrageously expensive, concrete coffee table adorned with a white orchid dish garden. "It's simple really. I wanted children. Dom didn't."

"Ah. Well, that sounds painfully familiar." She wore a sad smile. "I wish to God Larry had agreed to have a child with me. Then at least there'd be… well, it's a kind of immortality, isn't it, your genes surviving into future generations?"

"I never thought of it that way," I said, "but it makes a kind of sense."

Dom's two subsequent marriages had produced three children, while I was still hoping to become a forty-something first-time mother. Martin, meanwhile, was due to become a grandfather in a few weeks, at age forty-three. Several of my female friends had kids who were in college, and one had a brand-new granddaughter. I was really lagging behind on the procreation front.

Dom had been engaged for more than a year to our local police chief, Bonnie Hernandez, until she met someone else and called off the wedding. That was when the tables turned, with my ex trying to convince me to remarry him. Three months ago, however, I'd made it clear it was too late for us. I'd let him down as gently as I could, but I knew he was still smarting from the finality of it.

He'd find someone else soon enough, I had no doubt. That man needed a mate in his life. He could not tolerate being alone for long. Truth be told, I was surprised he hadn't gotten serious with anyone yet. Of course, it was entirely possible he was biding his time, patiently awaiting the inevitable failure of my new relationship. He'd never made a secret of his dislike, and distrust, of the man who was now officially my significant other. And while it was true Martin had a sketchy past, he'd explained his troubled youth to my satisfaction. My ex-husband had absolutely no say in the matter.

I asked, "Did you know Josie well?"

"I know what you're thinking," Madison said, "that we didn't have much in common, and I can't argue with that. But anyone who knew Josie also knew that she had such a big heart. After I moved in with Larry, I didn't know anyone else in Crystal Harbor, and I felt kind of adrift. One evening this loud, jolly stranger drops by with a bottle of vodka and some oysters, conducts a tarot reading to discover what kind of lizard I should adopt—gargoyle gecko if you're interested, and no I didn't—and hauls me off to a karaoke bar."

"Oh brother," I said.

She grinned. "I know, but it was the start of a close friendship. I even learned to toss back the occasional vodka oyster shot—and if you tell anyone that, I'll deny it. Plus I finally got up the nerve to try karaoke." In response to my raised eyebrows, she added, "Fully clothed."

I reached across the table to squeeze her hand. "That's a great Josie story."

"I'm going to miss her."

"Listen," I said, "I'm so sorry you had to endure that nasty business with Nina. The woman's a piece of work. Always has been."

"Larry knew that better than anyone," Madison said. "I didn't enjoy confronting her in public like that. It's not, well, it's not my style. But it had to be done. I couldn't let her continue to trash Larry's memory that way."

"Are you planning a funeral?" I asked. "I haven't heard anything."

"There will be a memorial service sometime within the next month or so," she said, "at the Unitarian church Larry attended. His parents were members, too, and so were his paternal grandparents. I don't have an exact date yet. I'm waiting to hear from the minister. I'll let you know."

"Louise said Larry had none of the usual risk factors for sudden cardiac arrest," I said.

"That's what she told me, but she also said that sometimes there's just no explanation. I tried so hard to get him to adopt a healthier lifestyle."

"And with some success," I said. "I know you improved his diet and got him exercising."

She smiled. "I also introduced him to daily meditation."

My eyes widened. "Larry? Why can't I picture that?"

"He agreed to give it a try—just to humor me, of course. After a while, though, when he began to feel the effects, he actually looked forward to it." Her smile faded. "Nina was no help where his nutrition was concerned. One thing she *wasn't* lying about was the pastries. She snuck that junk to him every chance she got. Larry couldn't resist and then it would trigger his carb cravings and we'd be back to square one."

"So one thing I was wondering about," I said, "and forgive me for prying…"

"Pry away," Madison said. "I owe you one."

"Well, that day at the cook-off," I said, "when it was clear Larry wasn't feeling well, I was surprised to see that his pupils were dilated."

She frowned. "I didn't notice that."

"That's not surprising," I said. "We were sitting in the shade when you joined us, so it wouldn't have been obvious. I was just wondering, and again, it's none of my business, but was he on any kind of medication that would cause that?"

She shook her head. "He used to take a drug for prediabetes, but Louise took him off that after he switched over to clean eating and his sugar levels improved."

I remembered something. "He was wearing that scopolamine patch for the nausea. I wonder…" I withdrew my phone from my purse and quickly looked up a list of side effects. "Yep. It can cause widened pupils."

"Mystery solved. Ah. My knight in shining armor."

I looked up to see Dom approaching with a waiter's tray laden with two glasses of red wine, two water goblets, and several small plates filled with what Madison would call "clean eating": cut-up fruit, mixed nuts, and raw veggies with hummus for dipping.

Immature Jane threw an internal tantrum over the lack of anything deep-fried or cheesy (or both), while Mature Jane smiled serenely and said, "How thoughtful of you, Dom. This looks delicious."

Which didn't fool my ex for an instant. He held my gaze just long enough to remind me that he knew me far too well to buy that baloney.

And speaking of baloney, would it have killed him to include a few slices of salami for his meat-eating ex-wife? A little pâté, maybe?

"I haven't felt much like eating lately," Madison said, as he deposited the drinks and food on our table, "but this looks very appetizing. Thank you, Dom."

Before he left us, I asked him, "Did you happen to see Phil? I need to touch base with him."

"He's in that big living-room area off of the indoor pool. He's kind of holding court there."

"Great. I'll swing by in a few minutes." With any luck, Josie's widower would have made peace with her decision to be enshrined as an edible work of art.

When we were alone again, Madison said, "I'm glad we ran into each other, Jane. I was thinking about giving you a call."

"Is there something I can help you with?" I took a sip of excellent cabernet.

"It's just that there are so many details to manage right now, so many things that need to get done. I find it… overwhelming."

"I know it can seem that way now," I said, "but it's only been six days. Take it one step at a time. I'll help in any way I can. As a friend."

"I wouldn't dream of taking advantage," she said. "I want you to bill me for any services you render."

"Larry was such a special guy." My eyes stung. I cleared my throat. "He did so much for Crystal Harbor. The least I can do is make a few phone calls for you, run interference, gratis. I'm doing it for Larry. I won't take no for an answer."

She scooped up some hummus with a carrot stick, smiling her thanks. "You drive a hard bargain, Jane."

"I have to ask," I said, "but I think I know the answer. Can't Liddy help with some of this?"

Madison's expression said, *You have got to be kidding.* "Larry told me that when their father was in his final illness—this was about fifteen years ago—Liddy was worse than useless. Far from helping, she made the whole situation worse, playing up her role as the distraught daughter, constantly demanding attention. He couldn't even get her to visit their dad in hospice because she found it distressing. Actually, the word she used was 'yucky.' Finally he just gave up. The entire burden fell to him."

"I wish I could say I'm surprised, but from what I've observed of Liddy…" I shrugged.

"So no, I'm not going to involve my sister-in-law," she said. "That kind of help, I don't need."

"Did you happen to catch Liddy's, um, performance Monday evening on *The Romano Files?*"

"I'm not a fan of that show," Madison said, "but a friend called and told me Liddy and Rex were on it, so I decided I'd better tune in. I missed the beginning, but at least I got to learn what a 'stingy bitch' I am, and how jealous I was of Liddy's close relationship with her brother. Let me tell you, if I could turn back the clock, I wouldn't do anything differently."

"So then it's true that you persuaded Larry to stop bankrolling her?"

"I made him see he wasn't doing his sister any favors in the long run," she said, "giving her money anytime she asked—and she asked constantly, believe me. He was infantilizing her, ensuring she would never take responsibility for herself."

"On the show," I said, "Liddy mentioned that she sells designer handbags on eBay. That can't be much of a living."

"It's not," Madison said. "Ever since Larry cut her off, she's been dating a string of losers, trying to find some man who's both willing and able to support her in her accustomed lifestyle."

I popped a grape into my mouth. It was pretty good. I should probably buy fresh fruit once in a while. "Think it'll work?" I asked.

Madison shook her head. "What does Liddy have to offer a man? She's an immature fifty-eight-year-old woman with no education, taste, or marketable skills. It's clear she's in denial about her age and lack of sex appeal."

Wow. Harsh, but accurate as far as I could tell. I couldn't help drawing an uncomfortable parallel between Liddy and Madison—not in terms of personality or physical attributes, of course, but in how the two of them chose to provide for themselves. After all, hadn't Madison herself snagged a wealthy husband capable of supporting her in style? For the past four years she'd had no career aside from being Mrs. Larry Kool.

I said, "Can I ask if Larry provided for his sister in his will?"

She nodded, reaching for her water goblet. After a couple of sips of wine, it would seem she'd reached her limit. "Larry knew better than to drop a chunk of cash in her lap. She'll receive a modest monthly allowance for life, with cost-of-living adjustments."

I wondered how she defined "modest." If the allowance was *too* modest, or even if it wasn't, I could see Liddy quickly burning through it and begging Madison for more, their fraught history notwithstanding.

As if reading my mind, Madison said, "My sister-in-law will have to make do with her annuity. She's not getting any handouts from me."

I happened to know Larry had pulled down some serious bucks during his long and eclectic entertainment career, and invested it wisely. He'd owned the stately old manse in Crystal Harbor that had been in his family for about two hundred thirty years, as well as a villa in Tuscany and a vacation home in Puerto Vallarta. Knowing Larry, I assumed he'd made bequests to various relatives and charities, but his young widow had no doubt inherited the bulk of his estate.

I tried a little hummus. Eh. Still not a fan. "So, what do you make of that bombshell Liddy dropped on Leonora Romano's show last night? Or did you already know about it?"

Her brows pulled together. "Bombshell?"

"You know." I rooted around in the nut bowl for a cashew. "Her and Rex."

"Oh. That." Madison wagged her hand. "Ancient history."

I did some quick mental arithmetic. Madison had been born about ten years *after* Rex and Liddy's long-ago affair. Ancient history indeed. "Did Larry ever mention how he felt about his costar, um, getting involved with his little sister?"

"*Former* costar," she corrected, "and *half* sister. He thought it was pretty sleazy of Rex to take advantage of a young girl's infatuation with a handsome TV star. He and Rex had a falling out over it."

"I was under the impression they remained friends," I said.

"They did eventually reconcile. But then a few years ago, when Larry and I started seeing each other, well, their relationship never really recovered from that." At my questioning look, she said, "I thought you knew. Rex and I dated for a little while. That's how I met Larry. Rex introduced us."

"Oh." I blinked in surprise. "I had no idea. So Larry, what, stole you from Rex?"

"Oh, nothing so dramatic. Rex and I went out for only a few weeks, and it was very casual. We hadn't even... we weren't, um..." Madison glanced around, wary of eavesdroppers.

"I get it," I said. "But I take it Rex wasn't exactly okay with you dropping him for Larry."

"You know men," she said. "They get all territorial, even if they never, you know, *occupied* the territory in question."

"Well, it certainly wasn't casual between you and Larry," I said.

She bit back a smile. "I know 'love at first sight' is considered a cliché, but let me tell you, it doesn't feel like a cliché when it happens to you. Larry and I had this deep connection right from the start. Like we were waiting our whole lives for each other."

I refrained from mentioning that Larry had experienced a longer wait than his bride did—forty-something years longer.

As much as I wanted to believe her romantic version of events, I found it impossible to ignore the obvious. Which is that after dating Rex Noble, even casually, for several weeks, Madison must have deduced that he wasn't exactly rolling in dough. Then along comes Larry Kool, who's worth... well, who knew what he was worth? Something in the tens of millions would be my guess.

And it's love at first sight.

Not that money necessarily had anything to do with it, but you know me. I can be a tad cynical at times. Or as I prefer to think of it, realistic.

I said, "Rex must've gotten over his, um, territorial issues at some point, because he seemed friendly enough with Larry at the cook-off."

"That wasn't friendliness," she said, "it was desperation. Rex was always trying to get Larry to help jump-start his career."

"How?"

"Mainly by putting in a good word with the right directors and producers," she said. "Larry is—*was* very well respected in the industry. People in power valued his opinion."

"Did he come through for Rex?" I asked. "I mean, it sounds like the guy didn't have much acting work in recent years."

"He didn't have much acting work since *Chase & Knabbe*," Madison said. "What Leonora Romano said on her show last night was true, though she didn't have to be so brutal about it. Rex is his own worst enemy. There was only so much Larry could do, and then he stopped trying for fear of being tainted by association."

"Well, it looked like Rex was still at it during the cook-off," I said. "He was talking to Larry about someone named Sawyer."

"That would be Llewellyn Sawyer," Madison said, "an up-and-coming movie director Larry once worked with. Lew's thing is British period pieces with a modern spin. I heard he has some Jane Austen project in the works. Or is it one of the Brontës? Anyway, they say it's going to be his breakout film. Are you telling me Rex was still badgering Larry about this right before he… collapsed?"

"What do you mean, 'still'?" I asked.

"Rex insisted on meeting Larry at Murray's Pub the night before the cook-off—just for a friendly drink, supposedly. Of course, he spent the whole time trying to persuade Larry to use his influence with Lew Sawyer to get him an audition for the new film."

"Rex wasn't the only one twisting Larry's arm last Friday," I said. "He had a run-in with Frank Martinez that day, too."

Madison's eyes widened. "How did you know about that?"

"I was with Larry at Frank's chili booth," I said, "and Frank was harassing him about how unfair the judging was, yadda yadda, and Larry said they had the same conversation the day before."

"That man actually came onto our property, uninvited," Madison said. "Larry was doing laps in the pool. I'd just brought him a kale protein shake and was back in the kitchen rinsing out the blender. It was a mild day and the windows were open, and after a while I heard what sounded like a heated conversation. I went out there and found Frank standing at the side of the pool, giving Larry a hard time about the cook-off."

"I knew Frank took the whole thing too seriously," I said, "but that's really rude."

"I started to give him a piece of my mind, but Larry assured me everything was okay, that Frank was just leaving. Which he did. But I have to tell you, the whole thing left me a little unnerved."

"Were you concerned for your safety?" I asked. "For Larry's?"

"You had to have been there," she said. "Frank was so… intense."

I thought of all those who'd expected Larry to provide for them in some fashion. His sister. His long-ago costar. Nina Wallace. Frank Martinez.

It seemed everyone wanted something from Larry Kool.

7

She's a Real Dog

MURRAY'S PUB WAS hopping, no surprise for a Friday night. Think multicolored strobe lights, fog machine, and wall-to-wall revelers dancing to earsplitting techno music.

Just kidding. Murray's was a homey neighborhood watering hole that had been operating in the same location on Main Street since the late nineteenth century. It had changed little over the years, aside from light bulbs supplanting gas in the vintage fixtures. Electricity also made possible the muted television over the bar, now showing a closed-captioned game at City Field between the Mets and the Nationals. The battered wooden booths and tables were filled nearly to capacity.

I paused inside the entrance, letting the familiar sense of peace and belonging suffuse me. It was the look of the place, from the antique woodwork worn to a smooth patina, to the hand-forged bronze foot rail and coat hooks, to the hoary collection of framed paintings, posters, photographs, and historic newspaper articles crammed into nearly every square inch of wall space.

It was the sound of the place, animated conversation and laughter against a backdrop of subdued bluegrass music.

It was the smell of the place, a heady blend of good draft beer and spicy Cajun fries.

And last but far from least, it was the presence of Martin McAuliffe behind the bar, greeting me with a wink and a private smile as he blended a batch of slushy, green drinks for a trio of giggly twenty-somethings.

Georgia Chen was the other bartender on duty that evening. When she wasn't baking fancy French pastries at Patisserie Susanne (or disturbingly realistic, life-size memorial cakes at the request of yours truly), she could often be found at Murray's, providing a second pair of hands when the place was busy.

"Oh my Gawd, it's Jane!" Georgia's New York twang sliced through the chatter, causing heads to turn my way. I offered a queenly wave in acknowledgment of shouted greetings and raised glasses from friends and neighbors celebrating the start of the weekend.

At the moment Georgia was putting the finishing touches on a cocktail called Sybbie's Punch, a popular local libation that had originated right there in Crystal Harbor back in the seventeenth century. Georgia herself had resurrected the drink a few months earlier, based on nothing more than a list of ingredients and her own considerable skills as a mixologist.

She was making the drink for Veronica Sheffield, one of my favorite clients by virtue of the fact that Veronica could envision no worthier use for her mountains of moola than to hire the Death Diva on a startlingly regular basis. Every time anyone in her vast extended family—not to mention her wide orbit of friends, friends of friends, and *their* extended families—kicked the bucket, Veronica would put on her thinking cap and devise some outlandish way to memorialize the dearly departed.

Just last week she'd engaged me to arrange a sort of scavenger hunt in which her cousin Ava's ashes were divided between one hundred tiny hourglasses, which were then concealed in various locations all around town. Ava's friends and family had to follow written clues (quite cleverly crafted if I do say so myself) to locate them. The person with the most hourglasses at the end of the hunt was the winner.

And let me tell you, the competition was cutthroat. Which might seem kind of surprising if you didn't know the grand prize was a portrait of a young Cousin Ava painted by Andy Warhol back when she'd been a teen supermodel and muse to a steady stream of rock stars. Even those who weren't particularly close to the deceased ("Cousin who?") tripped over one another in their zeal to snag an original Warhol, guaranteed to bring beaucoup bucks at auction.

Happily, those jackals were no match for Ava's devoted young dog walker, Bianca, who came equipped with serious running shoes, a six-pack of energy drinks, and a bloodhound's nose for her late employer's cremated remains. Bianca had been saving up for college, and the Warhol would help put that goal within reach. It wasn't hard to imagine Ava saluting the girl with a fist pump from the great beyond.

I made my way over to where the padre was chatting with his trio of comely customers, who appeared in no hurry to bid him adieu. You will be less than shocked to learn that I bulled past the flirtatious trio to claim both the last vacant barstool and the padre, who leaned across the bar to bestow a brain-melting smooch that left no doubt as to his relationship status.

With a sigh, the young ladies lifted their frosty drinks and drifted away.

Martin reached into a secret cabinet under the bar, withdrew a bottle of my favorite añejo sipping tequila, poured a generous shot into a small snifter, and slid it across to me. No charge.

That's right, he kept the high-end liquor on hand just for *moi*—with the full approval, I might add, of the pub's owner, Maxine Baumgartner, who happened to like me. Which I'll admit might have more to do with a sticky situation I once handled for her gratis than my winning personality, but whatever.

Okay, I know you're wondering about the sticky situation. Seems three years ago when Max's dad died, she and her mom learned that Whispering Willows Cemetery had accidentally planted another couple in the side-by-side double plot Mr. Baumgartner had carefully selected and paid for decades earlier.

The cemetery's administrator, Frank Martinez, had the unenviable job of breaking the news to the family and relaying his boss's slimy fauxpology ("We regret that an error occurred…").

The cemetery owner's name was Arlo Pleasant, a misnomer if ever there was one. Arlo doubtless assumed he'd have no trouble placating a middle-aged female barkeep and her elderly mom. Clearly he didn't know this particular irascible, strong-willed barkeep, or that she was good pals with a certain local Death Diva, who had a history of not taking crap from him.

Mr. Baumgartner had chosen a plot in the desirable Green Valley section of the cemetery, marked by gentle hills, shade trees with benches, and handsome upright headstones. Arlo's response to his cemetery's grievous error was to offer a replacement plot in Serene Meadow, the newest, cheapest section where the land was unrelievedly flat, with minimal landscaping, and only flush grave markers were permitted.

Oh, and? No side-by-side companion plots were available in Serene Meadow, only double-depth plots where two caskets are buried one on top of the other to save space. Nothing wrong with that, but it wasn't what Mr. Baumgartner had wanted, planned for, and paid for all those years ago.

To Frank's credit, he was clearly embarrassed, not only by his boss's failure to take responsibility, but by the man's smarmy attempt to cheat a grieving family.

As you can imagine, I was outraged on behalf of Max and her mom. I told them I'd see what I could do, as a friend. Then I called Sten Jakobsen, local general-practice lawyer and all-around good guy. Sten was seventy-three, and the closer he got to retirement, the more he enjoyed bare-knuckling it for the little guy. He offered his legal muscle pro bono before I could even ask.

Long story short, by the time Sten and I finished double-teaming Arlo, the man had sweated right through his pale-gray silk-and-linen Tom Ford suit. Not only had the replacement cemetery plot miraculously morphed into a side-by-side in the coveted historical section (a huge step up from even Green Valley), but Whispering Willows had picked up all costs associated with the interment, including a swanky granite headstone and perpetual care.

Martin saw me look toward the doorway as he filled small bowls from a giant canister of honey-mustard pretzels. "Waiting for someone?"

"Liddy Kool asked to meet me. Wants to hire me for some kind of Death Diva thing."

"She asked to meet you *here*?" he said. "I wouldn't have thought this place would be on her radar."

"The pub was my idea." I took a sip of the smoothest tequila in existence, golden nectar of the gods. "Whatever she has in mind, she wouldn't discuss it over the phone. My gut told me to meet her someplace neutral, rather than her place or mine."

"I'd say your gut is giving you sound advice. For what it's worth, I'd be wary of doing business with that flake."

"I'm way ahead of you. Figure I can always tell her I'm too busy or something, but no harm in hearing her out." I glanced around and lowered my voice. "Want to know the first thing that popped into my mind? You know, that Liddy might want to discuss?"

He paused while screwing the lid back onto the pretzel canister. Whatever rascally remark he was about to deliver died on his tongue when he saw my expression. He frowned. "What?"

"Never mind, it's stupid. I shouldn't even…" I made my hand into a stop sign.

"Jane." Martin tipped my chin up and made me look him in the eye. "It's me. Whatever you're thinking, it's not stupid."

I took a deep breath. "Okay, well, I was just wondering if Liddy might've gotten it into her head that her brother's death wasn't, um, natural. I mean, you know how overdramatic she is about everything."

His frown deepened. "You think Larry was murdered?"

"No! I just thought Liddy might… you know, because she's so…" I dropped my head into my hands and groaned. Finally I looked up and said, "All right, I admit I've had a few crazy thoughts. In the middle of the night. When my mind just won't be still. But what do I know? I'm no detective."

"Maybe not," he said, "but you've had more experience

with homicides than many actual detectives have."

I shrugged. "Comes with the territory when you're the only Death Diva in town."

"Try the only Death Diva, period. So what are you going to do?"

"Do?" I swirled the tequila in my snifter. "There's nothing *to* do, Padre. Larry died of natural causes. That's what Louise Holliday said, and she was his personal physician for as long as I can remember."

"But that dependable gut of yours is telling you something doesn't add up," he said. "Tell me, have you spoken with Louise since the autopsy was performed?"

"No, but—"

"But nothing," he said. "Go see her. Find out what the medical examiner said."

I thought about it. "Well, I guess it couldn't hurt to give her a call."

"Listen to you, you big kidder," he scoffed. "No phone calls. You want to find out what's what, you meet Louise in person."

This was a recurring theme with Martin, who believed there was no substitute for a face-to-face discussion.

"All right, all right," I said, "I'll see if I can get together with her this week. Listen, I've been meaning to ask you—"

"Maker's Mark!" a familiar voice barked, over my shoulder. "Double. Rocks."

"You got it." Martin reached for a lowball glass.

While the padre poured bourbon, I turned and gave Arlo Pleasant a big, jolly Death Diva grin. "What a coincidence! I was just thinking about you."

He flinched. "How are you, Jane?"

"Just swell, Arlo. Double-book any graves lately?"

He stared fixedly at his drink in progress, probably wishing he'd ordered a triple. "You need some new material. That line wasn't funny the first twenty times you said it."

"Aw, don't be like that. After all, if you can't laugh at yourself—" I mock-punched his shoulder "—I'm happy to do it for you."

Martin gave the man his drink. "Want to open a tab?"

Arlo slapped his credit card on the bar and stomped off.

"I'm beginning to think he doesn't like me," I said. "Did you get that, too, or is it all in my head?"

Martin's lopsided grin made him even more devilishly handsome. "You are one wicked woman."

"You say that like it's a bad thing."

He took an order for a pitcher of Blue Point Toasted Lager. As he worked the tap, he said, "What did you want to ask me, Jane?"

"Huh? Oh. It's about that dog. The big black one at the adopt-a-pet thing. The one who only had eyes for you."

"Layla," he said.

"Right, Layla. Sweet pooch."

"You'll get no argument from me. What about her?" he asked.

"Well, I was just wondering whether she's been adopted yet," I said.

"Not yet." He handed over the pitcher and made brief small talk with his customer before returning his attention to me. "Black dogs, especially large black dogs, don't get adopted as readily as the cute, little, lighter-colored ones."

"Really? That's so unfair."

"So she's still available," he said, "if you're interested."

"Me? I'm not in the market for another pet, and anyway, you're the one she's in love with."

His wry smile told me he'd known all along where I was going with this. "You seem to be forgetting one minor little detail." He pointed at the ceiling, indicating his apartment located directly above our heads on the second floor. "You want to know what would *really* be unfair? Keeping a big, lively dog like that cooped up in a one-bedroom walk-up. She'd go stir-crazy with no yard to run in."

"The town dog park is five minutes away, Padre. Drive a little farther and you've got tons of parks and beaches. And don't forget, I have five acres where Layla can run to her heart's content."

"You know, you've got a point," he said. "I could buy her a little motorcycle helmet, and for me, one of those T-shirts that says, 'If you can read this, the bitch fell off.' Only it wouldn't be sexist because…" He gestured for me to fill in the rest.

I rolled my eyes. "Because Layla is an actual bitch, ha ha."

"Of course, if I could get her on my Harley," he said, "she'd be a bitch on wheels."

"You're forgetting, I happen to know you also own an automobile." A sexy 1966 candy-apple-red Mustang convertible. "So enough about the Harley. How do you know she's still at the animal shelter?"

He hesitated a nanosecond too long.

I sprang off my barstool and stabbed a finger at him. "I knew it! You've been sneaking off to spend time with that bitch. Do not even *think* about lying to me."

I heard a sharp gasp and turned to see Liddy Kool standing behind me, looking like she'd just overheard the tastiest morsel of gossip and couldn't wait to spread it around. Everyone else within earshot—most of whom knew both Martin and me—appeared stunned, embarrassed, or both.

Liddy patted my arm. "You go ahead and let it all out, honey. All three of my husbands were cheaters. I know just how you feel."

"Oh. Wait. No no no…" I wagged my hands as if to erase the last thirty seconds. "You see, the bitch I was talking about happens to be a real dog."

"Doesn't matter how ugly she is," Liddy said, "it still hurts. Take it from me."

"You don't underst—"

"And *you!*" Liddy got in Martin's face. "What do you have to say for yourself?"

"What can I tell you?" He shrugged. "Layla gets me. Why, if I let her, she'd spend hours on end just licking my hair."

Those sitting nearby exchanged uneasy glances.

"Martin, you are not helping, dammit!" I said. "Tell them Layla's a, uh… tell them she's not human."

This was met with a low rumble of disapproval from the crowd, who clearly felt I'd gone too far in maligning my competition.

Liddy said, "Let him have the bitch, Jane, and good riddance. Where's your pride?"

This from the fifty-eight-year-old woman standing there in micro cutoffs and a midriff-baring baby-doll top from the juniors department.

A young man standing nearby tentatively raised his hand. "Uh… can I get a Lagunitas IPA and a glass of rosé?"

"Sure thing." Martin produced a wineglass and started pouring.

"Trust me," I announced to anyone who'd listen, "I *want*

Martin to be with Layla. I want them to *live* together. She'd be good for him. They'd be good for each other. And just so you know, Layla is a… she's a…" I groped for an explanation that would put this nonsense to rest.

"Oh my Gawd, you people, she's a *canine*," Georgia said, while working a martini shaker. "As in an honest-to-Gawd dawg. Martin, show them the picture."

Martin obediently hauled out his phone and tapped the screen.

I gaped at my boyfriend. "You carry around a picture of her?"

"Oh, he's got it bad, trust me." Georgia filled a martini glass and garnished it with a blue-cheese-stuffed olive. "He talks about that pooch awl the time."

"That's enough from you, Georgia," the padre grumbled as he held out his phone to display a close-up of Layla's big, doggy face wearing what appeared to be a big, goofy doggy grin.

As everyone crowded around to gush over the lovely Layla and tease me about my furry rival for Martin's affections, I spied a booth in the process of being vacated. I gave Liddy a shove in that direction. "Hurry, go grab that table. I'll buy you a drink. What'll you have?"

Martin was busy showing off Layla's glamour shot, and now Liddy gave the other bartender a dubious look. "Think that Oriental girl knows how to make a skinny mojito?"

That question was wrong on so many levels. As if I needed another reason to dislike Larry's half sister. I managed to keep my tone civil. "Georgia knows what she's doing, Liddy. I'm sure she can handle it."

When I joined Liddy in the booth a few minutes later, I

couldn't help but notice her making eyes at a table of four good-looking guys in their thirties. Alas, the gentlemen either hadn't picked up on her interest or were fixedly ignoring her. My money was on that second thing.

I set her diet cocktail on the table. I was still nursing my tequila. As I slid onto the bench across from her, I asked, "So, what can I do for you, Liddy?" I was in no mood to prolong our meeting.

"It's just been so… so…" The grief-stricken hitch in her voice was pure amateur hour. So much for Rex Noble sabotaging a promising acting career. "I still can't… can't believe Larry's gone."

She stared at me, my cue to launch into a flurry of platitudes. Instead I offered a simple but heartfelt, "My condolences, Liddy. We'll all miss him."

"But *I'll* miss him most of all!" she cried. "He was my big brother!"

"What did you want to speak to me ab—"

"I'm all alone in the world now." Liddy blinked hard, clearly trying to squeeze out a few tears. "There's no one left who cares about me. *No one!*"

It had been a long week. The last thing I wanted was to be drawn into The Liddy Show. Still, I had to say something. "I know it seems that way now, Liddy, but, um, time heals all wounds." So much for avoiding platitudes. "Now, if we can get back to the reason you asked to meet—"

"Larry always looked after me." She took a big gulp of her drink. "Like when Daddy was dying. He was in this yucky hospice place, and Larry knew I was too young and emotionally fragile to deal with it, so he insisted I stay away and remember Daddy the way he used to be."

Let's see, Madison had told me her father-in-law died fifteen years ago, which would've made Liddy forty-three at the time. And for the record, I'd visited many hospices and had yet to find one that could be described as anything close to yucky.

Before I could draw a breath to respond, Liddy barreled on. "I always did my best to please Daddy, but I was never good enough in his eyes. He always compared me to Larry, and how fair was that? Larry's acting career was in full swing before I was even born! And then when my mom entered me in all those child beauty pageants, Daddy was so negative. He said the makeup and costumes made me look like a little *hooker*, can you believe it? And don't get me started on what he said about the dance moves."

"Liddy, if we could circle back around to—"

"It was sexism, pure and simple." She tipped back her glass and drained most of her mojito. "Daddy wanted another boy, but he got me instead. It's why I spent my adolescence acting out. I was always trying to earn his love, but it never worked. Daddy's the reason for my three failed marriages. *He's* why I always pick losers. It's not my fault."

I had to ask. "Did your father ever offer you any career guidance?"

She rolled her eyes. "He tried to get me to go to college. So did Larry. They said it would help me 'find myself.' Help me 'grow up.' They wanted me to settle down and get some kind of business degree. Can you believe that crap? But I didn't fall for it. I knew they were just trying to keep me away from Gary."

"Gary?"

"Husband number one," she said. "We got married the day after I graduated high school."

"And, um, how long did that marriage last?"

She wagged her hand. "Like, nine, ten months. Gary kept insisting I get some crummy job! Like my acting career didn't count."

"Did you land any acting gigs?"

"That's not the point," she said. "He should've been supportive. Meanwhile, he refused to put in for more overtime at the poultry plant, claimed he was 'exhausted.' Not too exhausted to knock up the receiving clerk during his lunch break. The cheating bastard."

"Wow," I said, "that's, um... Didn't you tell Leonora Romano that you got involved with Rex when you were eighteen?"

"Yeah, so?"

"So that would've been during the time you were married to Gary, no?"

She scowled. "Are you judging me?"

"No, I was just wonder—"

"Because I have *had it* with everyone judging me. First Daddy, then my husbands. Even Larry, once that horrible wife of his got her claws into him. She's the reason he cut me off without a dime. But I got the last laugh, didn't I?"

Don't ask, don't ask, don't ask... "What do you mean, the last laugh?" *Dang!*

Liddy wore a smug smile. "I can't wait to see Madison's face when she finds out Larry left everything to *me*."

"Um..." Madison had told me just that morning that her sister-in-law's inheritance would take the form of a modest annuity. It would appear Liddy had yet to get the memo.

"Well, maybe not every last nickel," she continued. "I mean, he probably had to leave a little something to that snooty bitch. But they were only married for, what, a measly four years, and I've been his sister my whole life. I'm his closest blood relative. First thing I'm going to do is redecorate the mansion."

"The mansion?" I said. "You mean Larry and Madison's house?"

She leaned across the table and hissed, "It was never *her* house. My great-great-whatever-grandparents built that place over two hundred years ago. No way would Larry leave it to some cheap gold digger. You'll see."

Time to change the subject. "Liddy, you asked to meet me about a possible Death Diva job. If you've changed your mind, then I really have to get going. I have, um, another appointment to get to."

"Yeah, yeah, hold your horses." She polished off her drink and stared pointedly at the empty glass. Then at me. Then at the glass again. Subtle.

I started to rise. "So if there's nothing else—"

"I need you to steal Larry's ashes."

I dropped back onto the bench and sat there replaying her words in my mind, trying to make them sound like something other than *I need you to steal Larry's ashes.*

Finally I said, "I don't get it."

"I think I was pretty clear." Liddy lifted her glass and sucked down some melted ice before casting her forlorn gaze toward the bar. In case I hadn't gotten the message the first time. Did this routine work on guys? When I didn't respond with the offer of a refill, she said, "It's simple, Jane. She has them. I want them. Just tell me what it'll cost."

"By 'she,' I assume you mean—"

"That bi—"

"—Madison." Liddy needed to expand her vocabulary.

She said, "You know about that yucky thing she let them do to my brother, right?"

Everyone who watched *The Romano Files* last Monday knew how Liddy felt about the autopsy. *They chopped Larry up into little pieces!*

I said, "I'm afraid that had to be done for legal reasons, Liddy."

She recoiled. "Since when is there a law that says you have to dissolve someone's body in acid?"

"Oh. I thought you meant… To be clear, alkaline hydrolysis has nothing to do with acid."

Her tone couldn't have been more patronizing. "I don't know what movies *you've* been watching, but trust me, they always use acid."

I tossed the last of my tequila down my gullet. "Anyway, I happen to know Larry himself made that decision, so if you're unhappy about it—"

"Oh, I don't care about that." She flapped her hand. "I mean, it's yucky, but what are you gonna do? You've got to get rid of bodies *somehow*."

Said the sister who had objected strenuously to a postmortem intended to explain her brother's sudden death. Then again, this was Liddy Kool. Who could say how her mind worked?

I said, "So this is about the pulverized remains, or ashes if you will. I'm assuming they were given to Madison."

"Yeah, they were," Liddy said. "Any normal person would just put them in a whatchamacallit, an urn. Maybe stick it on the mantel or whatever. But not Madison, oh no. That weirdo says she's going to plant a *tree* on top of them. Like my brother's only good for *fertilizer*. Have you ever heard of anything so… so *disrespectful?*"

I thought but did not say, *Oh, honey, you cannot begin to imagine the things some of my clients have done with cremated remains.* Nor did I mention that when my friend and former employer Irene McAuliffe died a year and a half ago, I planted a pink dogwood, her favorite tree, in my backyard in her memory, and yes, her ashes are helping to nourish that young tree.

Instead I said, "That's actually not at all uncommon, Liddy. Many people find it a meaningful way to commemorate a loved one's passing."

"Well, I don't, and I'm his sister. So here's what you're going to do."

"Liddy—"

"You're going to rescue Larry's ashes from that money-grubbing bi—"

"Nope." I raised my palms. "You're talking about theft, which in case you don't know, happens to be illegal."

"Not if you replace his ashes with, like, fireplace ashes. She'll never know."

"Okay, still illegal, and I don't break the law for my clients," I said. "Period."

Now, I know what you're thinking. What about those legal*ish* assignments I mentioned earlier? I'm not going to pretend there weren't a few, shall we say, borderline jobs over the years. But I think you'll agree there's nothing borderline about swiping a dead man's remains from his grieving widow.

I said, "Have you considered asking Madison for, say, half of the ashes? Perhaps she'd be willing to share—"

"Oh sure," she sneered, "like that greedy bitch wouldn't

try to cheat me out of my portion by giving me, I don't know…"

Fireplace ashes? "Well, my answer is final, Liddy. This is between you and your sister-in-law."

"I want those ashes!" Liddy snapped. "All of them. I have a right. You're the Death Diva. You're supposed to do stuff like this."

"I don't know who you've been talking to, Liddy." I stood and grabbed my purse. "But the Death Diva does *not* do stuff like this."

She snatched up her leopard-print Dolce & Gabbana (yeah, right) handbag and stomped off, hollering, "Some Death Diva you are! I'm going to sue you for… for malpractice." As she slammed through the doorway, she collided with a teenage boy just entering the pub, screeching at him to watch where he was going.

By now the crowd had thinned out a bit. I crossed the room and collapsed onto a barstool while Martin closed out a customer's tab. When he was finished, he reached into the magical cabinet again and waved my bottle of tequila at me.

"No, thanks," I muttered. "Driving."

He shoved a bowl of honey-mustard pretzels in front of me, along with a glass of club soda. "If your little meeting had gone on any longer, I was going to give you an 'emergency' phone call so you could run far, far away. Liddy didn't seem too happy on her way out."

I leaned across the bar and whispered, "She wanted me to steal Larry's ashes."

"That is actually not the nuttiest thing I imagined her asking you to do. So no mention of the M word?"

"Murder?" I shook my head. "Nope, and I sure as heck

wasn't about to bring it up."

He looked behind me. "You need something, son?"

I turned to see the youth who'd had the bad fortune to be entering the pub while Liddy was exiting. He was tall, close to six feet, with brown eyes, wavy blond hair, and a nice summer tan, casually dressed in T-shirt and shorts.

The boy looked grim. "I'm not your son."

"Whew! That's a relief." When the kid didn't return his smile, Martin said, "I hope you're not planning to make me card you. I don't care how good you think your fake ID is, we both know you won't be twenty-one for another four years or so."

In response, the boy tossed his license onto the bar. I could see it was a learner's permit. Martin examined it briefly and handed it back. "Make that five years, Nathaniel. I can't give you anything stronger than a Coke. Are you meeting someone here?"

"No one calls me Nathaniel. It's Nate." He shoved the card in Martin's face. Still no smile. "Robbins."

I was getting a bad feeling about this.

"Listen, son—uh, Nate," Martin said, "if I'm supposed to know who you are, I mean, if we've met before or something, then I apologize. Care to clue me in?"

"Oh, you have plenty to apologize for," Nate said. "The way you treated my mom for starters."

I watched Martin go on high alert, but Nate had already denied being his son. "Who's your mom?"

"Claudia McAuliffe Robbins," Nate said. "Your sister."

8

In Which Jane Has S'more Questions

"WE NEED A national holiday," Louise said, "to celebrate the genius who invented this."

"You'll have to be more specific." I nudged the charred and half-melted marshmallow off my skewer onto a graham cracker, slapped a square of milk chocolate onto it, and topped it with another cracker. "Are you referring to the s'mores or the firepit?"

The droll look she gave me said we both knew the answer to that one. As she impaled another marshmallow and positioned her skewer over the flames, she said, "You've got to figure firepits have been around in some form for a couple of million years, since early humans first harnessed fire. Good luck singling out the first caveman—more likely cave*woman*—who came up with that."

"Weren't s'mores invented by the Girl Scouts?" I took a big bite of my gooey dessert sandwich and made the appropriate yummy noises.

She nodded. "About a hundred years back. You just know it was some enterprising Brownie who put it all together, but of course, the whole Girl Scout organization gets credit."

"Well, that Brownie absolutely does deserve a national

holiday," I said, over a mouthful of s'more.

"With a parade."

"Well, duh."

It was a balmy Saturday night, close to ten p.m. and fully dark. No moon, just a dusting of starlight. We were in the backyard of the ridiculously huge property I (well, really Sexy Beast) had inherited from Irene McAuliffe, sitting under a cedar pergola illuminated by rows of string lights. The freeform patio under our feet and the wood-burning firepit at its center were crafted of pale fieldstone, as were the pair of semicircular benches with backrests that surrounded the firepit. A couple of dozen thick cushions patterned in muted oranges and grays turned the space into a comfy outdoor living room.

I'd called Doc Holliday that morning and invited her over for dinner. Not trusting my questionable cooking skills, I'd ordered our meal from a local Mediterranean restaurant: an appetizer assortment of falafel, stuffed grape leaves, baba ghanoush, and spinach pie, followed by lamb kebabs with rice pilaf and grilled veggies.

We'd eaten our dinner on the large redwood deck that abutted the back of the house and spanned its length. The deck had a dining area at one end, cushioned rattan seating with umbrellas at the other end, and an abundance of planters and railing boxes overflowing with multihued flowers.

The teak dining table and chairs sat in the shade of a big, beautiful oak tree, which had already been big and beautiful when the house was built nearly fifty years ago. After Irene had inherited the property from her late husband, Arthur McAuliffe, and decided the place needed a deck, she'd simply had it built around the tree. A small set of stairs and a stone pathway led from the deck to the patio where we now lingered over our dessert.

And yes, somehow we still had room for s'mores after all that delicious food. While we're handing out parades, let's not forget the brainiac who came up with elastic waistbands.

The smell of woodsmoke competed with the perfume of fresh-cut grass and late-flowering honeysuckle. Crickets and katydids provided nature's white noise, interrupted by occasional rustles in the shrubbery as something small hunted something smaller.

Sexy Beast and Luci, Louise's Jack Russell terrier, lay curled up together on a cushion between their two humans, having exhausted themselves doing zoomies in the gargantuan, tree-studded yard. The six-foot-tall stone wall surrounding the entire back portion of the property meant we could let them run free. We'd given the dogs a few nibbles from our dinner, but they'd soon discovered that the s'mores were reserved for alpha females only.

I tapped my chin. "You have some marshmallow on, um…"

Louise reached for a napkin as Luci lifted her head, her dark little eyes locked on the sticky goo. The dog licked her lips. "Don't even think about it," Louise warned her.

"You have to admit," I said, "Luci's tongue would do a more efficient job. And you know what they say. A dog's mouth is cleaner than a human's."

"'They' are wrong, as usual. Did I get it all?"

I appraised the job she'd done with the napkin and offered a thumbs-up. Though on the short side, Louise was fit and always took care with her appearance. That evening she wore a teal silk tunic, slim white ankle pants, strappy sandals, and a chunky gold necklace. The only thing that gave away her fifty-something years was her silver hair, which she wore in thick goddess cornrows that culminated in a braided bun at her nape. Her hair and eyeglasses glinted in the warm glow of the firelight and overhead string lights.

I'd invited Louise over for the express purpose of picking her brain about Larry's sudden and shocking demise. The evening was winding down and I had yet to broach the subject. In truth, I was a little embarrassed by my suspicions, and wary of looking like a fool in front of someone I respected.

Also, I was finding it difficult to focus. My mind kept detouring to that scene at Murray's Pub the previous night when Martin's nephew, Nate Robbins, had confronted him.

Did I really want to know what Nate meant by his accusation regarding Martin's treatment of the boy's mother? It was just vague enough to send my imagination into overdrive. The little I knew about Martin's family background brought up more questions than answers.

Nate's mother, Claudia, was Martin's older half sister, the legitimate daughter of Irene's stepson Hugh McAuliffe and his wife, Diane. Four decades ago, Hugh had had an extramarital affair with an exotic dancer named Stevie Borden, and nine months later, Martin was born—which makes him Irene's step-grandson if you're, you know, drawing a family tree.

Not only did Hugh, as ruthless as he was wealthy, ignore his out-of-wedlock son and keep the boy's existence a secret from his family, but he used his financial resources and legal muscle to smear Stevie's name and avoid any paternal responsibility.

Nate hadn't lingered after lobbing his verbal grenade, and Martin and I had yet to find a private moment to discuss it. I couldn't say whether I was looking forward to that conversation or dreading it. Probably a little of both.

Louise set aside her napkin, leaned back against the cushions, and gave me a no-nonsense look that told me I was about to come clean whether I wanted to or not. "Okay, what's up, Jane?" she said.

I opened my mouth to deny that anything at all was up, only to sigh in defeat and mumble, "Am I that transparent?"

"If you're sick and this is your way of breaking the news, I have to warn you, your medical insurance does not cover lamb kebabs and rice pilaf."

Sexy Beast seemed to detect my discomfort. He abandoned Luci to crawl onto my lap and lean up against me for a soothing doggie hug.

"Okay," I said, "it's just… I don't know where to start. It's about Larry."

"You want to know whether his heart gave out on its own, or did someone give it a little nudge in that direction."

My jaw sagged. "How did you know?"

"Because I've been wondering the same thing, of course." Luci had rolled over to present her plump belly for rubs, and Louise complied. "And since you ask, yes, you are that transparent."

"I had no idea you were having the same… misgivings," I said. "I mean, no one else seems to think there was anything strange about his death."

"No one else was his personal physician for the past seventeen years. He didn't have the usual risk factors for sudden cardiac arrest. It just doesn't make sense."

"Can't it sometimes just happen, though," I asked, "with no real explanation?"

"Yes," she said, "but I'm all about the science. When a

patient of mine suddenly drops dead, I like to know why."

"Has that ever happened to you before? You know, that you had unanswered questions about a patient's death?"

"Never." She scowled. "And it turns out I don't like it one little bit."

"Well, let me ask you this." I reached across SB to lift the iron poker and revive the flames in the firepit. "Do you think some sort of poison might've been involved?"

She exhaled deeply and stared into the inky darkness beyond the patio. "That's the question that's been keeping me awake nights."

"Kind of a relief to know I'm not the only one who's been losing sleep over this," I said. "I assume you've spoken with the medical examiner?"

"Of course. Magda performed the postmortem just a few hours after Larry died. We talked beforehand, and again the next morning."

"Toxicology tests are standard, right?"

Louise nodded. "The basic tox screen mainly tests for drugs of abuse—opiates, weed, alcohol, that sort of thing."

"Correct me if I'm wrong," I said, "but no way was Larry into recreational drugs. And I've never known him to be a heavy drinker."

She shrugged. "He used to enjoy the occasional social drink, like most of us, but after his marriage to Madison, he barely touched a drop. And you're not wrong about the drugs. He was never into any of that."

"I can tell you he had scopolamine in his system the day he died," I said. "He was feeling sick to his stomach and didn't want to hurl onstage."

"Yeah, I saw that patch behind his ear," Louise said. "Larry used to get seasick, but Madison wanted to go on an Alaska cruise last year, so I prescribed scopolamine patches to prevent nausea."

"So tell me. Did Magda find any suspicious substances in his system?"

She waved away the question. "It's not like on those TV crime shows, Jane. Forensic toxicology is much more complicated and time-consuming in real life. There are literally thousands of drugs out there, and you have to know which one you're looking for."

I growled in frustration and jammed three marshmallows onto my skewer. "Well, it's too late now. Larry's already been liquidated."

Louise blinked at me over her glasses. "Excuse me?"

I explained aquamation. Happily, this woman of science did not need to be told the difference between acid and alkaline. "So that's it," I said. "There's nothing left to test."

"Not so fast," Louise said. "When I spoke with Magda before the autopsy, I shared my doubts about manner of death. She promised to take plenty of tissue and fluid samples for the county's forensic toxicology lab. They'll do more sophisticated testing there, using liquid chromatography with tandem mass spectrometry."

"Oh yeah, thank goodness for liquid chroma-whatsit and that tandem, um…" *Don't say bicycle!* "But didn't you say they need to know what they're looking for? I'm assuming you don't have a particular toxin in mind."

"You assume correctly. It could be any number of things— *if* he was even poisoned. I discussed his symptoms with Magda, and she said she'd share the info with the lab. That's the best we can do."

"So how long until they have results?" I asked.

"It can take several weeks. Usually a month or more." Correctly anticipating my reaction, she raised her palm and added, "I asked Magda to put a rush on it. I'm not ashamed to say I used Larry's celebrity status to nudge him closer to the top of the list."

"Why, Doc Holliday, I'm surprised at you," I teased. "Employing such unscrupulous Hollywood tactics."

"Yeah, that's me," she said, dryly. "I am *so* Hollywood. I would only have done it for Larry. But don't expect miracles. Magda seemed unimpressed by the whole celebrity thing. She has this crazy idea that all her deceased patients are entitled to equal treatment."

"Pretty radical," I said.

"But she likes me," Louise said, "so maybe she'll hurry it along as a personal favor."

Sexy Beast yawned, leapt from my lap onto the patio, and stretched luxuriantly. Luci joined him, and together they sprinted off into the dark, barking at some unseen critter scrabbling along the stone wall. I didn't want to know what they'd do if they actually caught something. Somehow I couldn't picture my pampered little lapdog sinking his fangs into some hapless bunny's jugular. I told myself the doggos simply enjoyed the chase.

I said, "I keep thinking about all that stuff Larry ate right before he died. He sampled chili and side dishes from every booth."

"And it was all right there in his stomach contents, according to Magda," Louise said. "And nothing there that didn't belong. But of course, the lab will have the final say. Are you thinking one of the cook-off contestants might've adulterated his food?"

"It would've been easy enough," I said. "They all had ample opportunity, and I have to tell you… well, maybe I shouldn't."

"Oh, you have got to be kidding me." She made a beckoning gesture. "Spill."

I exhaled forcefully. "Well, it's just that there were a couple of contestants who were less than pleased with Larry."

"Who?"

I hesitated, but after all, Louise and I were in this together. And I already knew the doc was no gossipmonger. "Just between us?"

She crossed her arms. "Ask me that again and see what happens."

"Okay, well, Nina Wallace was clearly disgruntled. Seems that for some time she'd been trying to—"

"Do the dirty with Larry. Not exactly breaking news."

"And then there's Frank Martinez," I said.

"He works at the cemetery, right?" she said.

I nodded. "The administrator. He's really upset that he never won the cook-off, thinks there's some kind of conspiracy or something and that Larry was behind it."

"Well, I tried almost all the chilies that day," Louise said, "and in my humble opinion, the judges got it right. Sounds to me like Frank needs to get another hobby."

"And get this," I said. "Kyle Kenneally actually tried to bribe me to use my influence with Larry."

"You mean that miserable letch who owns The Harbor Room?" She made a face. "I stopped going there. Just setting eyes on that fool was enough to put me off my feed. And that was *before* he grew that ridiculous beard."

"Here's the thing that doesn't make sense to me, though. Why would an angry contestant poison Larry *before* finding out whether they'd won? You'd think they'd wait until after they lost to take their revenge. After all, if there's even a chance you'll be taking home that trophy—" I executed an elaborate shrug "—where's your motive to off a judge?"

"Unless," Louise said, "the poisoner was certain from the get-go that the odds were unfairly stacked against him and that he had no hope of winning. Then it's a kind of preemptive revenge for what you know is about to happen."

I thought about Frank. He'd seemed to know he wasn't going to win, even before handing Larry his little bowl of chili.

"As much as I loathe Kyle," I said, "I'd have to take him out of the running since he fully expected to win—through out-and-out bribery, but still. *Dang!*" I was so distracted by our conversation, I'd let my marshmallows melt off the skewer. I watched the gooey stuff metamorphose into bubbling black lava in the flames. Smelled pretty good, though.

"From what I understand," she said, "Nina had been running after Larry for a couple of months at least."

"Without success," I said. "And this is a woman who does not take well to losing. So yeah, she could've gone to that cook-off with every intention of getting even with the man who'd rejected her."

I asked myself if this coldblooded behavior was consistent with the Nina Wallace I'd known for years. Based on my previous experiences with her, I had to admit that yeah, I could see her slipping a little something into Larry's portion of the chicken and white bean chili she'd made. Thinking back, however, I recalled that he'd eaten only one bite and ditched the rest.

Louise said, "So at least a couple of the contestants had it in for Larry. That would have to be one fast-acting poison to kill him so soon after he ingested it."

"But don't forget, he was feeling lousy before he sampled any of those chilies. You and I both noticed it."

She nodded. "For sure he put that scopolamine patch on before he left the house. That's not the kind of thing you carry around in your pocket. Who knows how long he was feeling sick?"

"Probably only a day or so. He said he had one of those twenty-four-hour bugs. Either that or food poisoning."

"And maybe he did," she said. "But if something more sinister was causing his nausea, then he would've been better off getting it out of his system. In that case, antinausea medication would have been the last thing he needed."

9

Warts and All

MARTIN LOOKED UP from the plate Cheyenne O'Rourke had just plunked in front of him. "I ordered the black bean and beet burger, Cheyenne."

"Nah, you asked for this thing." She didn't even try to hide her disgust as she gazed upon the thing in question, which I recognized as a tofu scramble wrap, something the padre wouldn't order if you said to him, *Hey, Padre, here's a check for a million bucks with your name on it if you order and consume one tofu scramble wrap.*

Needless to say, Martin, being an unrepentant omnivore, was not the target demographic for Janey's Place, the chain of vegetarian cafés Dom owned. It was only as a last resort that he'd ordered the veggie burger, and only because it had *burger* in the name and he was hungry. I suspect part of him was praying the ground legumes and beets would magically morph into USDA prime on its way from the grill to his mouth.

It was Sunday afternoon, and I'd dragged Martin to Janey's Place because I'd been jonesing for the only thing I ever ordered there: a delicious, creamy papaya-ginger smoothie. I was dreading the day when the Health Food Police would break down the door and arrest Dom for selling milk shakes and claiming they were good for you.

It was the lull between the lunch rush and dinner, and most of the café's customers tended to order takeout, so we were the only ones seated at the moment. A handful of tables, blond wood and chrome, occupied the space in front of the big picture windows overlooking Main Street. We'd chosen my favorite spot in the place, a quiet, sun-drenched corner away from the food-service counter.

"Cheyenne," I said, "I heard him. He ordered the burger."

She turned her flat stare on me, and I came this close to waving my hand in front of her eyes and asking if anyone was home.

Cheyenne was a nineteen-year-old slacker who'd nevertheless managed to hold down a job at the Janey's Place flagship store on Main Street for more than a year. Her dad, Patrick, was the manager, which explains why she'd been hired, but even he had become so fed up with her laziness and incompetence that he'd tried on several occasions to fire her.

My ex-husband, however, being the nicest guy in the world, believes in giving one more chance. And then one more, and maybe a few more after that. Suffice it to say, there were times when I wished Dom were a little less nice.

Today Cheyenne had paired her apple-green Janey's Place T-shirt—knotted high on her doughy midriff as usual—with white leggings patterned with purple cartoon dragons. Glittery red platform sandals made the eye-catching getup just that much more special.

"Also," I told her, "I've been waiting twenty minutes for my papaya-ginger smoothie. Maybe you could bring it out with Martin's burger."

"Yeah, whatev." She tossed back her lank, highlighted hair,

the better to display her three amateur tattoos. The names *Brian* and *Sean*, inked on the sides of her neck, had been defaced with tattooed *X*'s to denote the gentlemen's status as former paramours, while *Neal* had pride of place on the front of her neck. Which meant that either she and Neal were still an item three months after I'd first spotted that tat, or she had yet to X out that particular ex.

Cheyenne began clopping away on her high platform sandals. I said, "Aren't you forgetting something?" and handed her the plate with the tofu wrap while she rolled her eyes.

Nina Wallace entered the café with her eldest daughter, Julia, who was about to start her junior year at Crystal Harbor High. Nina acknowledged us with a perfunctory finger flutter before choosing the table farthest from ours. Which, unfortunately, wasn't far enough away to keep us from overhearing their conversation, if it could even be called that. Julia never once looked up from her phone as her mother launched into a tiresome diatribe about disappointing grades, an abysmal PSAT score, and the looming shame of community college.

"How will I ever be able to face Gloria Faber?" Nina fretted. "Her Brittany was accepted early decision to Northwestern."

Martin leaned forward. Quietly he said, "You know I'm never getting my burger, right?"

"Well, I really want that shake, I mean smoothie," I said, "so let's just give it a few more minutes."

"Okay, but then we're heading over to that new barbecue joint for some brisket and ribs."

"Sold. So listen." I, too, kept my volume down. Nina might not mind sharing family drama, but I certainly did.

"About your nephew."

"We don't need to talk about—"

"Yes, we do, Padre," I said. "There's a reason that kid came looking for you."

"Yeah, so he could tell me what a sleazebag I am and then vamoose without waiting for a response."

"What would your response have been?"

His pale-blue gaze drifted toward the window. Traffic on Main Street was light. Sunday shoppers ambled past on the sidewalk. He leaned back in his chair. "I never mistreated his mother, Jane. Claudia and I have nothing to do with each other. We never have. We're strangers."

"You met your half sister just once that I know of," I said. Martin had told me that when he was a troubled teenager—what used to be called a juvenile delinquent—he'd broken into his father's home in the middle of the night, just to mess with him. Never having met Hugh before, he'd had to identify himself as the man's bastard son. Which he'd done in front of Hugh's wife and daughter.

His father's response had been to threaten him with a shotgun. Claudia had been home from Harvard at the time, and it was she who'd persuaded Hugh not to call the cops or, you know, kill her half brother.

"That's the only time I ever laid eyes on Claudia,'" Martin said. "She didn't say one word to me."

"From what you told me, it sounds like she had her hands full that night trying to keep you alive and out of jail."

"Well, she's had more than a quarter century since then to get in touch," he said.

"So have you."

"Why would I?" He folded his arms over his chest. "No

one in her family has any use for me."

"Until now."

"What, you mean the kid?"

"Your *nephew*," I said. "Have you thought about how hard it must've been for Nate to seek you out like that?"

Martin barked a mirthless laugh. "To ambush me at my place of work, you mean. Maybe you didn't notice, but he wasn't exactly looking for a heartfelt family reunion."

"Weren't you about that age," I asked, "when you pulled that stunt at your dad's house?"

"So?"

"*So,*" I said, "are you going to sit there and tell me you don't recognize yourself in Nate? Not even a little bit?"

The padre sighed. He didn't try to deny it. Finally he said, "Find me a kid that age who isn't angry about something."

"You have good reason to resent your father," I said. "Your mom told you how despicably he behaved toward her, how he refused to contribute to your support or even acknowledge you."

"Your point?"

"That kind of thing goes both ways," I said. "You've got to figure Hugh's family got an earful from him about you and your mom. He would've cast you two in the worst possible light."

"Only after I showed up uninvited," he said. "Until then, I was this big, shameful secret."

"Except you told me Hugh's parents had already found out about you. By accident. That happened when you were about eleven, right?"

His expression softened. "I've often asked myself how two such loving people could've raised a man like Hugh McAuliffe."

I knew that Martin's paternal grandparents, Arthur and Anne, had died when he was still in his teens. But during the few short years they'd had together, they'd been very close.

"Why was it only your grandparents who knew about you?" I asked. "Where was the rest of the family?"

"Hugh made his folks promise not to tell his wife and daughter," he said. "For the sake of his marriage, supposedly. Grandma and Grandpa hated keeping me a secret, but they respected his wishes."

"But you had other plans." In the form of a middle-of-the-night break-in. "That must've been a shocking way for Claudia to find out she had a half brother, and Diane to discover her husband had fathered another child during their marriage."

"So what you're saying is, once they knew about me, Hugh poisoned their minds against me and Mom. You think I didn't figure that out a long time ago?"

"It wouldn't have taken much convincing," I said. "I mean, you did break in to their home, Padre."

"By that point I'd already learned how to tell when only the doors were connected to the alarm system. That window in his home office was just begging for a skinny sixteen-year-old to shimmy through it."

"You're only reinforcing my point," I said. "You made it all too easy for Hugh to paint you as this dangerous criminal. And to ask what kind of mother would raise a kid who excels at breaking and entering at such a tender age."

Martin looked at me.

"Stop it," I said. "You know I adore Stevie. She raised you just fine. All that nonsense you got up to when you were young, that's on you, not her."

"Damn right."

I already knew that Martin had turned his life around after his daughter, Lexie, was born. He'd used a modest inheritance from his grandfather to earn a degree from John Jay College of Criminal Justice. When he wasn't bartending, he was taking freelance gigs as a private investigator and executive protection specialist (a fancier way of saying bodyguard).

I leaned across the table. "Who knows what lies Hugh told Claudia and Nate about you? If it was me, I'd be trying to set the record straight."

At the only other occupied table, Nina had finally given up trying to politely signal Cheyenne to come take their order. Of course, she could have gotten up and ordered at the counter, where Cheyenne was busy texting on her phone. Instead Nina hollered, "Excuse me, young lady! We're still waiting over here. *Hello?*"

Only then did Julia look up from her screen, mortified. She stage-whispered *"Mom!"*

"Oh, don't you 'Mom' me," Nina said. "You have to learn to speak up for yourself in this world, Julia, or everyone will just walk right over you. *Young lady!*" Nina screeched, as her daughter slid down in her seat, trying to make herself invisible. *"We are ready to order!"*

Cheyenne texted for another minute, then clopped over to their table and stood there digging around in her ear. "What?"

Nina invited her daughter to order first.

"I'll have the vegan Cobb salad," Julia said. "Butter lettuce instead of romaine, pumpkin seeds instead of sunflower seeds, cannellini beans instead of chickpeas, quinoa instead of brown rice, make sure the grilled asparagus is super skinny with no tough parts, make sure the roasted beets are cut in slices, not chunks, extra avocado, hold the green beans, hold the tomatoes, and chipotle-lime vinaigrette on the side instead of champagne vinaigrette. No, you know what? Give me lemon-basil vinaigrette and mix it in, but only a little so there's just the thinnest coating on the greens."

Cheyenne waited out this recitation with the patience of a saint—a vacuous, apathetic saint with a history of poor decision making. She did not write anything down. Nina ordered the Thai coconut vegetable curry. Cheyenne returned to the food-service counter and picked up her phone.

Martin returned his attention to our discussion. "So, what exactly would you have me do about Nate?"

That was the big question. "I don't know, it just seems… My gut tells me he's hurting. Like something in his life is out of whack."

"That famous gut of yours." He gave me a teasing half smile. "Not to belabor the point, but again, the kid's sixteen. He's still figuring things out. The transition to adulthood is messy. It sure as hell was for me."

"Do you know anything about his family situation?"

He shook his head. "And that's the way I intend to keep it. After I walked out of Hugh's house that night, I washed my hands of all of them."

"But you're an investigator, Padre." And a darn good one, which I'd learned the hard way, having been the object of his snooping back when he knew me only as Irene McAuliffe's hired lackey. "You're telling me you were never tempted to do a little digging?"

"Never."

"Well, I think the whole thing's really sad. Especially with your first grandchild about to arrive." Martin's daughter, Lexie, and her husband, Dillon, had chosen to go the old-fashioned route and wait until the birth to learn whether they were having a boy or a girl. The baby was due in a few weeks.

The padre and Lexie's mother had been seventeen-year-old friends with benefits when their daughter was born. Despite his youth, he'd been an involved father from day one and never shirked his financial responsibility. The polar opposite of his own father.

I said, "Lexie has never met her aunt Claudia or her cousin, Nate. Who knows? There might be more cousins we know nothing about. Now, with your grandchild on the way, well, you could look at it as a fresh start."

"I know you mean well, Jane." Martin reached across the table and squeezed my hand. "But I'm asking you to let this go."

After a moment I nodded. He knew how I felt. It would have to be enough.

He said, "You haven't told me how it went with Doc Holliday last night."

My mood did an abrupt one-eighty. I sat up straight. "Turns out—" I glanced at Nina and reduced my volume to a whisper. "Turns out Louise has been having the same suspicions. Thinks it might've been poison."

His eyes widened. "Really?"

"That doesn't mean it was," I said. "It's just, you know, something that's got to be checked out. We'll know more in a few weeks, maybe sooner. Louise is trying to light a fire under the forensic lab techs."

The door opened and Rex Noble sauntered into the café. He appeared so jarringly out of place I almost didn't recognize him at first.

He whipped off his sunglasses, looked around, and gave us

a huge grin. He pointed as if aiming a gun. "Jane, right? And Marvin."

"Martin." The men shook hands, and Rex gave me a peck on the cheek.

The padre pulled another chair up to our table and invited him to sit. "I don't know what brings you here, man, but I've got to warn you, the service today is…" He wagged his hand.

"I already ate." Rex set his leather attaché case next to his chair. "Just came from Larry's house—well, it's Madison's house now. We had vegetarian fajitas. They were pretty good."

"Dom should've been there," I said. "My ex. He loves veggie fajitas. It's one of his specialties."

"If you're talking about Dom Faso," Rex said, "that's who made them for us. Nice guy. You two were married?"

I nodded. "Back in the Stone Age. What was he doing at Madison's?" The instant the words escaped my mouth, I wished I could take them back. I felt my face heat. "Not that it matters, I'm just, you know, curious."

"He went over there to change a couple of ceiling light bulbs for Madison," he said. "She has a thing about heights. Hates getting up on a ladder."

"Oh, that was nice of him." What I refrained from saying out loud was, *What's Dom doing hanging out with Larry's widow? The two of them barely know each other.*

Of course, it was none of my business, and since I never butt in with stuff that's none of my business, I didn't give it another thought.

Oh, please, you think you know me so well?

Okay, so maybe I gave it one or two more thoughts, and maybe one of those thoughts was to wonder how the heck Dom had gotten so friendly with Madison Kool over the past few days, friendly enough to change her light bulbs and whip up veggie fajitas in her kitchen. Didn't she have a handyman for stuff like that? The ladder thing, not the fajitas.

Thought number two: Which one of them initiated this sudden friendship, my ex-husband or the Widow Kool?

Happy now?

Rex said, "As to what *I* was doing over there, it has to do with a new project of mine. I've been conducting video interviews with some of the townspeople here in Crystal Harbor."

"What for?" Martin asked.

"I'm planning to pitch a documentary to Netflix about Larry's life," he said. "His early years, his multifaceted career, his relationships, everything. The *real* Larry Kool, warts and all. At this point I'm just gathering some footage to show the right people, generate some buzz."

"Let me guess," Martin said. "This documentary would be hosted by Larry's onetime costar, Rex Noble."

"Who better?" Rex winked. "I've already talked to a bunch of his friends and relatives, plus anyone I can track down who used to work with him. You know Larry was the spokesman for KrunchWorks snack foods, right? Well, I found out this old guy named Norman Butterwick owns the company."

I assured Rex we were well acquainted with Norman.

"We chatted this morning," he said. "Quite the character, that Norman. Short-term memory's shot to hell, unfortunately, so I doubt we can use him. He didn't even remember that Larry died, and he was right there when it happened."

"Is that what you were doing at Madison's?" I asked. "Interviewing her for your documentary?"

He nodded. "Dom, too. He didn't know Larry that well,

but he knows this town. He's the one who suggested I swing by here, scout the place out. He said Janey's Place is a kind of neighborhood gathering spot and an ideal location for impromptu interviews. Cute place," he said, taking in his surroundings. "At the very least, we can shoot some B-roll here."

Dom was, first and foremost, a businessman. I knew how his mind worked. If this documentary actually got made, and if it included shots of the Janey's Place flagship store, that could only help drive business to all thirty-four locations in the Northeast.

Rex produced his phone and tapped the camera icon. "You two knew Larry pretty well, right?"

"Um, yeah," I said, "but—"

"Who wants to go first? You know what? Scratch that. It'll be more fun to interview you both at the same time." He reached into his attaché and withdrew two sheets of paper and two pens, which he placed in front of us. "These are standard release forms. You're just consenting to appear in the video. Entirely routine."

I glanced briefly at the form. By signing it, I'd be allowing Rex to use the video "for any lawful purpose," waiving all my rights and releasing him from all liability.

I looked at Martin. He looked at me. We came to an unspoken agreement.

"I have to be honest with you," I said. "I'm not really comfortable signing that. Or even, you know, being interviewed on video."

Rex appeared taken aback.

Martin said, "No offense, man. The documentary sounds terrific and we wish you luck getting it off the ground, but at this point we'd rather not be involved."

"Well, that's a shame." Rex failed to mask his irritation. "All your friends and neighbors have been very enthusiastic. How can I put your minds at ease? You know what?" He made a show of slipping his phone back into his pocket. "No video for now. Let's just chat and get better acquaint—"

"Excuse me!" Nina trilled, this time addressing Rex, not Cheyenne. Like us, she and her daughter had abandoned any hope of getting served. She wore her most coquettish smile. "You're Rex Noble, aren't you?"

"Guilty as charged." He returned her grin, preening under the attention. "And who might you be, lovely lady?"

"Nina Hannigan Wallace." She approached our table. "I'm president of the Crystal Harbor Historical Society. My family's lived in this town for five generations. Isn't that right, Julia?"

No response. Nina's daughter remained glued to her phone. The girl had probably never watched an episode of *Chase & Knabbe*, and wouldn't have been impressed if she had. How could some old TV actor compete with the allure of the hottest social media influencers?

"Five generations? Wow." Rex gave Nina a playful wink. "Didn't know I was in the presence of Crystal Harbor royalty."

It took all my willpower not to roll my eyes at this exchange. In case you were wondering, or even if you weren't: Larry Kool's family settled here in the late eighteenth century, more than a hundred years before Nina's great-grandpa, the Prohibition-era gangster Hank "Hokum" Hannigan, decided that our charming waterfront burg was the ideal location from which to launch his criminal activities.

Said activities included, but were not limited to, bootlegging, rum-running, operating gambling dens and brothels, and being an all-around scary dude. Nina was so inexplicably proud of her infamous relative that she'd turned the basement of the Crystal Harbor Historical Society into a Prohibition museum for the express purpose of displaying Hokum's gangsterly memorabilia.

Larry's Crystal Harbor ancestors had been sadly boring in comparison, a respectable assortment of farmers, merchants, and pastors. No one had created a museum in their honor.

Nina said, "I didn't mean to eavesdrop on your conversation, Rex, but did I hear you say you're making a documentary about Larry Kool?"

Nina claiming she didn't mean to eavesdrop on your conversation was like a lioness claiming she didn't mean to take down your gazelle. It's what she does.

"That's the plan," he said, "if the stars are aligned. Did you know Larry?"

"Did I know Larry! No one in this town knew him better." She gave him a significant look. "And I mean *no one,* if you catch my drift."

Oh, brother. Martin and I shared another silent communication. We rose as one, and Martin offered Nina his chair.

"Unfortunately," he said, "we have to get going."

I said, "It was great seeing you again, Rex. Good luck getting your documentary made."

Warts and all, huh? Why did I have the feeling it would be warts and little else?

10

Killin' It

MADISON STIRRED A spoonful of raw, unfiltered honey into her hibiscus tea. "I guess I just don't understand what the holdup is."

"I know it's frustrating, but this kind of delay is fairly routine," I lied.

We were in her living room, which occupied one large corner of the ancestral home she'd inherited from Larry, a home that had existed in that spot for well over two hundred years. It was late morning, and the early-autumn weather was glorious, following an overnight thunderstorm. Sunlight streamed in through massive, multipaned windows set into the pale-taupe walls and high, slanted ceiling, as well as the two sets of wide French doors.

Madison and I sat facing each other on matching sofas upholstered in striped sage-green and cream linen. A vintage Isamu Noguchi coffee table from the 1940s sat between them, a functional work of art with its sculptural wooden base and gently rounded triangular glass top. Several antique Scandinavian rugs lay scattered as if by happy accident across the original wide pine plank floor. Fresh-cut flowers in an assortment of vases adorned the tables and fireplace mantel, perfuming the air.

The room was a pleasing mash-up of the old and the new, thanks to Madison's keen eye. Before she'd moved in four years earlier, the decorating style in this old house could best be described as Early Benign Neglect. It wasn't that Larry hadn't cared what the place looked like, he'd simply become used to it. Plus he was, you know, a guy.

She set her pottery mug on a coaster. "Larry's been gone nearly a month, Jane. You'd think by this time the county could issue a completed death certificate."

"It'll be updated to reflect the medical examiner's final decision," I said. "Unfortunately, that sometimes takes time."

"But why? We all know he suffered cardiac failure. His own doctor said so, and she was right there with him." Emotion roughened her voice and glazed her eyes. She looked past the French doors to the beautifully landscaped backyard with it elaborate wooden gazebo, surrounded by a profusion of bird feeders and nesting boxes. Finally she cleared her throat and said, "The certificate says, 'pending further study.' Does the medical examiner really have doubts about cause of death?"

"Actually, it's the *manner* of death that's at issue." I tried not to squirm as I said, "Meaning natural or, um, unnatural."

She stared at me for a moment. "Unnatural? Such as…?"

"Such as accident," I said. "Or suicide."

"Well, we all know Larry didn't die by accident or suicide. So that leaves what?" She frowned. "Murder?"

"Well, yes, homicide would be one possibility." I tried to sound casual. "And then there are cases like Larry's where the manner of death isn't immediately apparent. Which is why the ME wrote, 'pending.'"

Madison sat back against the cushions as she absorbed the

implications. Finally she said, "Are you trying to tell me they think Larry might've been murdered?"

I waved away the absurd notion as nervous sweat gathered under my arms. "This ME, she's real persnickety. Pulls this nonsense all the time, making families wait." Another lie. I was really racking them up today.

I hadn't shared my suspicions with anyone aside from Louise and Martin, and I certainly wasn't going to burden Larry's widow with them at this point, when it was entirely possible—no, make that *probable*—that Larry had indeed died of natural causes. I only hoped the forensic tox lab would hurry up and provide an answer, preferably one that would let the ME check the box marked "natural."

"Meanwhile," she said, "the life-insurance company is refusing to release the funds."

I said, "I had the insurance company request a letter stating there was no foul play. Unfortunately, the ME's office wasn't prepared to provide that yet." Which I'd known would be the response. I was just buying time until the tox lab finished their work.

"It's not that I'm in a hurry to receive the money," she said. "I'm far from destitute. It's just one more thing hanging over my head."

"Well, I'm on top of it," I said, "so try not to give it another thought."

Madison had taken me up on my offer to help with some of the dreary chores she was facing, and working with the insurance company was one of them. Heaven knew I was an old hand at it.

She got misty-eyed again. "I can't thank you enough, Jane. It means more than you know, being able to rely on your expertise in these matters. I still wish you'd let me pay you."

"I wouldn't think of it," I said. "We're friends." We were getting there, anyway. I'd been good pals with Larry for years. Not so much with Madison, who'd entered his life relatively recently. But I could see that changing, now that I was spending more time with her.

"Well then," she said, "I'll have to put on my thinking cap and find a more creative way to thank you."

I shook my head in mock exasperation, while privately I wondered what kind of gorgeous, or delicious, thank-you gift my new friend had in mind.

Larry's memorial service had been held the previous Saturday at the Unitarian church he'd attended. A string quartet played some of his favorite classical pieces. Family and close friends delivered moving eulogies and readings. Altogether it had been a lovely and fitting celebration of his life.

"Are you sure I can't offer you anything?" she asked. "I know you're no fan of herbal teas, but I do keep some coffee beans around for guests. I could grind some and make you a cup."

"Oh no, please don't go to the bother," I said. "I've had more than enough caffeine already today."

Madison looked past me and said, "You know Jane better than I do. There must be something we can offer her."

Startled, I turned and watched my ex-husband enter the room, carrying a dessert plate and cloth napkin. "I knew you were coming, Janey, so I stopped by Patisserie Susanne on my way here." He placed a fragrant chocolate croissant in front of me. My favorite pastry in the whole wide world.

I was so flummoxed by Dom's sudden presence, it took me

a moment to recover. "Wow. Thanks, Dom. Am I allowed to eat this thing in your house, Madison? We're talking serious butter and sugar here."

She grinned and pretended to cover her eyes. "What pastry? I don't see any pastry."

Dom sat on the other sofa. Not on the other *end* of the other sofa, mind you, but right next to Madison. He placed his arm on the sofa back behind her. Just like he used to do with me.

He turned to her. "Any progress with the insurance company?"

She shook her head. "Jane's tried. It seems the medical examiner isn't ready to rule out homicide."

"What?" He appeared genuinely shocked. "That's nuts. What are they smoking over there?"

"It's just a formality," I said.

That's right, Jane, keep fibbing. Do it enough and you might even get good at it.

"You know," Madison said, "maybe it's a good thing they're, well, looking into all possibilities. I'm not saying I think anything like that happened, but it's good to know the ME's office doesn't just rubber-stamp cause of death."

Okay, it was *manner* of death, but I wasn't going to correct her again. I know it's confusing for laypeople.

Dom said, "They're just doing this because Larry was a celebrity. It makes them feel important. If he were some Joe Shmoe off the street, this thing would be wrapped up by now."

She patted his thigh. "Jane has it well in hand. There's nothing more I can do, so I'm going to spend a little extra time today meditating and try to clear my mind of all this unproductive noise."

"Good plan." His hand, the one connected to the arm on the sofa back, settled on her shoulder. "Are we still on for dinner? I thought I'd grill up some of those portobello panini you like so much."

"Dom!" She gave his thigh a playful slap. "When are you going to let *me* cook for *you* for a change?"

Yeah, I was paying close attention. So sue me. And no, it wasn't because I still secretly pined for my ex. I'm happy to report that our relationship was now one of uncomplicated friendship. Martin was the only man I loved, and he loved me right back.

The thing is, it had been three and a half weeks since Larry died. Now, don't get me wrong. I'm not one of those people who feel you have to wait a certain prescribed amount of time before getting involved with someone new.

But I mean, three and a half weeks?

And by the way, when I say *involved*, I'm not implying what you might think I'm implying. I know Dom. He's not the kind of man to take advantage of a grieving widow so soon after her husband's death. I very much doubted they'd already become lovers. But watching them, I took note of the myriad telltale signs. If they weren't serious yet, they soon would be.

And as I've mentioned, Dominic Faso had a deep aversion to being alone. He was happy only when he was in a relationship, and he hadn't been in one of those since Bonnie Hernandez dumped him back in April. As for the two of us getting hitched again, I'd long ago made it clear that wasn't going to happen. Bottom line: Dom had to be getting antsy after nearly a half year with no significant other.

I should be happy for them. I *was* happy for them. Dom and Madison seemed like an ideal match. He'd finally found someone who shared his commitment to a boring, I mean healthy lifestyle. It didn't hurt that Madison was also young, beautiful, and sophisticated.

Of course, if I were being cynical (which you know I never am), I'd bring up the fact that Dom was wealthy, which seemed to be a trait Madison appreciated. I recalled Liddy referring to her sister-in-law as a cheap gold digger. *Look in the mirror, Liddy.* And while I'm willing to admit Larry's wealth might have played a role in Madison's decision to marry him, clearly it had been a love match, as well. The two are not mutually exclusive. If she was indeed a gold digger—and the jury was still out—she was certainly a far classier one than Liddy.

And then there was the fact that Dom was a devoted father, and hadn't Madison told me how disappointed she'd been that Larry hadn't wanted children? As determined as my young groom had been to remain childless back when we tied the knot, time and three great kids had altered his perspective. Dom had embraced fatherhood in a big way and was eager to bring more little Fasos into the world. So he and Madison were compatible in that way, as well.

I couldn't help it, though. My gut told me this budding romance was a tad precipitous. But you know me. I don't butt in.

Oh, shut up.

The doorbell rang. Dom said, "Are you expecting someone?"

"No. It's probably a delivery." Madison started to rise, but Dom gently pushed her back down.

"I'll get it." He strode out of the room.

Madison and I sat in uncomfortable silence. Finally she

asked, "How's your pastry?"

"Oh, *so* good," I chirped, with more enthusiasm than even a chocolate croissant merited. "Dom really shouldn't have. I mean, the *calories*."

"He's very considerate," she said, with a polite smile. "One might even say *devoted*. To cater to your preferences even when they represent the exact opposite of his own healthy choices."

"Well, yeah, he's... a nice guy. You know?" I glanced toward the front of the house, where muted conversation could be heard, suddenly wishing the nice guy would reappear and dispel the tension that had descended like an icy fog.

"Dom told me all about your relationship," she said. "How the two of you remained close even after your marriage ended." Her expectant expression seemed to demand a response.

I sprayed croissant crumbs as I blurted, "Oh, well, sure, we've always been close. But I mean, not *that* close, you know what I mean? I mean, not since our divorce. Which was, you know, eighteen years ago—eighteen and a half, actually, but who's counting?" My chuckle came out as a piggy snort.

To be fair to Madison, the current situation had to be more than a little awkward for her. Here she was nurturing a budding relationship while at the same time becoming friendly with her new man's ex-wife. Not only that, but the ex-wife was doing her some major favors. All things considered, I had to admit she was handling it better than I would have.

Unhurried footfalls could be heard now, growing progressively louder as Dom and the mystery visitor made their gradual way toward the living room. Couldn't they walk any faster?

It might have been my imagination, but Madison's smile now looked more brittle than polite. "One thing I've learned about Dom, which I'm sure comes as no surprise to you, is how honest he is about his feelings. He still cares deeply for you."

"Well, see, that's exactly what I'm saying. I think. Wait, if you mean—"

"*Heeere's Liddy!*" a shrill female voice hollered.

That's right, the new arrival was Larry's half sister, sweeping into the room like a coquettish hurricane in high-heeled boots, skintight jeans, and a hot-pink belly shirt that proclaimed in block letters that its wearer was *KILLIN' IT*.

"Now, don't start in about how I should've called first. Life's too short for that Emily Post BS. Hey, Jane! How's it goin'?" Liddy leaned down for an air kiss. "Holy guacamole, is that a chocolate croissant? Thank God you finally gave up that health-food crap, Madison. I'll have one of *those*." She threw herself onto the sofa next to her hostess, in the exact spot Dom had just vacated.

One look at Madison's steely expression confirmed what Liddy had no doubt surmised: that if she'd called ahead, her sister-in-law would have concocted some excuse to keep her from dropping by.

Liddy seemed unaccountably thrilled to see me. Did she even remember that the last time the two of us met, she'd threatened to sue me for Death Diva malpractice?

Dom seated himself on the sofa I occupied, and surprise! I did not get the cuddly, draped-arm routine. He squeezed himself into the corner farthest from me while studiously avoiding eye contact.

Which only shows how dense men can be. If his intention was to demonstrate to his new ladylove that he no longer cared *that* deeply for me, he would've treated me like the platonic pal

I am and chosen a nice, comfy spot with plenty of space on either side. Maybe thrown in a little manspreading and scratching for good measure.

Liddy pouted. "You're so far away, Dom. There's plenty of room over here." She patted the space next to her.

Okay, really? The two of them hardly knew each other, and while Dom was without doubt a studly specimen, common sense should have told Liddy to scope out the situation before getting all frisky.

I suspected she was here to try and wheedle a heftier allowance from her sister-in-law. If so, then horning in on said sister-in-law's new fella might not be the best way to go about it. But hey, what do I know?

Dom wisely ignored the invitation. "I'm afraid that was the only pastry, Liddy. But we do have some delicious fruit salad. Apples, pears, and grapes with a pomegranate balsamic dressing. Can I bring you a bowl?"

We? I distinctly heard him say, *We* have some fruit salad. An obvious Freudian slip.

On second thought, maybe not. That *We* might have been Dom's way of informing their clueless visitor that she was barking up the wrong hunk.

Oh, you know what I mean.

If that was his message, it was far too subtle for Hurricane Liddy. "No fruit for me," she purred, while giving him the once-over. "I'm in the mood for something much sweeter."

I looked at Dom. Dom looked at Madison. Madison looked at Liddy, and said, "Give it a rest, Liddy. Dom and I are seeing each other."

Well, that was one way to handle it, and I have to admit I found Madison's bluntness refreshing. Clearly it was the only thing Larry's sister understood.

Liddy gaped at Madison. *"My brother's barely cold!"*

And here we go.

She leapt to her feet and aimed a long acrylic fingernail (blinged out with a spray of tiny rhinestones) at Madison. "How could you even *think* of shacking up with someone so soon after your husband's death? You're supposed to wait a year!"

Said the woman who has no use for "that Emily Post BS."

"We're not shack—" Dom started, until I hurled a wadded-up napkin at his noggin at high speed. (Did I mention I was a high-school softball champ?) I would've thrown the last half of my croissant, but you know. Priorities.

I watched him get the message: *Let Madison handle it. She's the one with the experience.*

Madison's voice broke ever so slightly as she said, "You know how much I loved your brother. But he's gone and there's nothing I can do about that." When Liddy started to object, she cut her off. "Do you seriously believe you have any say in how I conduct my personal life?"

Liddy was flushed, her hands fisted, as she stood over her sister-in-law, the person who controlled the purse strings. I could almost hear the gears turning as she weighed her response. "Well. I just think you should take Larry's feelings into consideration, that's all."

Madison cocked her head slightly, as if pondering that statement. "Larry's feelings."

Liddy struck a pose, hand on hip. "I mean, not his feelings *now* because, um…"

"He's dead," her sister-in-law helpfully supplied.

"I meant his feelings when he was alive, duh. He would've

wanted you to wait a year, like I said."

"And you know this how?" Madison asked.

Liddy aimed a sparkly fingernail at her own chest. "Because I knew my brother, that's how. Better than *you* knew him. Obviously."

"I see." Madison folded her hands in her lap. "And the two of you discussed how he wanted me to conduct my personal life after he was gone?"

"Yeah. No. Not… not specifically." Clearly Liddy didn't know when to quit. "But I *knew* him. We were so close, we didn't have to, like, talk about every little thing. I just *knew*."

"How nice for you." Madison's tone was frosty. "I myself am not telepathic. Can you tell what I'm thinking at this very moment?"

I could. It was a four-word sentence (okay, maybe five words) that began with "Mind" and ended with "business." Gee, maybe *I'm* telepathic.

"Huh?" Liddy frowned in confusion. "Don't change the subject."

I was having a swell time eavesdropping on this juicy family squabble, but Mr. Nice Guy had reached his limit. "Maybe Jane and I should leave," Dom said.

Madison motioned to us to stay put. "You're not the ones who need to leave, Dom. The two of you are here by invitation."

"Unlike *me*, right?" Liddy flung herself onto the sofa once more. "That's the thanks I get for coming here to *warn* you. Can I get a drink? Oh, I forgot. You don't keep filthy old booze in the house."

I suspected Madison did indeed keep filthy old booze in the house, being an accommodating hostess. However, there was a time to be accommodating, and this wasn't it. Dealing with a sober Liddy Kool was enough of a chore. Liddy Kool all liquored up would've been even more gosh-darn delightful.

Madison turned to her sister-in-law. "I don't owe you an explanation, but if it will put your mind at ease, here it is. After this, I will consider the subject closed. Larry was a pragmatist. Naturally we discussed the probability that I would outlive him, considering the difference in our ages. He was adamant that if and when that happened, I should move on with my life. He actually said—" She gave a half laugh, her eyes misty. "He said, 'If Mr. Right turns up at my funeral, go for it.'"

I smiled. "That sounds like Larry."

Liddy looked skeptical. "Well, I just think—"

"I don't care what you think." Now it was Madison's turn to point a finger. "I mean it, Liddy, I will not hear another word about it."

This resulted in much eye rolling and huffing.

Someone had to ask; it might as well be me. "What did you want to warn Madison about, Liddy?"

She executed a dramatic sigh and examined her rhinestones, no doubt aiming to prolong the suspense.

"Oh, for heaven's sake," Madison said. "You need to leave now, and next time call before—"

"It's about Rex," Liddy said. "He's back in town. Doing more interviews."

"So what?" I said. "He wants to make a documentary. This is not news."

"No, but *this* is." Liddy sat forward. "It started out as a biopic, this project of his. Now it's turned into one of those true-crime specials."

"About Larry?" Madison's eyes widened as color leached

from her face. She turned to me. "I thought you said the delay at the ME's office was routine, that there was nothing to worry about. Why would Rex be making a true-crime program about Larry?"

"Not about *Larry*." Liddy's tone said, *Try to keep up.* "Everyone knows his heart gave out on him. This show would be about all the *murders* that have occurred in Crystal Harbor."

"Well," Dom said, "there's no denying we've had more than our share. I wonder why that is."

"Oh, I don't know," I said. "There haven't been *that* many murders in this town."

Okay, you know what? This would be a perfect time for you to keep your opinions to yourself.

Madison exhaled on a little laugh. "Well, that's a relief. I just assumed, since his original focus was on Larry, that Rex had gotten some crazy notion—" She wagged her hand as if to shoo away the ridiculous thought.

"But don't you get it?" Liddy said. "Rex isn't done with my brother, not by a long shot. Why do you think he's zeroing in on Crystal Harbor? It's not because of the murders. It's because of *Larry.*"

"I'm not following," I said.

"Rex hated my brother," she said. "He blames him for tanking his acting career, which, *hello?* He did all by himself. He says Larry bad-mouthed him to directors and producers, but that's a rotten lie. Larry tried to *help* him. But that's not the only beef Rex had with him." She turned to Madison. "He never got over Larry stealing you from him."

"That's just silly," Madison said. "It wasn't at all like that."

"Well, I'll bet Rex thinks it was," Liddy said, "and if I know him, he's still steamed about it."

Madison had told me her relationship with Rex had been brief and casual, while acknowledging that his masculine pride might've been bruised when she'd taken up with his old costar. Maybe he was more upset than he let on.

"*And,*" Liddy said, "I'm sure Rex knows the *reason* Larry stole you from him was revenge for sleeping with *me* all those years ago. My brother was always very protective."

"More nonsense," Madison said. "But be that as it may, if Rex is switching the focus of his project to the local murders, I still don't see what that has to do with Larry."

"It's about getting the show picked up," Liddy said. "True crime sells. Everyone loves those gory programs. They're on, like, twenty-four seven. Rex decided to cash in on the craze."

I was beginning to get it. "Because he'd have a better chance selling Netflix on a true-crime documentary than on one about Larry Kool's life."

"Right," she said. "So it'll be about the murders, *supposedly*, but his real target is the town's biggest celebrity. Rex is gonna use the show to trash my brother. Who's, like, dead and can't defend himself."

"I don't know," Dom said. "That sounds kind of farfetched."

"Trust me, I know the guy," Liddy said. "He comes across as all sincere and everything, saying how much he loved Larry, but he's a devious son of a bitch. We've gotta stop him *now*, before he demolishes my brother's reputation."

Madison said, "How would you propose we go about that?"

"I don't know, like, sue him or something."

"For what?" Dom said. "He hasn't done anything illegal."

"*Yet.* Isn't there a law against saying bad things about people?"

"About living people, yes," he said, "if the things they're saying aren't true and if the slander causes harm. But you can't sue a person for *thinking* about slandering someone. The law doesn't work that way."

Liddy flopped against the cushions, arms crossed. "Well, there must be some way to stop him."

"What I want to know," I said, "is how Larry ended up making so much more from *Chase & Knabbe* than Rex did. If what Rex said on Leonora Romano's show is true."

Madison answered. "Oh, it's true, all right, and there was nothing underhanded about it. When Rex was tapped for the show, he was a bigger name than his costar. He'd had some recent success, minor heartthrob roles in a couple of movies and a soap opera. Everyone assumed he was on his way."

"Including Rex himself, apparently," I said.

"He saw *Chase & Knabbe* as just one more stepping-stone to superstardom," she said. "Of course, to him it sounded like your basic dopey detective show. He anticipated one season at most before it sank into oblivion."

"In other words," Dom said, "Rex failed to predict the program's enduring appeal."

"Which brings us to the critical error he made in negotiating his contract," Madison said.

"I think I see where you're going with this. It's about the residuals," I said, referring to the royalty payments actors receive from reruns, DVDs, streaming, and so forth.

She nodded. "Rex managed to get the studio to cough up an extravagant, ego-stroking salary, but that only lasted while new episodes were being produced. After that, he received the rock-bottom royalty rate, and even that decreased sharply over time. When Leonora called his income from the show pitiful, she wasn't exaggerating."

I said, "So he went for the big initial paycheck over decent residuals because he was so sure *Chase & Knabbe* would be a flash in the pan."

Dom gave a low whistle. "A costly mistake, and one I assume his costar didn't make. But who could've predicted *Chase & Knabbe* would enjoy a decades-long cult following? Did Larry have a crystal ball?"

"You don't need a crystal ball," Madison said, "when you have a decent head for business and a modicum of humility. Larry had been a child TV star, but as an adult, he struggled to be taken seriously in the biz. One thing he'd learned early on was how important residuals can be. And unlike Rex, he took nothing for granted. When he was offered the role of Eddie Knabbe, he knew he had no hope of receiving Rex's star-level salary, so he made sure his bulldog of an agent held out for top-level royalties that would remain stable and not diminish over time."

I said, "And the studio went along with it because...?"

Madison shrugged. "Because *no one* had a crystal ball, including the studio execs. They were as shortsighted as Rex."

"So the bulk of Larry's income from *Chase & Knabbe*," I said, "came during the four decades after it was canceled."

"You bet it did," Liddy said. "Because my brother knew what the hell he was doing, and that loser Rex didn't. But on Leonora's show, he made it sound like Larry ripped him off or something."

"Did you know," Madison asked, "that Rex tried to reprise *Chase & Knabbe*? Just a couple of years ago."

"You're kidding," Dom said. "How would that even work, resuming the show after so much time has elapsed?"

"The idea was, they'd be playing the same roles as before," she said, "Samson Chase and Eddie Knabbe, only now the retired homicide detectives would be going rogue to solve the cold cases that had bugged them for all those years."

"Let me guess," I said. "Larry told him to take a hike."

"My husband was a busy man," Madison said. "He'd carved out a successful career for himself, with various income streams. And anyway, by that point he never would've considered working with Rex Noble. I got the feeling he just didn't trust the man."

At that moment my purse, sitting on the floor next to the sofa, began playing the zippy, Latin-inspired song "Tequila," which was my cell phone's custom ringtone.

I grabbed the phone, fully intending to dump the call—until I saw who was trying to reach me. "Sorry, I have to take this."

As I hurried toward the hallway, I heard Liddy start to whine about money. Wish I could say I was surprised.

I answered the phone. "Hi, Louise. What's up?"

"We were right, damn it," she said. "Larry was murdered."

11

Shame on Yew

NO, OF COURSE I didn't share the jaw-dropping news with the others. I claimed an emergency (convincing enough since I no doubt appeared as rattled as I felt) and skedaddled.

That evening found me in the family room of my house, performing yet another Death Diva favor for Madison. This one, however, was far more interesting, one might even say *entertaining*, than dealing with the insurance company and ME's office.

It seems Larry had amassed quite a collection of souvenirs from his three years on *Chase & Knabbe*. He'd made a habit of commandeering assorted props and ephemera that were headed for the trash bin. The result was a treasure trove of *Chase & Knabbe* memorabilia that, while considered worthless forty years ago, had transformed into valuable collector's items. Gee, maybe the guy *did* have a crystal ball.

Larry had given much of it away over the years to superfans, and donated several special pieces to the Museum of the Moving Image in Astoria, Queens, located across the East River from Manhattan. The museum is situated on the campus of Kaufman Astoria Studios, where *Chase & Knabbe* had been shot all those years ago, and where many movies and television programs are still made.

Larry's widow had been left with a dozen cartons filled with assorted souvenirs from the show, only a couple of which she felt compelled to hold on to. She could have sold the rest, of course, but she wasn't hurting for money. When she asked me for ideas, I suggested an auction benefiting one of Larry's favorite causes, The Actors Fund, a charitable organization that provides a financial safety net for actors and other professionals in the performing arts.

Madison thought that was a swell idea, so I got the ball rolling by contacting Randall Bishop, a charity and fundraising auctioneer I'd worked with on several occasions. The next order of business was inventorying the contents of those cartons. Sophie had already offered to swing by that evening to help me go through them, and when I informed Louise of the game plan—a *Chase & Knabbe* paraphernalia-fest with Buffalo-chicken pizza and beer—she asked what time and could she bring Luci.

Seven p.m. and yes, of course.

By eight-thirty we'd inhaled the pizza, were on our second beers, and had already emptied three cartons. As tempting as it was to linger over every little item Larry had saved (and I mean really, how many monogrammed whiskey flasks did one hard-drinking TV homicide detective really need?), we quickly found a rhythm and became efficient at sorting the haul into two piles: auction-worthy treasures in one, and questionable tchotchkes only a hard-core fan could love in another. I compiled a master list as we went, while Sophie snapped photos of each item.

Louise and I had lost no time getting Sophie up to speed on our initial suspicions regarding Larry's sudden demise and the startling confirmation of those suspicions by the Suffolk County toxicology lab. And no, we didn't hesitate to share what little we knew with the mayor of Crystal Harbor. Not only was Sophie discreet, but she knew more about what went on in our town than anyone. We were eager for whatever insights she might provide.

My family room was a grand yet comfortable space dominated by an oversize, horseshoe-shaped ivory leather sofa and a television to rival the screen in the home movie theater located in the basement, next to the gym and wine cellar.

How very fortunate that the owner of these fancy digs, Sexy Beast, allowed little old me, his official guardian, to live there with him. All he asked in return was regular scritches and the occasional Vienna sausage.

The dogs snoozed in a cuddle puddle on a nest they'd constructed from pillows and downy sofa throws, while we superior life-forms chose to sit cross-legged on the thick, slate-blue carpet amid the growing piles of vintage detective-show props.

Louise reached into carton number four and produced a chipped blue-and-white coffee mug adorned with the phrase *#1 DAD*. "Did this land in here by accident?"

"Doubtful," Sophie said. "Larry didn't have any kids that I know of."

"Didn't you guys watch the show?" I added this latest item to my list. "That's the mug Detective Eddie Knabbe kept at the police station. He always drank his coffee from it. This definitely goes in the auction pile."

"Eddie had kids?" Sophie positioned the battered mug on Irene's six-thousand-dollar coffee table (you read that right) for its glamour shot. "I don't recall that."

"Okay, this rings a bell," Louise said. "Eddie was divorced, right? But it was a contentious divorce and he almost never got to see his kids."

"But he still has this mug from when they were little," I said, "and he refuses to get rid of it, even though the other cops tease him about how beat-up it is. He's superstitious, like if he throws it out, he'll never see his kids again. That chip was there from the very first episode."

"So to get back to this poison that killed Larry," Sophie said, as she peered into the box. "You say it's from the yew plant?"

"That's right," Louise said. "It's called taxine and it's a powerful cardiotoxin. Turns out just about every part of the yew is highly poisonous. Well, except for the arils."

Sophie looked up. "The what?"

"The fleshy coverings around the seeds. The arils look like red berries. They're literally the only part of the plant that won't kill you. But if you don't remove the seeds from them first?" Louise mimed hanging herself.

"Yikes," Sophie said. "But aren't yew trees and bushes fairly common?"

"They sure are," I said, "especially in cemeteries. There's a lot of mystical symbolism associated with them. They're considered the tree of the dead. They can live a very long time. There are yew trees in Europe that are thousands of years old." I'd done a bit of online research after Louise told me what kind of poison the lab had found.

Sophie said, "So when you say every part of the plant is toxic, you mean not just the seeds but the leaves, too?"

"They're more like needles," Louise said. "Yew is an evergreen. And yeah, the needles will do you in. So will the bark."

"So why did it take so long to find out that's what killed him?" I asked. "You'd think they would've found plant parts in his stomach. Even if someone, I don't know, chopped them up and mixed them with his food."

"If there'd been anything like that in his system," she said, "it wouldn't have gotten past Magda, trust me."

"Can't see how it would've gotten past Larry either," Sophie said. "Someone slips bits of tree bark and what all into your chili, you're gonna notice."

"In the absence of identifiable plant materials, taxine poisoning can be overlooked, and the death chalked up to natural causes."

"So how did someone poison Larry with yew," I asked, "without feeding him parts of the plant?"

"The lab techs think it was a tincture," Louise said. "Someone went to the trouble of processing the needles, seeds, what have you, into a concentrated, alcohol-based liquid. The plant parts get filtered out and you're left with a little vial of poison."

I was beginning to get it. "Which can be added to anything the victim eats or drinks."

"As it happens," she said, "one of the lab techs had encountered a case of yew poisoning before. A suicide, sadly, who showed symptoms similar to Larry's. They didn't know to test for taxine until a family member found the bottle of tincture the poor guy had made. That's what gave this tech the idea to test for it in Larry's tissues. Otherwise we might never have learned the truth."

"I'm thinking this poison's got to be pretty vile," I said. "The killer would need to find something flavorful enough to mask the taste."

"I'll tell you what would mask the taste," Sophie said. "Spicy chili con carne, that's what."

"And maybe someone did spike Larry's chili," Louise said, "but he was feeling sick before he arrived at the cook-off. He put on a scopolamine patch to ward off the nausea. Which worked against him, as it turned out. He would've been better off getting the toxin out of his system."

"Larry's pupils were dilated that day," I said. "I blamed the scopolamine, but could it have been the poison?"

She nodded. "Taxine can cause enlarged pupils."

"Listen, ladies," Sophie said, "we're falling down on the job. What do we do with this?" She unfolded a handkerchief to reveal a stack of Detective Eddie Knabbe's business cards, loosely held together with a disintegrating rubber band.

We all took a moment to consider.

"Auction," Louise said.

"Superfan giveaway," Sophie said.

"I vote for auction. Two against one." I logged it in.

Sophie fanned out the cards, snapped a picture, and reached into the carton for the next item. "Whoa." She lifted out a big crystal ashtray, handling it as if it were a holy relic. "Is this what I think it is?"

"Sure looks like it." I took the ashtray from her, turned it this way and that. The thing had heft. "I could certainly see this caving in someone's dome."

"What?" Louise said. "What am I missing?"

"You didn't watch *The Romano Files*?" Sophie asked her. "The episode right after Larry died? Leonora showed a clip from the episode of *Chase & Knabbe* where some poor schlemiel gets dispatched with this thing. Turned out the secretary did it."

"I can't abide *The Romano Files*. I gave it a pass."

I lifted up the ashtray and we all pronounced, "Auction!" in unison.

We concentrated on emptying that carton and moved on to the next one, which held Eddie Knabbe's dress uniform, trench coat, and ketchup-stained necktie. Sexy Beast and Luci took a sudden interest, jumping off the sofa to sniff the musty garments, all of which went into the auction pile, natch. The dogs decided it was a good time to head into the kitchen for a drink and to ensure they hadn't missed any errant scraps of pizza crust.

We were halfway through the next carton (Eddie's desk blotter, nameplate, Rolodex, and doodle-filled detective notebook) when Sophie said, "I'm going to come right out and say what we're all thinking. Whispering Willows Cemetery has a yew hedge growing along the rear fence."

Louise said, "Frank Martinez is there every day. He's the administrator." She turned to me. "You told me he resented Larry, that he seemed to know he wasn't going to win the cook-off even before the winner was announced."

"Sure, Frank has access to yew," Sophie said, "but so does everyone else in town. That boneyard's open to the public."

"You don't even need to be on the cemetery grounds to get to that hedge," I said. "It's growing on the outside of the fence. Plus I'm willing to bet it's not the only yew in town. But there's something else. Something Madison told me about. The day before the cook-off, Frank showed up uninvited in their backyard. Larry was swimming laps in the pool. Madison had just brought him a kale protein shake."

Sophie made a gagging noise. "Sorry. Proceed."

Louise said, "Was Madison still outside when Frank arrived?"

"No," I said, "she'd already gone back into the house. She had no idea he was there until she heard them arguing. She went to check it out, and Frank left."

"So that shake was just sitting there when he let himself into their backyard," Sophie said.

"While Larry was swimming laps. Chances are, he didn't realize at first that Frank was there."

"Meaning," Louise said, "he wouldn't have noticed if Frank took the opportunity to add a little something to his shake."

"Is a kale protein shake—" Sophie grimaced. "Ugh, just the thought. Anyway, would the taste of all that scrumptious kale mask the flavor of the yew tincture?"

"I suppose it's possible," I said. "It would depend on what other ingredients it had. And what that tincture actually tastes like. These are things we have no way of knowing."

"If it *was* Frank who killed him," Louise said, "he could've delivered the coup de grâce the next day by putting more poison in Larry's portion of chili. Particularly if it looked like he wasn't succumbing to the first dose."

I said, "Dom told me that at the cook-off he overheard Frank telling Maxine Baumgartner that Larry won't get away with it again."

"Which only shows what a sexist troglodyte the guy is," Sophie said. "Everyone knew that Larry was one of three judges. He didn't have any more influence over the outcome than Maia or me. But he's this famous *male* celebrity, and we're just a couple of spineless little females, so of course it must be his fault when someone loses 'unfairly.'"

"Well," I said, "Larry was the public face of the cook-off, the front man if you will. That might've led some people to assume he was the decider."

"Yeah," Louise said, "*small-minded* people."

"Okay," Sophie said, "here's something you probably don't know about Frank. As in you definitely don't know because no one else in town does."

"Except you," I said. Now do you see why I had to include her in our little get-together?

"This stays just between us," she said.

"No problem." Louise mimed zipping her lip.

"Wait." I turned to the doc. "*I* say 'Just between us' and you practically bite my head off. *She* says it and you're all like, sure, Sophie, anything you say, Sophie."

She shrugged. "It's Sophie."

The mayor glared at me. "You want to hear this or not?"

I rolled my eyes and motioned for her to continue.

"Frank was expelled from college for attacking a professor."

"Attacking him how?" I asked.

"Beat him up or something," she said. "Don't know the details."

"It must've been serious," Louise said, "if they expelled him for it."

"Well, that's intriguing," I said, "but I don't know how relevant it is. I mean, a lot of people do stupid things when they're young."

Not that *I* ever did, but that's what I've, you know, heard.

"Then how about this?" Sophie said. "When his last boss fired him, he destroyed the man's car."

Louise said, "Destroyed as in…?"

"As in he went to town with a baseball bat, and when that didn't do enough damage, he found a reciprocating saw in his boss's garage and started in with that."

"Wow," Louise said. "That's one angry ex-employee."

"When did this happen?" I asked.

"Well, let's see," Sophie said. "He's been working for Whispering Willows for about three years, right?"

"Four," I said.

"It happened a few months before Arlo hired him."

"So not when he was young and stupid," I said. "More like when he was in his 'should've known better' early thirties and stupid."

"Was he arrested?" Louise asked. "For either incident?"

"Not for the thing with the professor," Sophie said. "But they did arrest him for taking apart his boss's car. There was some sort of settlement and the charges were dropped."

"Okay," I said, "I have to ask how you know all this."

"I prefer not to divulge my sources." It was a common refrain.

"Well, I have to admit these revelations are disturbing. I've had a lot of dealings with Frank, and for sure we've had our differences, but to be honest, I have a hard time picturing him being violent."

"Antisocial individuals don't always advertise that aspect of their personality," Louise said, "particularly when they're trying to blend in to society."

"Or trying to keep their new job at the cemetery," Sophie said. "Jane, you of all people should know how skillful psychos can be at concealing their true nature."

She had a point there. I'd dealt with more than my share of them.

"Based on these two incidents," Louise said, "it sounds to me like Frank feels entitled, and when things don't go his way, he snaps—lashes out at those who would deny him what he believes is rightfully his."

"One thing I don't get, though," I said. "Why would he have been so open about how much he hated Larry? I was right there when he got into a tiff with him at the cook-off. And that thing he said to Max, about how Larry wouldn't get away with it again? He didn't seem to care who heard him. I mean, if he was planning to kill the guy, wouldn't he have tried to keep a low profile?"

"Most criminals aren't all that smart," Sophie said, "and based on Frank's prior actions, he seems to lack impulse control."

"Well then, I'm glad I never got him *really* angry."

Louise had started poking through the next carton. "Well, will you look at this." She held up a gold detective's shield, prompting a chorus of *Oooh*'s. We passed the little treasure around.

"No need to vote on this one." Sophie took a picture and placed the shield in the auction pile while I added it to the list.

I said, "Remember that episode when Eddie was made to turn in his gun and shield?"

"Which one?" Louise asked. "Eddie got suspended two or three times each season."

"Check it out." Sophie extracted a crossbow from the box.

"Ah yes," I said. "The crossbow murderer, remember her? This gizmo showed up near the end of season three when the writers were trying to come up with creative new ways to commit homicide."

"Auction," Louise said, and Sophie and I concurred.

Next came a padded envelope containing a thick stack of glossy eight-by-tens: Detective Eddie Knabbe in trench coat and stained necktie, the ubiquitous unlit cigar jammed in his mouth. On each black-and-white photo, Larry had scrawled not just his autograph, but his character's well-worn catchphrase: *It's time to turn up the heat!*

"There must be tons of these out there in the wild," Louise said. "Forty years' worth. They're not exactly rare."

"Save these for the superfans." Sophie placed them on the pile not headed for auction.

"I'm curious," I said. "Has Rex Noble approached either of you for the documentary he wants to make?"

They both raised their hands. Well, that made sense, that he'd target the mayor of Crystal Harbor as well as Larry's personal physician.

"He tried to interview me," Louise said. "I insisted on knowing what kind of questions he intended to ask, and that was the end of that. I'm sorry, but I am not about to violate a deceased patient's privacy to help Rex Noble pitch his little career-salvaging project."

"Tried to get me to sign this one-sided release," Sophie said. "I had Amanda escort him out of my office."

Louise laughed. "When I objected to the release, he explained it to me in insultingly simple terms, nice and slow."

"And he still has all those lovely capped teeth?" I said. "I'd say you showed commendable restraint, Louise."

Sophie said, "You know Rex is now talking about making a true-crime special about all the homicides in Crystal Harbor, right?"

This was news to Louise. "Good grief. And now that it turns out Larry was poisoned, that'll give his program a whole new focus."

"Rex is no fan of Larry's," I said, "no matter how much he praises him publicly."

"Well, he wasn't praising him on *The Romano Files*," Sophie said.

"He was, until Leonora pushed the right buttons," I said, "then his true feelings came out. He blames Larry for his own lousy career choices. He must be getting pretty desperate at this point. He even tried to revive *Chase & Knabbe*." I watched a metaphorical light bulb blink on over Louise's head. "What are you thinking, Doc?"

"Just that if I were a washed-up actor," she said, "with no prospects and forty years' worth of grievances, I just might be tempted to tilt the odds in my favor."

Sophie and I took a few moments to follow her reasoning.

"Oh," Sophie said.

"You mean…?" I said.

"It's kind of brilliant," Louise said. "First you commit the murder. Then you let it be known you plan to honor the dearly departed with a documentary."

"Then," Sophie said, "the documentary turns into a true-crime special about Crystal Harbor's murders. An easier sale."

"Rex assumed his victim's death would be chalked up to natural causes," Louise said, "but suddenly there's a surprising new development, courtesy of the Suffolk County tox lab. Larry was poisoned."

"No problem," I said. "As long as fingers don't point at Rex, this could be even better for him. His true-crime special now has a 'ripped from the headlines' angle. The town's most famous celebrity is also its most famous murder victim."

"A program that juicy is bound to be picked up," Sophie said, "if not by Netflix, then by a major cable network."

"What better way to exact revenge on the man you blame for all your woes?" Louise said. "Not only do you end his life, but you use the murder to resurrect your career."

"Speaking of Rex's woes," I said, "there's also the fact that Larry wooed Madison away from him."

Louise blinked. "Rex and Madison were a couple?"

"That might be overstating it. She says they dated casually for a short while."

"But let's think about this," Sophie said. "When would Rex have had the opportunity to poison Larry? You say he was sick *before* the cook-off."

"I'll tell you when he could've done it," I said. "He was with Larry at Murray's Pub the night before. He could've spiked his drink."

"I don't know," Louise said. "We've already decided that yew tincture must taste pretty nasty."

"Okay then, how about this?" I said. "Larry loved the nachos at Murray's. Fully loaded with all that spicy meat, jalapeños, guacamole, onions, pico de gallo, the works. If that wouldn't kill the taste, I don't know what would."

Sophie wore a crooked smile. "I assume this is something he indulged in when the missus wasn't around."

"I doubt Madison ever set foot in Murray's."

Louise said, "So Rex could've slipped a few drops of the tincture into his food when Larry was, what, in the little boys' room?"

"Have you ever seen Larry out in public?" I said. "He'd always spend time circulating, collecting hugs and handshakes. He was like a magnet—everyone was drawn to him. It would've been all too easy for Rex to slip the poison into his food."

"You know," Sophie said, "I did see Rex give Larry his soda at the cook-off. Larry drank a lot of it, trying to settle his stomach. What do you think? A few more drops of the tincture, a little extra insurance? Not enough to taste, just enough to tip his old costar over the edge."

I said, "When I met Rex earlier, at the adopt-a-pet area, he was already holding that cup, but I never saw him drink from it. And when his dog, Piglet, tried to lick it, he held it away from him."

"Nothing strange about that, but I see what you're implying. He wouldn't want to poison his pooch."

I said, "So let me ask you, Sophie. At any point, did you see Rex himself drink from that cup?"

"No," she said. "And in fact, when he handed it to Larry, he assured him that he hadn't drunk from it."

"Of course, they say poison is a woman's weapon." I turned to Louise. "Are you going to tell me again that 'they' are wrong?"

"It depends," she said. "Women are much more likely than men to choose poison as a murder weapon. The gentlemen like their guns."

"Aha!"

"*But—*" she raised a finger "—since men commit about ninety percent of the murders, they actually kill with poison more often than women do."

Sophie said, "So is there someone of the female persuasion we think might've done it?"

"Hold that thought," I said. "*First,* let's pretend we're still doing the job we got together to do." I reached blindly into the carton and pulled out another padded envelope from which I withdrew a sheaf of papers topped by a bright yellow cover and bound along one side with two brass brads. The words *CHASE & KNABBE* appeared prominently at the top, with *Detective*

Drama Pilot centered underneath, along with the writers' names and production company info. Two signatures had been scrawled across the cover in blue ink: *Rex Noble* and *Larry Kool.*

"How amazing is this?" I crowed. "The script for the *pilot!*"

"Autographed by both costars," Louise said. "This should bring a pretty penny at auction."

We spent a few minutes leafing through the typewritten pages, reading some of the dialogue aloud, and reminiscing about that very first episode. Suddenly it was as if Larry were in the room with us. My eyes stung. I cleared my throat and glanced at my companions, and saw I wasn't the only one missing our old friend.

Sophie looked us both in the eye, as grim as I'd ever seen her. "We need to get the cowardly dirtbag who took him from us."

12

Why the Heck Are We All Yelling?

LOUISE EXHALED LOUDLY. "I feel compelled to point out that that's a job for the Crystal Harbor PD."

"Chief Hernandez is more than competent," I said, "and so are her detectives, Howie Werker and Cookie Kaplan. They happen to be friends of mine."

"I hear a 'but,'" she said.

"But they're not above accepting a little help," I said, "as long as you don't step on their toes. Well, Cookie doesn't mind. Howie isn't exactly thrilled when civilians get involved."

Sophie raised an eyebrow. "One nosy civilian in particular."

I flapped my hand. "Howie's all bark. I can handle him. And since you asked about possible female culprits, Sophie, let's think like cops. Don't they always start by taking a good, hard look at the spouse?"

"Do they? Or is that just a TV thing? Okay, I'll play along. Did Larry leave everything to the lovely Widow Kool?"

"Just about," I said.

"But think about the age difference," she said. "Larry was seventy-four. And how old is Madison?"

"Twenty-nine," I said.

"Well, there you go. A forty-five-year difference. If she wanted him gone, all she needed was a little patience. Nature was bound to do the job for her."

"Not so fast," Louise said. "Larry was a pretty healthy seventy-four. Sure, he could stand to lose a few pounds, but he had no serious medical issues aside from his blood sugar, and he'd turned that around through dietary changes."

"Which, of course, was Madison's doing," I said. "I mean, if she wanted to become a widow, why push a healthy lifestyle on her husband? The swimming, the yoga and meditation, not to mention all those salads and kale protein shakes. Sophie, don't start!" I added, as the mayor shuddered in disgust.

"Okay, I see what you're saying," Sophie said. "It would've made more sense for her to encourage his junk-food habit, make sure he got plenty of cheeseburgers and ice cream."

"When I say he had no serious medical issues," Louise said, "I mean even before he met Madison. Well, except for the prediabetes, and we'd been controlling that with medication. His arteries were squeaky clean, even on a steady diet of bacon, cheese, and butter. Some people are just lucky that way. Routine diagnostic tests never turned up anything that needed attention. There was every reason to believe he'd make it to ninety and beyond."

"By which time," I said, "Madison would be in her mid to late forties."

"So?" Sophie said. "I don't get it."

But Louise did, I could tell. "By then," she said, "it might be too late for her to have a baby."

"She wanted a child," I told Sophie. "Larry didn't."

"Well, she must've come around to his way of thinking," Sophie said, "because Larry had a vasectomy a couple of months after the wedding."

"You know about that?" Louise said.

"Told me about it himself. I called to invite him to a poker game and he begged off. Said he'd just gotten snipped and all he planned to do that evening was pop Advil and ice his beanbag."

"Wait," I said. "Time out. Larry had a *vasectomy?*"

"Why does that surprise you?" she asked.

"It's just that Madison still seems so, I don't know, wistful about her childless marriage. I assumed she'd been hoping all along that Larry would change his mind. It's hard to believe she'd have agreed to a vasectomy."

Louise looked like she wanted to say something but was holding back.

"Whatever it is," Sophie said, "you know it won't go any further than these four walls."

"Okay, first of all," Louise said, "I should point out that you don't need anyone else's permission, and that includes your spouse, to undergo sterilization. Larry thought he and Madison had agreed not to have kids, that they were on the same page. Not at first, of course. She was up-front about wanting a baby. But once she realized he had no intention of becoming a first-time father in his seventies, she told him she was okay with it."

"Possibly hoping he'd change his mind down the road," I said. "Or even trick him into getting her pregnant? She wouldn't be the first."

"Well, all I know is that when she found out he'd gone ahead and made it permanent, she freaked."

Sophie's eyes widened. "He didn't discuss it with her beforehand?"

"Unfortunately, no," Louise said. "He really thought they were in total agreement. He did it as a kind of surprise gift to her, to spare her having to use birth control, which she considered unnatural. He thought she'd be pleased that he'd willingly gone under the knife for her."

"Oops," Sophie said.

I asked, "Do either of you know anything about Madison's background? What she did for a living before she met Larry?"

"She was a preschool teacher," Sophie said. "Loves kids, I guess."

Louise said, "Larry mentioned that she was real poor growing up. He was happy to be able to improve her standard of living. Loved buying her presents." She caught the look that passed between Sophie and me. "He insisted she wasn't greedy or acquisitive. He'd known women like that and was convinced Madison had nothing in common with them."

Sexy Beast and Luci rejoined us, making a beeline for the open carton. Louise and I corralled our pets on our laps to keep them from making off with any of the intriguing *Chase & Knabbe* artifacts it contained.

What's that you say? We were shirking our responsibilities? Big deal, the inventory would get done eventually. We were on a roll.

"Speaking of wealthy men and their love lives," I said, "did you know Dom and Madison are now an item?"

"I heard something about that," Louise said.

"That rumor mill's been working overtime," Sophie said. "Everyone in town has an opinion."

"I'll bet they do," I said. "For what it's worth, I just want Dom to be happy, and for him that means being in a committed relationship."

"Seems she likes her men older," Sophie said.

"Well, Dom's what, about your age, Jane?" Louise asked.

I nodded. "He turned forty last month. An eleven-year age gap, so what? Fun fact—Dom's second wife, Svetlana, is eleven years older than him."

"Did Madison know Larry was feeling lousy before he left home?" Sophie asked.

Louise shook her head. "He hid it from her. When I saw him at the cook-off, I could tell he was sick, but he was determined to see it through to the end. So I looked around for Madison and let her know what was going on."

"She seemed genuinely surprised when she found out," I said, "and very concerned. Tried to get him to leave."

Sophie said, "Jane, you mentioned that Madison had no problem with them doing an autopsy. You'd think if she had something to hide—like homicide—that she'd try to prevent it."

"Well, *Liddy* certainly objected," I said. "She was fine with the aquamation, which literally dissolved her brother's body, but she had a conniption over the autopsy."

"So I assume we're all wondering the same thing," Sophie said.

"Why did Liddy try to prevent her brother's autopsy?" Louise said. "Was she afraid of what they'd find?"

"Let's put ourselves in the killer's shoes," I said. "We would've gone to a lot of bother to make our victim's death appear natural. Obviously we want to avoid an autopsy because of what it might reveal. And we want him put in the ground pronto."

"Oh no, we don't," Louise said. "Think about it. Buried bodies can be exhumed. Some poisons can be detected months or even years later."

"Got it," Sophie said. "So we're big fans of cremation."

"Whether by flame or that newfangled aquamation," I said. "Same end result."

"But here's something your average killer might not know," Louise said. "Tissue samples from autopsies are usually saved for years, in case questions arise later."

"So what you're saying," I said, "is that the risk of discovery never goes away, even if the body was cremated."

Louise nodded. "As long as an autopsy was performed. But even then, many poisonings go undetected. Unfortunately, it happens all too frequently. We were lucky."

"Luck had nothing to do with it, Louise," I said. "You're the reason Larry's death certificate now has a check mark next to 'homicide.' You leaned on Magda hard. Admit it."

She wore a little smile. "Well, an invitation to one of Raymond Holliday's backyard clambakes just might've been involved."

"I knew it!"

Louise's husband, Ray, is legendary for his clambakes. We're talking lobsters (big ones!), mussels, clams, potatoes, and corn on the cob, steamed in layers on a bed of seaweed in the ginormous pot of a turkey fryer. And that's only the centerpiece of a feast that includes a beluga caviar station, exotic cocktails from the torchlit tiki bar, and an unapologetically retro baked Alaska for dessert. A popular local band plays beach-party tunes, and yes, everyone dances well into the night, when they aren't playing water-balloon volleyball or bending over backward to win at limbo.

An invitation to one of Ray's clambakes is a coveted prize, with attendant bragging rights. With incentive like that, Dr.

Magda Temple would've camped out in the tox lab to ensure the techs left no stone unturned in their quest to find out what killed Larry Kool.

"So to summarize," Sophie said, "Liddy objected to the autopsy, which ended up uncovering her brother's homicide."

"She did not, however," Louise said, "object to liquefying his body via aquamation."

"Viewed as a whole," I said, "'no' to autopsy and 'yes' to aquamation could signal a guilty mindset."

"Or," Sophie said, "it might have nothing to do with guilt or innocence and it's just Liddy being her typical flaky self."

"She dropped in on her brother often," Louise said, "and had ample opportunity to poison him."

I don't know," I said. "When he introduced us at the cook-off, I got the feeling they hadn't seen each other in a while. She was whining about him ignoring her texts and emails."

"That doesn't necessarily mean anything," Sophie said. "I could see Liddy texting Larry with requests for money even if they were sitting across the table from each other."

Louise said, "She can't be happy that her sister-in-law ended up with the house. It's been in the Kool family for countless generations."

"Madison didn't just get the house in Crystal Harbor," I said. "She also got the ones in Tuscany and Puerto Vallarta, along with Larry's sizable investment portfolio. Not to mention a hefty life-insurance payout. Liddy has to make do with a modest monthly allowance. She *assumed* she'd be inheriting the whole shebang, minus a token bequest to Madison. That's what she told me."

"Well, there's your motive if you're looking for one,"

Sophie said. "Her brother stopped supporting her in the style to which she'd become accustomed. She blamed his wife."

"With good reason," I said.

"But if he were to suddenly drop dead of presumed natural causes?" she said. "Liddy was laboring under the assumption that it would all be hers when he died, that she'd be rolling in dough. No doubt looking forward to the day when she could evict her sister-in-law and make *her* beg for money."

"Speaking of which," I said, "I was at Madison's when you called this morning, Louise. Liddy was there, too, and on my way out I heard her haranguing Madison about her annuity, how she can't possibly live on it. How, with the right clothes and jewelry, she'd be able to catch a rich husband and wouldn't even *need* any of Larry's money."

"Yeah," Sophie said, "'cause that plan's worked so well up till now."

"It's sad," Louise said. "From what I know of Liddy, it's clear she's terrified of ending up old and alone."

"I heard her wailing about how Larry promised to take care of her for life," I said, "which I find highly doubtful, and how the house rightfully belongs to her. Okay, on that second thing, she kinda has a point."

"But is she even capable of taking care of a historic old home like that?" Sophie asked. "Liddy's never owned real estate of any kind. She's been in the same rental apartment forever, and I understand she almost got tossed out more than once."

"Sounds like a recipe for disaster," I said. "To get back to Rex's documentary for a moment, Liddy is determined to stop him from making it. She's convinced its real purpose is to destroy her brother's good name."

"I hate to say it, but she could be right," Louise said.

"As troubling as that is, I'm more concerned about Rex's safety."

"What do you mean?" she asked.

"Let's say Rex starts digging into the murder, asking uncomfortable questions, doing a little investigative journalism. Assuming he's not the one who bumped Larry off, he could be in danger from whoever did."

"If he gets close enough to the truth, you mean," Sophie said. "You think that could be the real reason Liddy's trying to stop the documentary? Because she's afraid of what he'll find out?"

I shrugged. "It's possible."

Louise said, "Since we're working down the list of people who might've had it in for Larry, let's not neglect a certain local charmer with a taste for men who don't happen to be her husband."

"Ugh," Sophie said. "Do we have to talk about Nina?"

The mayor had a right to be bitter about the woman who'd nearly succeeded in stealing the last election from her.

"Bottom line," Louise said, "Nina wanted Larry, Larry didn't want her. But she couldn't accept the rejection. She went so far as to spread a false rumor that she was committing adultery with the town's most well-known, and well-loved, celebrity."

"Well, we all know Nina doesn't like to lose," I said, with a nod to Sophie, "and has been known to go to unethical and even illegal lengths to keep from doing so."

"So the question is," Sophie asked, "just how angry was she about being rejected?"

"Angry enough," Louise said, "to whip up a batch of poison along with all those cookies and pastries she bakes?"

"Speaking of the pastries," I said, "Nina claimed she was sneaking them to Larry, and Madison confirmed it. Who knows when she brought him his last batch?"

"Or whether it contained a special new ingredient," Louise said. "What kind of pastries were these?"

"Apparently his favorite was a recipe she came up with herself called café brûlot chiffon squares."

"What's café brûlot?" Sophie asked.

"It means 'burnt brandy,'" Louise said, "and it hails from Louisiana—spiced coffee with cognac that's set on fire."

"So I'm guessing," I said, "that any dessert made from this stuff is going to be pretty strongly flavored."

"Strong enough," Sophie asked, "to mask the taste of yew tincture?"

"Who knows?" I shrugged. "I should also point out that just like Rex and Frank, Nina could've given Larry another dose of poison at the cook-off."

Sophie pulled a face. "In that chicken-and-bean dreck she was serving, you mean. I managed to force down a single spoonful, and only because my role as a judge required me to taste all the entries."

"Larry also ate just one bite," I said. "But as we've established, he was already sick before he got there."

The faint sound of a key turning in my front-door lock brought our heads up. Sexy Beast and Luci sprang off our laps and raced toward the front of the house, barking like the big, scary guard dogs they were (shh, don't tell them).

Louise and Sophie gave me an inquisitive look. They knew I lived alone.

"Jane! Where are you?" The padre's excited voice rang through the house as he sprinted through the two-story foyer and into the living room before leaping over the two steps leading down into the family room, where we were. SB and Luci were right on his heels, yipping happily, having picked up on the newcomer's manic vibes.

Okay, yes, I'd finally relented and given Martin a key and the alarm code. I was tired of him using his skills as a (former) B&E artist to let himself in anytime he wanted.

He skidded to a breathless halt before us, wearing the biggest grin I'd ever seen on him.

He threw his arms wide. "Well, *hello,* ladies! And aren't you looking absolutely stunning this evening."

For the record, we were all sprawled on the carpet, wearing some variation of sweats. My hair was in a lopsided topknot from which most of it had escaped to hang limply on my neck.

"I must warn you, Martin," Louise said, "if you're experiencing some sort of psychotic break, that is not my medical specialty."

"Not to worry, Louise, I haven't lost my marbles yet. I'm just so…" He took a big breath and locked his eyes on mine. "I'm a grandpa."

I didn't know I could jump to my feet that fast—or squeal that loudly. He was in my arms in a heartbeat, receiving a rib-cracking hug and a big, smacking, congratulatory kiss.

Louise and Sophie took their turns while the canine pack members lost their little minds.

I'm yelling because they're yelling, SB, but why the heck are we all yelling?

The alpha male must've done something very, you know, alpha, Luci. We won't starve today!

"Boy or girl?" I asked.

"A healthy little boy," he said. "Eight pounds, three ounces."

"How's Lexie?"

"Dillon says she's doing just fine. A real trooper. That's my girl!"

Sophie said, "Pics or it didn't happen."

Martin pulled his phone from his jeans pocket. "I'm on my way to Harbor Memorial to see the little guy for myself, but in the meantime, Dillon sent me this." He tapped the screen to bring up a photograph.

We all exclaimed over the close-up of a squinchy newborn wearing a light-blue knit cap. The padre bent down to show the picture to the overexcited dogs.

What the heck is that ugly thing, SB?

Some old man wearing a dopey beanie, Luci. Keep yelling.

"I can't wait to pinch those little cheeks," I said. "Does he have a name yet?"

"Not yet."

"Get over to the hospital, Padre." I gave him a little shove. "You have a grandson to meet."

He wrapped me in a lingering hug, and I'll admit I indulged in a nanosecond of envy before firmly slamming the lid on that self-pitying nonsense. This wasn't about me. It was about Lexie and Dillon and their beautiful new son. It was about the man I loved experiencing the joy of a momentous life event.

His arms tightened and he pressed a gentle kiss to my forehead. My eyes stung. He could read me, could sense every shift in emotion, and it was okay. It was more than okay.

I cleared my throat and smiled up at him. "Give that little boy a kiss for me. And his parents, too."

A HALF HOUR LATER, I'd just said good night to Louise and Sophie (after making plans to finish our inventory the next evening) when my phone once again trilled the opening bars of "Tequila." Glancing at the screen, I saw that my caller was Martin.

I answered with, "So? Does he look like his grampy?"

"I thought you should know," he said, "that Madison is here."

"At the hospital? How does she know Lexie and Dillon?"

"No, that's not—They just brought her here by ambulance," he said. "She's been poisoned, Jane."

13

Flushing Out a Killer

"WELL, NOW I KNOW what it's like to get my stomach pumped." Madison sat against a nest of pillows, tucked under the covers of the old-fashioned four-poster bed she'd once shared with her late husband. She was nearly as pale as her ivory satin nightshirt, except for the dark smudges beneath those striking green eyes. "All in all, it's an experience I could've lived without."

Or not, I thought, considering the procedure very likely saved her life.

Dom sat on the bed next to her, holding her hand. I'd taken a seat on the upholstered storage bench at the foot of the bed, though I didn't plan to stay long. I'd offered to swing by Janey's Place and bring them dinner so Dom wouldn't have to cook, an offer he'd gratefully accepted. After letting me in to the house and stowing the food in the fridge, he'd insisted Madison would be upset if I didn't come upstairs so she could thank me personally.

It was midafternoon. She'd been released from Harbor Memorial Hospital a couple of hours earlier. Dom had stayed in her hospital room overnight and brought her home once the doctors had given her the all-clear.

He shifted so he could look over his shoulder at me. "Have the cops spoken with you yet?"

I nodded. "This morning. Howie and Cookie wanted to know all about my visit here yesterday."

They also wanted to know how jealous I might be feeling, now that Dom had taken up with Larry's widow. And yes, the detectives were my pals, and yes, they knew I was crazy about Martin and totally over my ex, but they had to cover all the bases. I didn't take it personally. For my part, I filled them in on what I'd learned about those who'd seemed to have it in for Larry, for one reason or another.

Dom said, "They interviewed me at the hospital last night. I have to say, I was surprised at how quickly the lab figured out what poison was used."

"Well, they knew what they were looking for this time," I said. "Or at least, what seemed the most likely."

The tests on both Madison's stomach contents and the fruit salad in her kitchen came back positive for taxine, the toxin derived from the yew plant—the same thing that killed Larry.

I turned to her. "Do you mind my asking when you realized you'd been poisoned?"

"I didn't." She shook her head at her own thickheadedness. "Not at first. I'd decided to have some of that fruit salad after dinner. I took a bite—a piece of pear—and thought I detected a bitter aftertaste. The dressing was made with balsamic vinegar, so the fruit should've tasted only sweet and sour. Then I tried a grape."

Dom said what I was thinking. "Why didn't you stop after the first bite?"

"I wasn't thinking about... well, I wasn't thinking," she

admitted. "And I remembered that you'd already eaten a big bowl of it, and you didn't say anything about it tasting strange."

"I didn't just *eat* some of that fruit salad," he said, "I actually made it at home and brought it here that morning. Do I have to tell you how long the detectives questioned me about that?"

Madison squeezed his hand. "They had to know you had nothing to do with poisoning me—or Larry, assuming the same person is responsible for his murder." It might have been my imagination, but she seemed a little more tentative as she turned to me and added, "The same goes for you."

"I don't think they consider either of us suspects," I said, "but they have to interview everyone who had access to your kitchen. It's their job. So how much of the fruit salad did you end up eating?"

"Four or five pieces. I thought, well, maybe it was the steamed kale I'd just eaten. Maybe its bitter taste was lingering."

Yay, more kale. I should've brought Sophie along so we could all watch her gag.

"I thought either that," she said, "or perhaps Dom put some strange herb or something in the fruit salad."

I said, "When did you begin to notice that something was wrong?"

"About an hour later," she said. "It started out as nausea and stomach cramps, and then my heart started racing. I felt foggy. Confused. I made some ginger tea, but it didn't help. That's when I called Dom to see if he'd felt sick at all after eating the fruit."

"I called nine-one-one immediately," he said, "and met her

at the hospital."

"Needless to say, I feel a little foolish." Madison brought his hand to her lips and kissed his knuckles. She held his gaze as she said, "Thank goodness one of us was thinking clearly."

"Don't beat yourself up." Dom brushed a strand of hair off her face. "Confusion is a symptom of this poison. I'm just glad you thought to call me."

"Madison," I said, "did you have any visitors yesterday besides Dom, Liddy, and myself?"

"No. And my housekeeper, Doris, isn't here on Wednesdays."

"Were you home all day?" I asked.

She started to nod, then caught herself. "The Rose Bookshop called to tell me a book I'd ordered had come in— *The Kale Lover's Complete Cookery Book*. I went there to pick it up at around two-thirty or three."

"Dom," I said, "I know you didn't have any of that fruit salad while I was here, so when did you eat it—before I arrived or after I left?"

"Before."

"Who was the last to leave here?" I asked. "You or Liddy?"

Madison answered for him. "Liddy stayed after so she could keep harassing me about money. I finally had to practically wrestle her out the door."

"And was she in your presence the whole time she was here?"

Madison and Dom exchanged a look. It was clear they'd discussed this. And for sure Howie and Cookie would have asked. "She used the bathroom at one point," she said. "And no, I have no way of knowing whether she detoured to the kitchen. But I, well, I just can't see it. Not Liddy."

Dom said, "Let's just wait and see what the detectives turn up."

"I mean, I'm not going to pretend she's my favorite person," Madison said, "but I just don't think she has it in her."

My phone chose that moment to ring. The lively musical ringtone had seemed like a swell idea back when I'd chosen it, but I was dreading the day when I'd forget to silence my phone, and my fellow funeralgoers would be treated to *"Tequila"* at full volume.

I glanced at the screen, and groaned. "Speak of the devil."

Dom's eyebrows rose. "Liddy?"

I nodded glumly. "Would it be terrible if I let it go to voice mail? I really don't feel like getting sucked into…" No need to finish the thought. We were all well acquainted with Madison's high-maintenance sister-in-law.

The look on their faces told me what I'd already surmised: that if I ignored the call, particularly in light of recent events, whatever drama Liddy was embroiled in would only snowball.

"Dang," I muttered, and connected to the call. Before I had a chance to say hello, she was screeching into my ear.

"My apartment is crawling with cops! You have to help me, Jane. They're tearing the place apart!"

THE COPS WERE NOT, as it turned out, tearing the place apart, any more than the medical examiner had "chopped Larry up into little pieces" last month, as his sister had put it. Liddy

Kool had never met an exaggeration she didn't love.

During the eight minutes it took me to drive to the Americana apartment building, my phone emitted at least two dozen notification pings—texts from guess who. For some reason, Liddy had decided the Death Diva was the go-to problem solver, her own personal equalizer, if you will.

The instant the elevator doors opened on the third floor, she lunged inside, seized my arm, and marched me down the hall to apartment 3H. "You have to make them stop!"

"I take it the police are searching your apartment?"

"Duh!" she said. "I never said they could."

"Well, do they have a search warrant?" I asked.

"Yeah, whatever." She flung open the door. "They're going through all my personal stuff. They're *destroying* my home!"

The living room was a mess, all right, but it wasn't due to the search in progress, unless the cops brought dirty drinking glasses and empty fast-food containers with them. Not to mention the leaning tower of yellowing fashion magazines that probably went back twenty years. A sour, stuffy smell pervaded the space, making me wonder if Liddy ever thought to open a window.

Can you imagine this person being responsible for her family's magnificent ancestral home, built when George Washington was president?

Somehow, I no longer felt so conflicted about Larry's young widow inheriting the place. At least I could be fairly confident it wouldn't turn into another Grey Gardens under her stewardship.

Detective Cookie Kaplan was lifting sofa cushions with her gloved hands and inspecting the assorted treasures entombed beneath them: sandwich crusts, cash (both coins and the green stuff), hair doodads, a credit card, and one, two, three, *four* pairs of sunglasses. I heard activity coming from the interior of the apartment. Cookie must have enlisted another officer to assist in the search.

"Hi, Jane." Cookie let the last cushion fall back into place, fanning her face against the cloud of dust and crumbs that erupted. "Liddy mentioned you were on your way. About a hundred times. Not sure why she called you."

"That makes two of us," I said.

Liddy gaped at the detective. "To *stop* you! You're violating my rights. I'm going to sue you *and* your whole police department. You'll be walking a beat when I'm through with you."

To Liddy's consternation, Cookie appeared most amused by this threat.

"You've been watching too many *Chase & Knabbe* reruns," I said. "Cookie, I assume you showed her the warrant."

"Of course." She nodded toward the paperwork sitting on a grimy end table. "Ms. Kool took no interest in it."

The detective was in her late thirties, with curly brown hair pulled back in an artfully messy bun. She wore burgundy-framed eyeglasses and, as usual, a pair of offbeat earrings. Today it was a grinning sun and a winking moon. I don't think I'd ever seen her wear the same earrings twice.

I scanned the first part of the warrant, and told Liddy, "This gives them the right to search your entire home and vehicle. It's legal. A judge signed off on it."

"But what are they *looking* for?" Liddy said, as Cookie strode down the hall to the bedroom. "I didn't *do* anything!"

I read the *Items to Be Seized* section. No surprises there. "They're looking for anything relating to the yew plant," I told her. "Specifically it mentions any parts of the plant, including but not limited to seeds, leaves, and bark, as well as any products created from the plant, including but not limited to liquid products."

"Yeah," Liddy said, "that detective with the stupid earrings told me Madison got herself poisoned. She asked me if I messed with that disgusting fruit salad."

"Disgusting?" I said.

"Well, it had some kind of vinegar in it, right? That's what her boyfriend said. That guy Don."

"Dom."

"Whatever. I mean, who puts vinegar on fruit, anyway? Yuck." Suddenly she gasped. "He tried to get *me* to eat it. You heard him! He tried to *kill* me! *Detective!*" She ran into the bedroom, hollering, "You have to arrest Madison's boyfriend. His name is Don something. He tried to kill me, too!"

As I scanned the search warrant for any other pertinent info, my eyes fell on the section labeled *Probable Cause*. It seems that when the detectives interviewed Liddy that morning, she complained bitterly about her greedy sister-in-law, yammering nonstop about Madison's hateful personality and destructive influence on Larry, even going so far as to accuse Madison of murdering her husband.

I wasn't surprised that Liddy lacked the sense to keep her big mouth shut when questioned by the detectives. I was surprised, however, to read that her fingerprints had been found on the refrigerator handle in Madison's kitchen as well as on the bowl containing the fruit salad. It seems Liddy had been arrested for DUI a few years back, which meant her prints were on file and available for comparison.

Well. This was a whole different kettle of fish. Or fruit. I'd been wondering what evidence the detectives had shown the judge to get her to sign the search warrant. Now I knew.

Cookie escorted Liddy back into the living room. Giving me a pointed look, she said, "I need Ms. Kool to remain in here until we're done."

I nodded to acknowledge my role as official Liddy wrangler. I steered her to the sofa. "Let's sit down. They'll finish faster if we're not in their way."

"Detective?" a female voice called from the bathroom. "I have something."

Cookie joined the other officer. Liddy looked questioningly at me, as if I had all the answers. All I could do was shrug.

Glancing around, I noticed small, pink-and-black labels on some of her belongings: WATER on a spray bottle. SPIDER PLANT on a flower pot containing dead, shriveled vegetation. NAIL POLISH on a clear plastic box crammed with dozens of bottles of guess what.

The detective returned a couple of minutes later, trailed by an officer I knew, Geri Marvin, a petite woman with a brown ponytail and a smug, self-important attitude. Geri and I offered each other cursory greetings.

Cookie held up a sealed, transparent police evidence bag, inside of which was a small, wet plastic baggie edged with silver duct tape. My heart stuttered when I saw what was inside the smaller bag: a tiny glass vial containing an amber liquid.

"This was found taped inside your toilet tank, Ms. Kool," she said. "Would you care to explain?"

"I have no idea what that is," Liddy said. "I've never seen it. Why would I tape something inside my toilet? That's disgusting."

Geri said, "Not in the *toilet*. In the clean-water tank *behind* the toilet."

The detective gave the officer a quelling look. Geri glared at Liddy.

"There's a label on the bottle," Cookie said, "the kind made with one of those battery-operated label makers. Like the one you own."

Geri held up another evidence bag containing the label-making device.

"Oh, cool! Where'd you find that?" Liddy actually reached out as if expecting the cops to hand it over. "I've been looking for that thing."

"Don't you want to know what the label on the bottle says?" Cookie asked.

Liddy gave an impatient sigh.

"It says 'yew.'"

"It has my name on it?" Liddy said. "That's weird, 'cause like I said, I've never seen—"

"Not *y-o-u*." I could tell Cookie's patience was at its breaking point. "It says *y-e-w*, as in the plant that's the source of the poison we're looking for." She held the evidence bag closer so we could see the little pink-and-black label, before handing the bag to Geri and producing a pair of handcuffs.

"Liddy Kool, I'm arresting you for the attempted murder of Madison Kool. You have the right to remain silent..."

Yeah, that'll happen.

14

The End of the Road

"NOT EVEN A HINT?" I asked.

"That would spoil the fun," Martin said.

"Translation—if you'd told me where we're going, I'd have refused to accompany you."

The padre just smiled.

It was Saturday, two days after Liddy's arrest. We were in Martin's vintage Mustang, ostensibly for an aimless ride on a gorgeous autumn afternoon. Yeah, right. This man did not do *aimless*. But I knew not to waste my breath demanding he reveal our destination.

I only hoped I was dressed appropriately. My outfit, in case you're wondering, consisted of black jeans, black suede half boots, and a pale-pink pullover with a pretty scarf in an abstract watercolor pattern. The jeans were new and reasonably fashionable, not old and faded for once. So I was okay for a restaurant as long as it wasn't superfancy. But it was about two p.m. and we'd both already had lunch, so…

Where the heck was he taking me?

The late-September weather had turned cool, but the leaves wouldn't change color for a few more weeks, so I knew this outing wasn't about leaf peeping. At first I'd hoped we were heading for the local animal shelter, that Martin had changed his mind about adopting Layla. But as we drove in the opposite direction, I was forced to relinquish that particular fantasy. It was so frustrating. I knew he loved that big, silly dog, and she was crazy about him. They were meant to be packmates.

And yeah, I checked every few days to see whether she'd been adopted. It seemed Martin was right. Large adult mixed-breed dogs, and in particular black dogs, weren't most folks' number-one choice.

As for where the padre was taking me, all I knew was that we were driving west, toward Manhattan, rather than east, toward the far end of Long Island. We'd already left Suffolk county behind and were in Nassau. I did notice that Martin was staying off the major highways, which told me we were almost certainly not headed for the city.

I said, "So is the little guy all settled in?" Lexie and Dillon had brought their new son home a couple of days earlier.

Martin grinned. "I got to hold him. A real armful!"

"As handsome as his grandpa?"

"Well, that's a pretty high bar, you have to admit," he said. "Give him time."

"I can't wait to meet him," I said. "As soon as his parents have gotten a little sleep and are ready for visitors, let me know." I'd already stopped in to Beatrice & Daughters, an upscale baby store on Main Street, to buy the newcomer an adorable little outfit. Okay, three outfits, a baby bathtub, and one of those complicated infant play gyms.

"They'd love to see you. So far it's just been close family. The grandmas have been taking turns staying with them to help out. My mom, too, of course." He decided to change the subject. "Anything new on the police investigation?"

"What investigation?" I said. "The cops stopped looking for suspects once they arrested Liddy."

All too aware of her garrulous nature, I'd advised her not to say anything—*not a goldarn word!*—until she'd met with her court-appointed lawyer. I had little hope that she'd heed my advice, but I had to try.

It wasn't that I necessarily thought she was innocent. As far as I was concerned, the jury was still out. So to speak. It's just that in some ways—whether due to narcissism, naïveté, or an unholy combination of both—Liddy Kool was her own worst enemy. If she *was* innocent, I could see her yakking her way to a wrongful conviction, just because she didn't know when to shut the heck up.

Unable to make the exorbitant bail (the only close relative in a position to chip in being her victim), Liddy remained behind bars.

"Did I tell you," I said, "that when the cops found the bottle of poison, it was labeled 'yew'?"

He shot me a dumbfounded look. "You're kidding. Because, what, otherwise she'd forget what was in the little vial she'd secretly taped inside her toilet tank?"

"They checked out the label. It definitely came from her own label maker. And the only fingerprints on the device were hers."

"You know Liddy better than I do," he said. "Does that seem like something she'd do? Carefully label the poison she uses on her sister-in-law? And most likely her brother, too."

"Who's to say? This isn't the first time I've asked myself how that woman's mind works."

"I assume they've tested the contents of the vial," he said.

I nodded. "It's a tincture made from yew—a concentrate of the toxin. Same thing that killed Larry."

"Which means the attempted-murder charge will be amended to include actual murder," Martin said.

"As long as they can connect her to Larry's death," I said. "Which, assuming she's guilty of poisoning his widow, is kind of a given."

"*Assuming* she's guilty?" He glanced at me. "Am I missing something? Seems pretty cut-and-dried to me." When I didn't immediately respond, he said, "Okay, so what does the famous Death Diva gut have to say about all this?"

"Something about it doesn't smell right."

"The famous Death Diva nose, then." He shot me a teasing smile, but I wasn't in the mood to return it.

"I know Liddy's a flake," I said, "and maybe 'flake' is too mild. Maybe loose cannon is more like it. But you weren't there, Padre. At her apartment. You didn't see how, well, how clueless she was. Like she didn't really grasp the trouble she was in, not until Cookie slapped the handcuffs on her."

"Could be she's just a good actor," he said.

"No one's ever accused her of being that," I said. "And it's not like anyone's going to buy an insanity defense, if that's what you're implying. The thing is, as self-involved as Liddy is, she doesn't know to leap out of the way when the proverbial freight train is bearing down on her."

Now it was Martin's turn to pause, thinking, as he made a right off of Piping Rock Road onto Frost Pond Road. We were in Old Brookville. Or maybe Glen Head. I wasn't that familiar with this area.

Finally he said, "She lives alone, right?"

"Right."

"No boyfriend?" he asked. "No close relatives?"

"No steady boyfriend, and the guy she was with at the cook-off is already history. Seems they never stick around for long. As for family, Larry was all she had."

"So we can assume no one else has a key to her apartment?" he asked.

"I thought of that," I said. "She told the detectives she has the only key."

"Meaning it's unlikely anyone else taped that little bottle inside her toilet tank."

"Unless they did it the same way she put the poison in Madison's fruit salad," I said. "*If* she did it. By slipping around without her hostess's knowledge."

"So you're saying someone could've visited Liddy and planted 'proof' of her guilt while they were in the john."

"It wouldn't be that simple. This 'someone' would've had to locate Liddy's label maker—which Cookie told me they found in a rat's nest of junk under her bed—labeled the vial of poison, planted the vial in the bathroom, and put the label maker back under the bed."

"All while Liddy is presumably within earshot in her small apartment," he said. "No, it would've had to be a break-in. How are her locks?"

I shrugged. "She lives in the Americana. Built fifty years ago and reasonably well maintained. Not sure about the locks, but I assume she has a deadbolt."

"If she even uses it," he said. "Not everyone is that diligent, plus I can picture Liddy forgetting to lock up when she leaves."

"What about Madison's house?" I asked.

"What about it?" Martin turned left onto Cedar Swamp Road for a short distance, then right onto Sea Cliff Avenue.

Which meant we were in the village of Sea Cliff, which meant we'd come to the end of the road.

No, I mean that literally. Sea Cliff is on the water. To reach the next town to the west, we'd need to ditch the Mustang and swim across Hempstead Bay. Or drive around the bay. But the swimming thing is, you know, more direct.

"Who do you know in Sea Cliff?" I asked.

He chose to answer my previous question. "If you're thinking someone could've broken into Madison's house and poisoned her fruit salad, then it's possible but unlikely. I'm betting that old place has excellent locks and a state-of-the-art alarm system."

"So does my house," I said, "but that never stopped *you*. Good grief, I must've been crazy to give you a key."

"No, just madly in love."

"What, a person can't be both? Oh."

"What?"

"I just remembered," I said. "Madison mentioned that she went out that day, to the bookstore, just a few hours before she ate the poisoned fruit. She wasn't gone long, so she might not have set the alarm."

Martin made a couple of more turns onto narrow, curving roads lined with Victorian-era homes. "So it's theoretically possible," he said, "for someone to have broken into Madison's house while she was out, poisoned the fruit, and then slipped into Liddy's apartment to tape the little vial of yew toxin inside her toilet tank."

"Emphasis on 'theoretically,'" I said. "You have to admit that scenario is pretty farfetched."

"Let's say it happened that way, for the sake of argument. Then how do Liddy's fingerprints end up on Madison's fridge door and fruit bowl?"

"I'll tell you what Liddy told the cops," I said. "She admits she *did* sneak into the kitchen after she used the bathroom, but only because she was curious about a fruit salad made with vinegar. She wanted to taste it for herself, but just a bite or two on the sly, not a whole bowlful in case she didn't like it. Which she didn't. It turned out to be 'yucky.'"

"Pretty lame explanation," he said.

"I agree, but hey." I shrugged. "That's Liddy."

"And she didn't get sick."

"Which, if she's telling the truth," I said, "means the fruit was poisoned after she left."

"Do you happen to know whether they found her fingerprints on the vial of poison?"

I half turned to face him. "That's the thing—they *didn't*! There were no prints on it or the baggie or the tape. I mean, are we supposed to believe Liddy took care to wipe her prints from the bottle of poison she hid in her home but didn't think to do that when she sprinkled some of it on her victim's food?"

"I agree, it doesn't make much sense, but again..."

We said it together. "That's Liddy."

He pulled to a stop in front of a three-story cedar-shake house perched on a high cliff overlooking the bay. Like many of its neighbors, this home looked to be at least a hundred years old, but lovingly maintained, with freshly painted yellow-ochre siding, maroon window frames, and sage-green shutters.

"Okay, so who lives here?" I asked, but Martin was already out of the car.

When he reached the front door, he turned and saw me still sitting in the passenger seat, arms crossed, treating him to a frosty glare.

He responded with his most engaging grin, the one he knew darn well I couldn't resist. It was a look that said, *You've made your point, I'm a rascally scamp and I don't know how you put up with me, but just humor me this once and I promise I'll never do it again. Until next time.*

I gave him another few seconds of The Glare, muttering some choice words it was just as well he couldn't hear, before letting myself out of the car, giving the door a good hard slam, and stomping up the brick walkway to stand next to him.

The padre leaned down and kissed me. He whispered, "Thank you," and for one charmed instant those blue, blue eyes swam with raw, unfiltered emotion and not a hint of guile.

And that's when I realized he needed me there, by his side. He just hadn't known how to tell me.

I squeezed his hand, then reached up and gave the brass door knocker a couple of polite taps. He took a deep breath, let it out slowly, and waited. A half minute later the door swung open.

Martin said, "Hello, Claudia."

15

I Know All About You

MARTIN'S HALF SISTER stared at us without recognition. Clearly he hadn't called ahead. "I'm sorry," she said, "do I know you?"

"I'm Martin McAuliffe."

Her eyes widened and she stifled a gasp. Her words were barely audible. "I—I should've known. You look so much like him." Meaning, I assumed, their father. Hugh McAuliffe.

No one said anything for long, torturous moments. When I could no longer stand the tension, I thrust my hand out. "Claudia, I'm Jane Delaney. Martin's girlfriend. It's nice to meet you at last."

Claudia's good breeding overcame her shock and whatever darker, more painful emotions lurked beneath the surface. She reached out on autopilot and shook my hand. She did not, however, invite us in.

Claudia McAuliffe Robbins was an attractive woman in her mid to late forties. She shared the padre's crystal-blue eyes. Her shoulder-length dark-blond hair was threaded with a few strands of silver. She wore jeans and a plaid blouse in muted tones.

She gave Martin a worried frown. "Has something happened?"

It was clear what she meant: something terrible along the lines of a death or grave illness. Which might have made sense if these two knew each other, but despite being half siblings, they were virtual strangers.

"No. Nothing like…" He shook his head.

"Then why are you here?"

He met her gaze unflinchingly. "It's time, Claudia."

She stood her ground. "Why now? It's been… too long."

"You're right," he said. "It's been much too long. It never should've been like this."

Her features hardened. "And whose fault is that?"

You would've been proud of me. I managed to zip my lip, through sheer force of will. It's your fault! *I wanted to shout.* You're the older sibling. You had all the advantages. You should've reached out to your younger, troubled half brother.

Martin had a different answer. "I think we both know whose fault it is, and he's not standing here. He doesn't get a vote in whether you invite us in or we get back in my car and drive away."

While she pondered his words, I heard a door creak open across the street. I glanced over my shoulder and saw a woman's face peeking out at us. To Claudia's credit, she ignored her nosy neighbor, who was obviously curious about why these visitors had gotten no farther than the Robbinses' front porch. I could almost hear her wondering what we were selling, and were we going to bang on her door next.

"What do you want?" Claudia asked Martin.

His expression was unguarded, his voice barely above a whisper. "I want to meet my sister."

After a moment she looked away, blinking. She let out a harsh breath.

I heard footfalls in the foyer behind her. "Mom, when's—?" Nate cut himself off when he spied Martin. "What the hell is *he* doing here?"

Startled, Claudia looked from her son to her brother. Her tone was accusatory as she said, "How do you know Nate?" Without giving Martin time to respond, she wheeled on Nate. "What did he do? Has he been bothering you?"

I said, "Oh, for heaven's sake—"

"Jane, it's okay." The padre and Nate had themselves a little stare-down. I realized he was reluctant to bust the kid. They must have reached an unspoken understanding, because Nate tossed his hand as if to say, *Whatever. Go ahead and tell her.*

Martin turned to his sister. "Nate introduced himself to me."

Now she really looked alarmed. She confronted her son. "You *introduced* yourself? Where? When did this happen?"

"It's no big deal," Nate said. "I just wanted to see him for myself, okay?"

Claudia seized his arm as he started to turn away. "It most definitely *is* a big deal. I'm your mother. Since when do you go behind my back?"

He jerked out of her grasp. "Since you treat your own relatives like some horrible secret. I wouldn't even have known you had a brother if I hadn't overheard you and dad that time. At least Grandpa *tells* me things."

Martin and I exchanged a look. So that was it. I could only imagine the things Hugh McAuliffe had told his grandson about wicked Uncle Martin.

"Your grandfather shouldn't be—" Claudia's lips compressed into a hard line. "If you have questions, you should come to me, not him.”

“Why?” Nate sneered. “So you can tell me again how it’s none of my business?”

“I never said that—”

“You said he’s not really family.” He jerked his head toward Martin. “He doesn’t care about us, so why should we care about him?”

Claudia closed her eyes briefly and expelled a ragged breath. “I’ll ask again. Where did this ‘introduction’ of yours take place?”

Nate mumbled, “Murray’s Pub. In Crystal Harbor.”

“A *pub*?” She shook her head. “This just keeps getting better and better. You’re sixteen, Nate. You had no business going into a pub.”

Martin said, “I tend bar there. Nate didn’t try to order any alcohol. I guess he just wanted to… put a face to my name.”

Claudia gave Nate a look that mothers have been giving their impertinent teenage sons since time immemorial. “So let me get this straight. You accosted your uncle at his place of business in front of his customers and other employees.”

“I didn’t…” Nate whined. “I mean, ‘accost’? It wasn’t like that.”

Excuse me, you little liar, but it was precisely like that. If I bit my tongue any harder, it would break in half.

Claudia’s expression was ominous. “We’ll talk about this later. Meanwhile…” She opened the door wider, stepped back, and gave a resigned sigh. “You’d better come in.”

It wasn’t much as far as invitations went, but we weren’t about to get all Emily Post on her. That was Liddy’s bailiwick, after all.

Claudia’s home had retained much of its original Victorian

character, from the gleaming dark woodwork to the parquet flooring, period wallpaper, and ornate brass chandeliers.

We passed through the foyer and into an octagonal parlor with old-fashioned maroon wallpaper, a tray ceiling picked out in sage-green and gold, and built-in, glass-fronted hutches displaying an eclectic variety of objects, including a basket filled with seashells, a child's clay sculpture of a bird, and a wooden box that might have been a humidor. Perhaps Claudia's husband was a cigar smoker. The sofa and armchairs were overstuffed brown leather, burnished from long use. Not from the Victorian era, but not purchased last week, either. Throw pillows in a variety of textures and patterns contributed to the cozy, welcoming feel of the room.

Claudia gestured toward the sofa. Martin and I obediently sat. Her ingrained politeness wouldn't let her leave it at that. "I'll put a pot of coffee on. Nate, do we have any of those brownies left?"

Brownies and hot black coffee sounded like the very definition of heaven just then, but I forced myself to say, "I won't hear of it, Claudia. Not after the way we barged in on you."

The look Martin gave me suggested I'd lost my marbles. *Brownies, Jane!*

"Well, I know *I* could use a cup," she said. "It won't take five minutes."

After she left us, Nate sprawled in one of the armchairs, treating us to what he no doubt considered an unnerving stare. We simply stared right back.

Finally he smirked at Martin "I know all about you, you know."

The padre's tone was perfectly agreeable as he said, "We

don't have to do it this way, Nate."

The boy spread his arms. "Do what? I'm just making conversation, *Uncle Martin.*"

He made it sound like a cussword.

"I know you *think* you know all about me," Martin said. "All I would say about that is, consider the source."

Nate straightened. "What does that mean? My grandpa doesn't lie to me."

I let my fingertips rest lightly on Martin's thigh. A subtle warning to tread carefully.

The padre retrieved his phone from a pocket and gave the screen a few taps. He held it so Nate could see the photo he'd pulled up. "This is my mom. Your great-aunt. Her name is Stephanie. Friends call her Stevie."

Stevie Borden didn't look like anyone's great-aunt—or great-grandmother, for heaven's sake, which she now was. She was sixty-two but looked at least ten years younger, thanks to good genes and an active lifestyle.

The boy took one bored glance and slumped back against the leather cushion. "So?"

"So Stevie enrolled at SUNY Stony Brook when she was a couple of years older than you are now," Martin said. "Her family couldn't afford to help—well, they didn't even want her to go to college, but that's another story—so she worked part-time to pay for tuition and books. Wanted to be a teacher."

Nate yawned ostentatiously. "Fascinating."

Maybe it was just as well I never had kids, because I doubted I'd be able to control my temper in the face of such insolence.

"She got a work-study job in the university's main library," Martin continued, "but that didn't pay much, so she supplemented her income by dancing at a men's club a couple of nights a week."

Now he had Nate's gleeful attention. "Your mom was a stripper? No way! Did she give lap dances?"

The padre had to grasp my wrist to keep me from springing up and giving this rude boy what for.

"I'm guessing your grandpa left that part out," Martin said, "about being a regular customer at a strip joint. Not a good look for a church deacon and good family man. Your mother would've been three or four when he got involved with Stevie."

Nate shrugged. "So your stripper mom got herself pregnant."

I couldn't restrain myself. "That's biologically impossible."

"Huh?"

"No woman can get herself pregnant," I said. "She needs help."

"Yeah, well, your boyfriend's mom, she had it all planned out," Nate told me. "She was looking for a well-off guy to trap. Grandpa had no intention of cheating on Grandma, but this stripper seduced him and got knocked up on purpose. Figured she could soak him for support, be set for the rest of her life. Threatened to tell his family if he didn't pay up. Only, she didn't count on him standing up for himself. In the end she didn't get a penny," he added, with a smug smile.

"Are you finished?" Martin said. "Would you like to know what really happened?"

"So is this where we do a 'he said, she said'?"

"This fiction your grandpa spun, about Stevie being some sort of calculating femme fatale, it's all BS. She was a poor student struggling to support herself, like I said. She caught Hugh's eye and he pursued her. They had an affair, her birth control failed, and she got pregnant."

"You're leaving out the part about her doing it with a married man," Nate said.

"Hugh told her he was single," Martin said. "When Stevie could no longer hide her baby bump, her folks kicked her out of the house. She was homeless and out of work. Had to drop out of college, of course. All she wanted was for her child's father to live up to his financial responsibility. Instead Hugh sicced a team of high-priced lawyers on her. He could've supported his son for less than he ended up paying those lawyers."

Nate said nothing for a minute as he digested his uncle's words. It was indeed a case of "he said, she said," but I had to wonder if Martin's truthful version of events might've gotten through to him, just a little, might've made him question what he'd been told. It was also possible this smart kid wasn't as credulous as Hugh assumed. Maybe, despite his love for the old man, Nate had begun to see through some of his self-serving prevarications.

Finally he said, "So how about you breaking into my grandparents' house in the middle of the night? I guess you're gonna tell me that never happened, huh?"

"No, that happened, all right," Martin said.

Nate's gaze snapped to his uncle's face. I could tell he wasn't expecting him to admit it.

"I was the same age you are now," the padre continued, "and a total screw-up. I became a father about a year later. That's what made me finally get my act together."

"Whoa, you had a kid at seventeen?"

"I don't recommend it," Martin said.

"Don't worry," Nate laughed, "I'm too smart to mess up like that."

Ah, the arrogance of youth.

"So what did your grandpa tell you about that night?" Martin asked.

"You broke in, like I said. With a gun."

A huff of laughter escaped Martin.

"What?" Nate demanded.

"Nothing," he chuckled. "Go on. I want to hear what else I did."

Nate wore a dubious frown as he said, "You woke everyone up—Grandpa, Grandma, and my mom—and threatened to shoot them all. Their dog tried to attack you, so you grabbed his collar and put the gun to his head and told my grandpa you were gonna blow away his pet."

"The dog's name was Whupper," Martin said. "That's what his tag read. He was the sweetest pit bull you could ever hope to run into during a home invasion. All Whupper wanted to do was play fetch and lick my face and steal doggie treats from the kitchen. That's what we were doing when your dad came downstairs. With his shotgun."

"No way," Nate said. "Grandpa would've told me if he was armed."

"Must've slipped his mind," the padre said. "Looked like a pretty old twelve-gauge from where I stood shaking in my sneakers."

I spoke up. "Nate, do you know whether your grandfather owns a shotgun?"

"Yeah. So? His dad gave it to him when he was a kid. They used to go duck hunting. He's shown it to me once or twice."

"Where does he keep it?" I asked.

"In his bedroom closet." He quickly added, "But that doesn't mean he had it with him that night."

"No, of course not," I said. "Why would a homeowner grab his shotgun when he hears an intruder in the middle of the night? That just makes no sense."

Nate did not care for my tone, I could tell. Too bad.

Martin said, "Let me ask you this, Nate. How many times has your grandpa told you this story?"

"I don't know." He shrugged. "Three or four times, I guess. When I was about twelve I asked him to tell me about you, 'cause my mom refused, like I said. So he told me how you terrorized his family that night."

"And were the details exactly the same," the padre asked, "each time he talked about it?"

I could read the answer on the kid's face. His shrug told us how totally bored he was with these awkward questions.

"I'll take that as a no," Martin said. "It's hard to keep the details straight when you're making a lot of them up."

"I told you, my grandpa doesn't—"

"I know," Martin said, "he doesn't lie to you. Here's what really happened, if you're interested. I crawled through the unlocked window of your grandfather's study and made a huge racket running around the house and playing with Whupper."

"You made noise on purpose?" Nate asked. "Why?"

"I wasn't there to rob or hurt anyone," he said, "I just wanted to jerk Hugh's chain, this so-called father who'd treated my existence like some minor inconvenience, to be dealt with by his legal team and then forgotten. I'll be the first to admit my actions that night were monumentally stupid, but for the record, I did not compound that stupidity by going in there armed. I wasn't packing so much as a nail clipper."

Nate fidgeted, staring into the cold fireplace. "Why should I believe you?"

"Because it's the truth." It was Claudia, entering the room with a tray holding a full coffee carafe, mugs, the usual etceteras, and yes, a plate of homemade brownies. She set the tray on the coffee table and said, "I wasn't trying to eavesdrop, but the kitchen is right over there and I heard most of your conversation."

She sat on the other stuffed chair and turned to her son. "I had no idea you were talking to Grandpa about all this."

Nate shrugged. "He didn't want me to tell you. Said it would upset you."

Somehow I knew all the adults in the room were thinking the same thing: Hugh didn't want his grandson to tell Claudia about their conversations because he knew she'd contradict him.

She seemed to be mulling this over as she poured coffee and urged us to try the brownies. "Nate made them," she said. "He's quite the baker."

I took a bite and declared, with all honesty, that it was the best brownie I'd ever tasted. "The chocolate is so intense, and it's the perfect texture. Not too cakey or too fudgy."

"Better than Patisserie Susanne," Martin declared, "and I always thought nothing could beat theirs."

Nate tried, and failed, to play it cool. "I use three kinds of chocolate in the batter. It's my own recipe. Must've taken twenty tries to get it right."

"He had plenty of willing guinea pigs," Claudia said, "when the girls were all home at the same time."

Martin paused with the coffee mug halfway to his mouth. "Nate has sisters?"

Her eyebrows rose. "Three of them. The twins, Stella and Olivia, are in college, and Ellie lives in Minnesota. I thought you knew."

"I know nothing at all about you and your family, Claudia."

"But you're a private investigator," she said. "I just assumed you'd been, well, keeping tabs on us."

He set the mug down. "Honestly, I avoided learning anything about any of you. When I decided it was time we got acquainted, I just looked up your address."

She nodded, and I could see she was beginning to comprehend how difficult it had been for him to finally take that step.

He added, "But it would seem you know a bit about me."

"What can I tell you?" She offered an embarrassed smile. "You're my brother. I was curious. I know you moved from Rocky Bay to Crystal Harbor a little over a year ago. That's when you left your job in Southampton and started working at Murray's Pub."

"I moved to be closer to a certain individual I'd grown kinda fond of." The padre gave me a playful elbow nudge.

I felt my face heat. "This is the first time you actually admitted that."

"I knew you'd figure it out." To Claudia he said, "I'm sure you know about what I will politely refer to as my misspent youth."

"Which ended around the time your daughter, Alexandra, was born."

"Everyone calls her Lexie," he said.

"I also know," Claudia said, "that you got a degree in criminal justice from John Jay."

"I do some bodyguard work in addition to investigations," he said. "Plus the bartending, of course. Keeps things interesting. What do you do?"

"I'm CEO of a marketing agency in Manhattan."

"Nice. And your husband?"

Before she could answer, Nate said, "My dad died in January."

"I'm so sorry to hear that," Martin said. "I had no idea."

Claudia said, "It was sudden. Thad had a stroke. Nate and his grandfather have spent a lot of time together since then."

I suspected she was trying to explain Hugh's outsize influence on the boy.

"Dad was never as close to the girls," she said. "He was so pleased when he finally got a grandson."

Nate turned to his mother. "You said Martin was telling the truth. About when he broke in to Grandma and Grandpa's house. For real?"

She gave an unhappy sigh. "Your grandfather... embellished a bit, Nate. And left some details out. I was home from college when it happened. I'll never forget that night."

"I'm sorry," Martin said. "I know it's far too late for apologies, but I never intended to frighten you or your mother."

"Once you told us who you were, it all made sense," she said. "I still thought you were a little hoodlum, but I got why you were there."

Nate said, "You mean you didn't know Grandpa had a son until that night?"

"He never told anyone," she said. "You know Grandpa. He's all about reputation. But once I laid eyes on Martin, I never doubted he was my brother. I mean, look at him. You've seen pictures of your grandpa when he was younger. And also, well, you might as well know, Nate. That wasn't the only time

Grandpa strayed. Grandma told me later about the women."

Nate looked stricken. It's hard when your heroes mess up. "If she knew, why did she stay with him?"

"Relationships are messy," she said. "Marriage is messy."

An angry flush stained his cheeks. "Did Dad ever do that? Mess around?"

Claudia shook her head. "No. I'm certain of it. And neither did I." When he responded with a sullen stare, she added, "I wouldn't lie to you about this, Nate. I know I haven't been very… forthcoming about certain things, but I will never lie."

"So Martin didn't have a gun?" Nate asked.

"No, he did not. Your grandfather did have his shotgun, and he was… well, I'd never seen him like that. Beyond enraged. I was afraid he might lose control and…" She didn't finish the thought.

"Shoot him?" Nate wore an incredulous frown. "His own son?"

Martin said, "Your mom deserves the credit for defusing him. She got the gun away from him and convinced him not to call the cops. Then she held the front door open, and I ran like the house was on fire." He addressed his sister. "Thank you for saving my brainless butt."

She gave a half laugh. "We'll never know if I actually did that, but you're welcome."

Something passed between the siblings then, as they sat smiling at each other, and I sensed there might be hope yet for this particular "messy relationship."

Martin said, "You asked me why I came here—whether something happened. I said no, but that's not strictly true. I meant nothing *bad* happened." He produced his phone again, gave it a couple of taps, and handed it to Claudia.

Her face lit up as she studied the screen. She smiled at me. "It would seem congratulations are in order, Jane."

"What?" I craned my neck to view the screen. "Oh! No, this little fellow isn't mine. His mom is Lexie."

Claudia gaped at her brother. "You're a *grandfather?*"

He grinned. "And here I thought you knew everything about me."

"I knew Lexie got married about a year and a half ago, but I had no idea she was expecting. How wonderful!" She passed the phone to her son.

Nate's features softened as he scrolled through the images. "He's so little."

"Only three days old. He's changing every day." The padre wore the sweetest, proudest smile as he added, "They named him Martin."

I gasped. Joyous laughter escaped me as I hugged my man.

Claudia's eyes shone. "You must be a heck of a dad to make your daughter want to name her son after you."

He acknowledged the compliment with an embarrassed little shrug as Nate handed the phone back. "Lexie was my number-one priority from the moment she was born. And now my little troublemaker has a little troublemaker of her own," he chuckled. "I feel like the luckiest guy alive. The instant I laid eyes on my grandson, I knew it was time to mend our family, Claudia. Or at least try."

"I'm glad you did. Does Lexie know about me?" When he nodded, she said, "I'd like to send a baby present."

"I have a better idea," he said. "We could all get together, once little Marty is ready to meet his adoring public. Ideally at a time when Nate's sisters can join us."

"Maybe at my place," I said. "I have the room, and we can have a nice brunch."

Which I'd have catered, of course. Something told me these folks would be less than impressed with Fruity Pebbles and toaster waffles.

"I'll bring brownies," Nate said.

"I'll hold you to that."

I heard the front door open and close. Claudia stiffened. Nate suddenly looked grim. I had a sickening feeling I knew why.

"Nate!" a male voice called from the front of the house.

Claudia raised her voice. "We're in here, Dad."

Martin asked, "Does he live with you?"

She shook her head. "But he has a key."

Moments later Hugh McAuliffe entered the room. He was in his early seventies, tall, with receding white hair and glasses. He wore neat khakis and a windbreaker over a red sport shirt. His features rearranged themselves into a welcoming smile when he noticed Martin and me. "I didn't realize you had company."

The padre stood and closed the distance between himself and his father. He uttered a respectful, "Sir," and held out his hand.

Hugh's hand started to come up even as he glanced around the room and saw that the rest of us hadn't moved a muscle. No one was smiling. Or even breathing, but maybe that was just me.

His gaze flew back to his son's face and he saw it then. Probably felt like he was looking into a time-travel mirror. The hand fell back to his side. The pleasant smile was history.

"You've got some damn nerve," he growled.

Claudia stood. "Dad—"

"Get out!" Hugh pointed toward the front of the house and commanded his son, "You get the hell out of here."

"This is my house, Dad," Claudia said. "Martin is my guest." She faced her father squarely, seemingly unmoved by his fury if you didn't count a wash of hot color in her cheeks.

Clearly this man was accustomed to being in control, and being obeyed. He turned to his grandson. Nate averted his gaze.

Hugh glared at his daughter. "You have no idea what you're doing, Claudia."

She straightened her spine. "I think I do, and it's something I should've done long ago."

He treated us all to one last caustic sneer and slammed out of the house.

16
Cheap Creep

"SO WHO'S COMING back here next month for Halloween?" I asked.

All five teenagers—the three girls and two boys who constituted Crystal Harbor High School's History Club—let me know they were totally stoked about the town's annual Halloween Cemetery Tour.

We'd just left the historical section of Whispering Willows Cemetery and were strolling toward the front gate under gray skies. The History Club had asked me to give a talk about the famous and infamous individuals from Crystal Harbor's past who'd been interred there beginning in the seventeenth century.

Arlo Pleasant, the boneyard's owner, had volunteered to do the honors himself, but the kids weren't interested in hearing that stiff (yeah, I said it) drone on in his self-important manner. Only the original, authentic Death Diva would do. Naturally, I took pains to make our little excursion through local history as entertaining as possible. Not a difficult task, considering most of the heavy lifting had been done for me by some of the wild and wonderful characters buried beneath our feet. The club's history aficionados couldn't get enough of their outrageous stories. Some things, you just can't make up.

Sunday afternoon had brought swollen clouds and cooler temperatures than the day before, when Martin and I had visited Claudia. I'd shoved a small umbrella into my purse, but thankfully, the rain had held off.

I know what you're thinking. *Enough about the weather, Jane. I want to know more about that Halloween Cemetery Tour.*

Well, if you insist. The tour was less than six weeks away, but preparations had been in the works for months. It was one of Crystal Harbor's most popular events, and every year those of us responsible for making it happen strove to outdo ourselves.

The Halloween tour took place in the historical section, but that was the only thing it had in common with the educational talk I'd just given. The festivities would commence at midnight on October 31. This year we planned to serve Sybbie's Punch to those adults who cared to imbibe, and apple cider to everyone else. The creepy snacks would include red velvet cupcakes topped with vanilla buttercream and drizzled with blood (otherwise known as raspberry sauce); cookies decorated with ghosts, zombies, and spiders; and mini mummy pizzas, complete with mozzarella bandages and black-olive circles for eyes.

The entire historical section and all paths leading to it would be adorned with skull-shaped pathway lights, fake spiderwebs, bats with glowing red eyes, and candlelit jack-o-lanterns (carved by local schoolchildren). Overhead string lights and strategically placed uplights at the base of the tombstones would provide illumination. And let's not forget the life-size skeletons, zombies, and horror-movie characters who would come to life at opportune moments, resulting in much shrieking, laughing, and wetting of pants.

My job as the official emcee—well, I *am* the one and only Death Diva, after all—was to spookify the crowd and prime them for the sudden appearance of assorted ghosts from the town's past who would leap, shuffle, or in some cases slither from behind monuments during the walking tour.

My costume varied year to year. This time I planned to do myself up as Adrienne Early, an infamous Crystal Harbor matron who'd died in 1843, but not before outliving five wealthy husbands, all of whom expired under questionable circumstances. Adrienne was one intimidating broad, and since the local constabulary never had any hard evidence, she was left undisturbed to enjoy a long and affluent life, finally succumbing to… wait for it… a bite from a black widow spider. My mid-nineteenth-century dress had a high neck, narrow sleeves and waist, and a full, dome-shaped skirt. A bonnet, shawl, and basket of "poisonous mushrooms" completed the fetching ensemble.

Every year the role of Jeremiah Nevins, who'd founded Crystal Harbor in the 1650s by purchasing the land from the Matinecock tribe, was played by Ben Ralston, a local private investigator and pal of mine. He did a darn fine job, too, managing to be both scary and historically accurate—if you overlooked the fact that Ben was far more Black than the melanin-deprived Jeremiah. No one cared, or if they did, they knew better than to bring it up.

This year Dom's eldest child, Karina, who'd just started her senior year in high school, would take on the role of Ruby Kirk, a Victorian teen whose parents forbade her to keep company with her ne'er-do-well beau. Ruby responded by setting her house on fire, resulting in the death of her entire family. Well, you know how touchy teenagers can be. But at least she got to run away with her fella, who decided she was a little too mouthy and promptly slit her throat. During the tour, I would point out Ruby's gravestone, which was Karina's cue to emerge from behind it in a white Victorian dress, very mouthy indeed as she runs around screaming, with fake blood dripping from her throat.

Rocky (first name only—*so* Hollywood) was our most popular local pet groomer. New customers waited a year and a half for their first appointment. He was going to play "Doctor" Archibald Nevins, a snake-oil salesman and last descendant of Crystal Harbor's founding family, who was run out of town in 1903. Several years later when Archibald died, the Town Council permitted his body to be brought back and interred in the cemetery next to his more respectable ancestors.

The padre would be transforming himself into Oswald Collingwood, a seventeenth-century con man who fled England and claimed to be the masked executioner who'd separated King Charles I from his head—a lie that eventually got him hunted down and shot behind his Crystal Harbor home by the king's men. Martin would wear a period costume, including a long auburn wig and fake Van Dyke beard, and carry an enormous executioner's ax.

Frank Martinez would play Percival Ruskin, a peg-legged reprobate who settled here around the same time as Oswald. Not only did Percival tip off the king's men and thus cause Oswald's death, he then proceeded to steal the valuable recipe for Sybbie's Punch from Oswald's widow, Sybille Collingwood. In retaliation, Sybille treated Percival to some poisoned punch and had him sealed up, still alive, behind a brick wall in her basement. The result of all this Colonial-era mayhem was a blood feud between the Collingwoods and Ruskins that persisted for centuries.

Frank would wear a fake peg leg and carry the punch bowl Percival had been walled up with. The highlight of the tour would be the ghosts of Oswald and Percival chasing each other around the boneyard, hollering threats and trying to do each other in, while Sybille—played by the irrepressible Mayor Sophie Halperin—runs after them, hurling verbal abuse while attempting to clock them with her rolling pin.

This year's Halloween tour wouldn't be the same without Larry, who'd always played the ghost of Nina's great-grandfather, the Prohibition-era gangster Hank "Hokum" Hannigan. Larry loved to ham it up, tipping his fedora to the ladies, bloviating about the hapless cops who could never pin anything on him, and dispensing cups of bootlegged spirits (aka lemonade).

After Larry's death, the Halloween Cemetery Tour committee voted to permanently retire the character of Hokum Hannigan.

I said good-bye to the History Club kids at the gate, and waved to the parents who were picking them up. I sensed a presence at my back and turned to see Frank.

"Any time, guys," he called to the departing students. "We love the history geeks!"

When said geeks had pulled away from the curb, I took note of Frank's steel-blue suit and striped tie in taupe and mauve, with a paisley pocket square in the same colors. He always looked so put together at work. "Do you ever go home?"

"When someone wants to come in and discuss the purchase of a family plot, and they can only do it on Sunday—"

he shrugged "—I make the time."

Quite a display of responsibility from a guy who once systematically destroyed his former boss's car.

He started to turn away, but something in my expression caught him up short. "Do you need something, Jane?"

"I just… Are you still waiting for your customer?"

"They already left." He loosened his necktie. "A couple in their seventies who'd never given a thought to burial arrangements. Never *wanted* to think about them would be my guess. Anyway, he recently had a health scare and…" Another shrug.

"And suddenly they're making you come in on a Sunday to sell them a plot."

"Come on." He led the way to the nearby administration building, a homey white clapboard structure with a pitched roof. He held the door open for me and we took seats in the reception area, which some wise person had designed to be as comfy as a living room, with potted plants, thick carpeting, and stuffed furniture in soothing shades of blue and green.

Now that I had his attention, I wasn't sure how to go about asking what I wanted to know. I wasn't even sure what I wanted to know. The only thing I *was* sure of, while visions of pummeled profs and battered automobiles danced in my head, was that I had to approach this discussion as tactfully as possible.

"When Larry and I stopped by your booth at the cook-off," I said, "you seemed to think the whole judging process was pretty unfair."

"To put it mildly. You can't convince me he didn't exert more influence than Sophie or Maia." He held up his hand to forestall my objection. "Look, I'm sorry about what happened to the guy, but you can't deny he was a dominant presence in this town. Too dominant. His opinions carried weight."

"I don't know how well you know Sophie and Maia," I said, "but they aren't the kind of people to just step back and let the famous guy call the shots, I don't care how dominant he was."

"I guess we'll never agree about that," he said, "and it's a moot point going forward. Someone else will be named as the third judge next year."

Frank did not appear broken up by that fact.

"So, um, someone I know happened to hear you talking to Max Baumgartner at the cook-off." I paused to give him time to recollect the conversation.

He appeared not to know where this was going. "Okay. I talked to a lot of people that day."

"They heard you say something like 'Larry won't get away with it again.'" I kept my tone neutral. "I'm just curious what you meant by that."

Frank stared at me. I forced myself not to squirm.

His voice was flat as he said, "It sounds like you've already decided what I meant by that."

"No. Really." Yes, really, but no way would I admit it.

"What I meant," he said, with exaggerated patience, "is that I intended to file an official complaint with the cook-off committee and try to have Larry removed as judge. Replaced with someone who cares more about choosing the best chili than scoring popularity points."

How did naming Maria Echevarría's chili the winner score Larry popularity points? I decided that question was better left unvoiced.

I also decided not to bring up Frank's uninvited presence

in Larry and Madison's backyard the day before the cook-off. *Say, did you happen to slip some poison into Larry's kale protein shake?*

A poison, I might add, that came from the yew plant, which grew in abundance along the cemetery's back fence. Frank must come in contact with that hedge every day. No doubt he was well aware of how toxic it was. But something he'd once mentioned in passing had been gnawing at me.

"That day you helped me bury Josie Evangelista's lizard," I said. "And thanks again for that. You went above and beyond."

He acknowledged this with a little nod.

"You told me about a conversation you had with Madison Kool," I said. "She was here and you tried to get her to purchase a side-by-side plot."

"I mentioned it might be time," he clarified, "to think about final arrangements. In case they'd been putting it off, like this couple that was here earlier."

"You didn't seem too happy that Larry had chosen aquamation."

Frank frowned. "What's your point?"

I chose not to tell him what my point was, but I have to tell *someone,* so listen up. Just how miffed was Frank when the town's biggest celebrity decided that being dissolved in lye was preferable to being interred in an exclusive piece of real estate under a fancy monument in close proximity to all his Kool ancestors going back more than two centuries? Could that have been the final straw that tipped Frank over the edge into homicide? What exactly was going through his mind when he learned about the lye?

"I was just wondering," I said, "what Madison was doing here if she wasn't interested in a plot. I mean, was there a funeral that day?"

His eyes narrowed. "Why do you care?"

"I don't really," I lied. "I'm too curious for my own good. Forget it."

Frank said nothing for a few moments. Probably trying to work out my real motive for asking. Finally he said, "She was visiting a grave, if you must know."

"Really? Madison isn't from around here. Who does she know who's buried—"

"Larry's ancestors," he said. "She said it was peaceful there, in that section of the cemetery. She sits on a bench and meditates or something."

"Huh. If she likes it that much," I said, "I'm kinda surprised they decided not to buy a plot. I guess doing it a greener way—you know, dissolving him in lye—was more important."

"I guess. I really couldn't say. I don't know the woman that well."

"So, um…" I felt my palms go clammy. "I was wondering about something else."

He sighed. "Sure, let's have it. I've got nothing better to do than satisfy your curiosity about stuff that's none of your business."

"You know how folks in this town gossip," I said.

"The official Crystal Harbor pastime."

"Yeah, well, I heard that you experienced some, um, drama," I said, "before you moved here."

"Drama." There was that flinty stare again.

I cleared my throat. "Something about you attacking one of your college professors."

"So that one's making the rounds, huh? For what it's

worth, this prof was no saint. He came on to my girlfriend. Had a history of messing with his female students. The school chose to handle the whole thing quietly. No cops, no publicity. They fired the guy and expelled me."

"Did you, you know, hurt him badly?" I asked.

He crossed his arms. "As badly as I could manage, considering how much vodka I'd tossed back," he said. "He wasn't hospitalized if that's what you mean."

"Okay, and I also heard," I said, "that you might've, you know, done something to your boss's car."

"Former boss. He fired me."

"For cause?" I asked.

He nodded. "I was a drunk."

After a moment I said, "Oh."

He smiled at my discomfiture. "I used to come to work drunk and leave the same way. And before you ask, I was drunk when I destroyed his vehicle. And even drunker when they arrested me for it."

"You don't seem..." I said. "I mean, do you still...?"

"No. I've been sober for four years, three months, and seventeen days. I will never stop going to meetings. AA saved my life. Unfortunately, it was too late for my marriage."

"I'm sorry," I said. "I didn't know you'd been married. But congratulations on your sobriety. I know it's a struggle."

"As for the guy whose car I clobbered," he said, "I paid for the damages—meaning I bought him a new ride—and the charges were dropped."

"So that brings up another question," I said.

"Jeez." He shook his head, with an incredulous smile. "You are something else."

I glanced around to ensure our privacy. "We both know

your boss is kind of a creep. Why did he hire you with your arrest record?"

"Arlo's not just a creep," he said, "he's a cheap creep."

"No kidding," I said. "Just look how he treated Max and her mom after burying someone else in their plot."

"He doesn't like to pay for background checks on new hires," Frank said. "Considers them a waste of money. Thinks he can do a quick internet search and get the same results. Which was good news for me, but one of these days he's going to hire someone dangerous."

17

The Cult of Larry

BY THE TIME I left the admin building it had started to drizzle, making me glad I'd brought the umbrella. I wasn't paying much attention to my surroundings as I headed out the gate toward my car, until I heard my name called. I followed the sound and spied Rex Noble hurrying toward me on the sidewalk. He squinted angrily at the sky, as if he could bully the clouds into holding it in.

"Do you have a few minutes?" he asked.

"How'd you know where to find me?"

"Someone told me they saw you come in here."

"Who?" I asked.

"Oh, that doesn't mat—"

"It does to me." I hated it when people were secretive for no reason. Plus, I wanted to know who considered it their business to report on my whereabouts.

Rex took note of my implacable expression, shot another dark look at the dark sky (he had not had the foresight to bring an umbrella, and I did not offer to share mine), and said, "It was Nina Wallace, okay? I just finished interviewing her again. Fascinating woman. Did you know her great-grandfather was Hokum—"

"Yeah, I know. Listen, Rex, I'm kind of busy."

"I'll be quick," he said. "Just a few questions. Only, let's get out of this downpour. My car's right over there."

It wasn't a downpour, it was a drizzle, like I said. The fact was, Rex wasn't the only one who had questions. I had a few of my own.

Yeah, I know, I'm "something else." And not always in a good way.

I agreed to join Rex in his car, figuring I could let myself out at any time. If we used my vehicle, heaven only knew how long our little confab would last.

I slid into the passenger seat of a light-blue BMW, well on in years but not old enough or pretty enough to be considered fashionably vintage. Just, you know, old.

Rex, sitting behind the wheel, reached into the backseat and grabbed his attaché case, the same one he'd had at Janey's Place three weeks earlier. "Before we get started—"

"Okay, I need to make something clear," I said. "No recordings and I'm not signing a release."

"But—"

"We're just having a casual chat at this point, Rex. If I change my mind about appearing in your documentary, I'll let you know."

He grinned. "You're obviously not up on the latest. Now we're talking a true-crime *series*. Since it turns out poor Larry was murdered, the first episode will be devoted to his case."

Oh, good. Another true-crime TV series. Because there aren't enough of those.

"I assume you're still planning to host it," I said.

"Absolutely. It's a natural tie-in, don't you think? The actor who worked with Larry—on a *detective* show, no less—

hosting the program exploring his murder. How perfect is that?"

Somehow I didn't think Rex's former costar would consider the whole idea so gosh-darn perfect, but he wasn't in a position to weigh in, was he? "I assume you'll want to wait until his murder is solved," I said, "before producing the show."

"News flash," he said. "His murder was solved. The killer left her fingerprints on the murder weapon. If you can call a fruit bowl a murder weapon."

"Liddy denies it. Vehemently." Her court-appointed attorney seemed competent enough, though she still hadn't been able to make bail.

"And you believe her?" he asked.

"I don't know. Okay, she probably did it, but what if she didn't? What if Liddy is cleared before the first episode airs and we still don't know who the killer is?"

"You're not thinking like a TV veteran," Rex said, with a patronizing smile. "In that case we present Larry's case as an unsolved mystery. Then, when the killer is caught, we get everyone tuning in again for the thrilling update."

"In which case the first episode will have a lot of unanswered questions," I said.

"That's right. We'll look into all aspects of his murder, concentrating on the candidates for whodunit. Plus we'll present as much of the *how*dunit as we know at that point."

"Have you considered," I asked, "that that kind of investigative journalism might be risky? If you, you know, get too close to the truth?"

"The only thing I'm concerned about," he said, "is the series getting canceled."

"I was thinking more along the lines of *you* getting canceled, if the murderer decides you need shutting up."

He chuckled. "That's quite an imagination you have."

I *imagined* Rex's blasé attitude might be attributable to the fact that he knew darn well who the killer was, and it was someone whose face he saw in his shaving mirror every morning.

The skies suddenly opened up. I peered through the rain-smeared windshield and noted with relief that there were plenty of pedestrians in the area, scurrying by under their umbrellas. Unless Rex pulled a gun, I didn't think I was in much danger.

I couldn't help myself. "How do you think Larry would feel about this series? You know, about being the focus of the first episode?" *Warts and all,* as Rex had once promised.

"I honestly don't care." His congeniality slipped a few notches. "I don't owe that man a damn thing."

"Because he wouldn't help you get roles?"

His hard gaze homed in on me. I forced myself not to reach for the door handle. "Who have you been talking to?" he asked.

I could hardly refuse to answer after demanding to know who *he'd* been talking to about me. "Liddy," I said. Well, and Madison, too, but he was only going to get one name out of me. "I didn't realize it was classified information."

"That woman's a blabbermouth," he said. "Always has been. Yeah, my old friend Larry flat-out refused to put in a good word for me. I would've done it for him."

From what Madison had told me, Larry did try to help his old costar, up to a point. *Rex is his own worst enemy,* she'd said. *There was only so much Larry could do, and then he stopped trying for fear of being tainted by association.*

Rex said, "You ever hear of a director named Llewellyn Sawyer?"

Yes. "No."

"He's a real up-and-comer," he said, "has a new project in the works. Supposed to be his breakout film. Anyway, Larry knows the guy, he's worked with him. Do you think he could be bothered to suggest my name to Sawyer, get me an audition?" His expression was now pure venom.

"So I have to ask," I said. "This true-crime project of yours, focusing on Larry and all. Is this your way of getting back at him? I mean, it doesn't seem like you're inclined to pull any punches where he's concerned."

"And why should I?" He leaned toward me, invading my personal space, and I found my fingers inching toward the door handle. "What kind of friend was he in the end? I'm looking forward to telling the world the truth about their precious Larry Kool."

"I assume you'll be paid handsomely for it," I said.

"And what's wrong with that?" he demanded. "Why *shouldn't* I jump at any opportunity to profit off that bastard's death?"

Rex stopped abruptly, his expression guarded. He eased back against the driver's seat and took a deep breath. "Not that money's the driving force behind this project. Let's call it a not-unwelcome side benefit."

Who did he think he was kidding? Revenge, move over and make way for greed.

I decided on a different tack. More flies with honey and all that. Plus I don't mind telling you, Rex was beginning to scare me a little. Maybe more than a little.

I said, "Well, I for one don't blame you one bit. You forget, I knew Larry real well. You don't have to tell *me* he wasn't the saint most folks around here consider him."

Rex studied my face. I wasn't the most accomplished liar, but all the practice I'd gotten lately must've paid off, because he visibly relaxed. "I just assumed you'd drunk the Kool-Aid along with everyone else in this town."

"*Kool*-Aid," I said with a grin. "I see what you did there."

"Huh? Oh!" Rex laughed. "That didn't even occur to me."

"Anyway," I said, "I guess that's the reason I don't want to be interviewed for your show. If I say what I really think about Larry, I'll make a lot of enemies around here. And I can't afford that. I run a small business that's dependent on referrals."

"Okay, I hear you," he said, "but it sure would help to showcase an honest voice from a respected member of the community. Something to cut through all the sentimental claptrap."

"I call it the cult of Larry," I said. And okay, maybe I was laying it on a bit thick, but Rex ate it up.

"Yes!" He slammed his palms on the wheel, making me jump. "Precisely! I think we have the title for our first episode. 'The Cult of Larry.' Or how about 'Drinking the Larry Kool-Aid'?"

Oh, brother. "I saw you talking with him at the cook-off," I said. "Up at the stage, right before the winner was announced. From where I stood, the two of you seemed to be on good enough terms."

"I'm an actor, remember?" he said, with a sly smile. "I was giving him one last chance to intercede on my behalf with Lew Sawyer."

One last chance. I didn't like the sound of that.

"I'm assuming he refused," I said.

"What do you think?" He gave a bitter headshake. "I'd asked him to meet me at Murray's Pub the night before. He loved that place. I figured a couple of beers and some nachos might help loosen him up, put him in the mood to help his old buddy. I should've known better. So the next morning I decided to contact Sawyer myself, which totally backfired on me. Larry had already trash-talked me to him."

"Did Sawyer say that?"

"No, but it was obvious."

Not to me. The Larry I'd known would never have been that petty. "Clearly you were a better friend to Larry than he was to you," I said. "For example, I saw you give him your soda."

"Yeah, he had a stomachache. I figured the Coke would help. No one knew at that point that he'd been poisoned. Well, one person knew." Rex snickered, and I stretched my mouth into the semblance of a smile. I was beginning to loathe this man.

If Rex had indeed poisoned Larry's nachos at Murray's the night before the cook-off, it was possible that initial dose had been enough to make him sick but not do him in. The next day when Larry failed to respond to his "one last chance" to help his old costar, he drank the soda Rex offered him and promptly died.

"So you're doing a whole new round of interviews in town," I said. "Did you speak with Madison again?"

He pulled a face. "She won't talk to me. Somehow she's gotten the idea that I don't intend to treat Larry fairly. She even threatened to sue me for slander if my show includes 'falsehoods that harm Larry Kool's good name and/or posthumous earnings potential.' That's how she put it. Sounds like she's been talking to a lawyer."

"Posthumous earnings potential?" I said.

"*Chase & Knabbe* is still bringing in the bucks, Jane. Well, for Larry's heirs now. Me, I'm making pennies on it."

It would appear Madison had been paying attention a few days earlier when the subject of slander came up. Since she couldn't prevent Rex from producing a mean-spirited tell-all show about her late husband, she was promising to take him to court if he didn't stick to the verifiable truth. And something told me Rex had no intention of sticking to the verifiable truth.

Madison had mentioned that Larry hadn't trusted Rex, so it was only natural for her not to trust him either—for good reason as I was discovering. I assumed her threat was the first salvo in an attempt to keep the series from being picked up. I could see her making the same threat to every person or entity involved in its production.

"Madison's threat seems kind of harsh," I said, "considering the two of you were a couple at one time."

"I wouldn't say were were a *couple* exactly," he said. "We only went out for a few weeks. It ended before we got really serious. Who told you about that?"

"Well, Madison herself." Should I say this next thing? Oh sure, why not? "Liddy thinks Larry stole Madison from you to get back at you for, um, being involved with his little sister way back when. And that you never got over losing Madison to him."

Rex barked a laugh. "Please tell me you don't believe that nonsense."

"Honestly? I don't know what to believe," I said. "But it's

really none of my business, so..." *Please fill me in on the stuff that's none of my business.*

"You might not believe this," he said, "but even now I have women coming after me because I used to be on TV or because they assume I must be loaded or... well, a whole raft of questionable reasons."

"Well, you're still a good-looking guy," I offered. "There's that."

He gave a little wink. "Thank you. That's nice to hear from a beautiful young woman such as yourself."

Maybe I didn't loathe him as much as I thought.

"Anyway," he said, "I got burned a few times, so years ago I started running background checks on women I date."

"The kind of checks you can do yourself online?" I asked, thinking of cheapskate Arlo (not so) Pleasant.

"Oh, hell no," he said. "I use a PI here in Crystal Harbor. Maybe you know him. Ben Ralston?"

"Oh sure, Ben's a great guy," I said. "He's helped me out with a couple of my Death Diva jobs."

"He gives me a fair rate, and it's worth every penny."

"So I think I see where you're going with this," I said. "You ran a background check on Madison that turned up something alarming."

"Not exactly. Ben told me about a boyfriend of hers who died in a fall down the stairs in his house."

"Sounds pretty alarming to me. Was she there at the time? Do they think she, you know...?" I mimed a push.

"No, no, nothing like that," he said. "Madison was in Kentucky at the time, visiting her grandparents. He was alone in the house, and he'd been drinking. There's no question it was an accident."

"So then, what's the problem?" I asked.

"Madison and I had already gone on about eight or ten dates when I learned about this," he said. "We'd had several long conversations touching on all sorts of personal subjects, past relationships included. I was beginning to think she might be the one. And that's what I was looking for, to be honest. A serious relationship. I'm way past meaningless hookups."

"Let me guess," I said. "She never mentioned her boyfriend's tragic death."

"Not one word. After I found out about it, I asked her some leading questions, gave her every opportunity to bring it up, but she never did, and finally I realized she never would. I could only wonder what else she'd been keeping from me. If someone's not prepared to be open and honest, well… I broke it off."

"Was she upset?" I asked.

"Not really," he said. "I treat my lady friends as well as I'm able, but let's face it, I don't have unlimited funds, and at a certain point I think she began to realize that."

"Is that when she took up with Larry?" I asked.

He nodded. "I'd introduced them while we were dating. There was no 'stealing' involved. As I understand it, she made the first move with him. No hard feelings on my part."

Madison had led me to believe she'd dropped Rex for Larry, and that it had caused a rift between the two former costars. Perhaps her ego wouldn't let her admit she'd been dumped.

"Well, the rain has stopped, or just about." I opened the car door. "Sexy Beast is going to be wondering where Mommy is."

"Give that cute little poodle a few scritches for me," he said.

"Will do. Same for Piglet," I said as I stepped into a puddle.

"I hope you change your mind about that interview," he said. "This project needs you, Jane."

18

A Little More Than Friendly

"THEY'RE UPSTAIRS IN a carton." Madison started to rise from the sofa.

"You stay put. You're still recovering," I said. "I'll get the carton. Where is it?"

"Oh, thank you, Jane." She lifted a mug of grass-colored tea. "It's in the sitting room off my bedroom. It's labeled. You can't miss it."

"I'll be right back."

It was the morning after my back-to-back chats with Frank and Rex. Madison had called the previous evening and told me she wanted to donate a few pieces from Larry's *Chase & Knabbe* paraphernalia collection—which I'd finally finished inventorying and returned to her a couple of days earlier—to the town's upcoming goods and services auction, held annually to benefit our local Friends of the Waterfront.

I liked that idea and told her I'd come by the next day to pick up the items since she said she was still a little weak five days after being poisoned. I didn't mind running them over to The Harbor Room, the venerable restaurant that hosted the auction every autumn.

Once upstairs, I let myself in to her large, high-ceilinged

bedroom, which looked darn elegant even with an unmade bed. Her housekeeper, Doris, was busy with the laundry and had yet to tackle the second floor.

As soon as I moved into the adjoining sitting room, I spied the medium-size carton, taped shut and marked *G&S AUCTION*. The contents rattled a little as I lifted it. Madison had mentioned that she'd included the #1Dad mug and a few other small items. One of the auction volunteers would package them prettily in a basket and write up a fun description for the printed program.

Back in the bedroom, I lingered for a bit, admiring the mixture of contemporary and antique furnishings, including the stately four-poster bed. Madison had quite an eye for decorating.

As I started for the door, something caught my eye—a scrap of cloth peeking out from between the foot of the bed and the upholstered storage bench I'd sat on a few days earlier after she'd been released from the hospital. Something about the color and design of the cloth looked familiar. I stepped closer to get a better look.

Setting the box on the bench, I lifted the cloth and spread it out, revealing a paisley silk handkerchief in taupe and mauve.

It was Frank Martinez's pocket square, the one I'd seen tucked into his suit jacket the day before.

I pictured Frank tossing his jacket onto the bench, pictured the pocket square falling out, pictured him putting the jacket back on—either late last night or early this morning—without noticing that his fancy silk hankie was missing.

I shoved the cloth into my jeans pocket, lifted the box, and carried it downstairs.

I smiled at Madison. "Is there anything I can do for you before I leave?"

"I'm fine. Doris will get me anything I need. Thanks so much, Jane." Her eyes misted. "I don't know how I'd have gotten through the last month without you."

"Oh, you'd have managed somehow," I said.

A BRISK BREEZE whipped my hair as I followed the path from the cemetery's maintenance building toward the low-rent Serene Meadow section. One of the groundskeepers had told me I'd find Frank there, checking on a grave opening.

I encountered him walking toward me on the path. Some distance away a backhoe sat idle next to a pile of dirt as a worker stood in the freshly dug hole, carving the edges.

"Nattily turned out as always," I said, as I tamed my windblown hair with a claw clip from my purse. Today Frank wore his beige suit, this time with a yellow-and-gray plaid necktie and charcoal-gray pocket square.

He grinned. "Why don't you just email me your list of prying questions. Save you the trip here."

"Can't put this in an email." I produced the pocket square, shook it out, and watched his grin fade.

After a moment he said, "What's that?"

"That's right, Frank. Play stupid. I've got all day." The breeze caught the hankie as I held it aloft, whipping it like an elegant paisley flag.

Frank glanced nervously around and spied a young family

strolling nearby. He snatched the cloth from me and shoved it into his pants pocket before offering a greeting to the visitors as they passed us.

Once they were out of earshot, I said, "Aren't you wondering where you misplaced it?"

His scowl told me he knew darn well where he'd misplaced it. "This comes under the category of things that are none of your business, Jane."

"Can't argue about that," I said. "And yet the more I thought about it, the more I began to wonder about something you and I discussed yesterday."

"I don't know where you're going with this, but I need to get back—"

"You told me Madison was visiting the graves of Larry's ancestors," I said, "that day you happened to run into her here. The day you suggested it might be time she and Larry... how did you put it? Thought about final arrangements."

He stared across the nearby rows of flush grave markers, and the grave digging in progress, with an exaggerated air of boredom. "So?"

"So that was a lie." His unwillingness to meet my gaze kind of clinched it. "What was she really doing here?"

"You're calling me a liar now?"

"I just did. Yes."

He drew himself up. "I don't have to stand here and be insult—"

"Then stop lying," I said. "It's that simple. Or you can keep pretending, but I must warn you that if you do, there's a good chance you'll end up regretting it."

Frank's expression hardened as he pondered my words. "I told you those things in confidence, Jane."

"What? I'm not follow—"

"My arrest." He scanned our surroundings and waved away a worker who'd begun to approach. "And that other thing. When I was expelled. I need this job."

"Good grief, Frank," I said, "do you think so little of me? Like I'd really go running to that creep Arlo and rat you out. Please."

His expression went from outraged to wary. "What then?"

"What I meant," I said, "was that if you persist in lying about what Madison was doing here that day, and it turns out to have something to do with Larry's murder, then you, Frank Martinez, can be held criminally liable for making a false statement. We could be talking obstruction of justice, even accessory after the fact. And don't get me started on perjury."

Okay, you got me. I'm not a lawyer, I just play one when I'm talking to someone who knows even less about legal stuff than I do.

"I'm not worried," he said. "I'd never lie to the police."

"Just to me. And so we're clear, I'd never lie to the cops either. I'd have to tell them that Frank Martinez told me Madison Kool was just visiting graves that day. If they ask me what I know."

Again he found the flat acreage in the Serene Meadow section of absorbing interest. Finally he sighed and said, "She's completely innocent, Jane. A grieving widow."

"And isn't it nice that she has you to help her through the grieving process."

He flushed. "I didn't take advantage. If you must know, it was Madison who… you know, initiated it."

"Starting when?" I asked.

"Starting that day when I ran into her here, as a matter of

fact," he said. "I barely knew her, but she was, well, friendly. Maybe a little more than friendly."

"And married," I said.

"Hey, I don't mess around with married women," he said. "It's not worth the trouble."

"So. Frank." I stared at him until he made full eye contact. "What was Madison doing here that day?"

"It sounds bad, but it was totally innocent. Trust me."

I waited.

"She was taking cuttings from the yew hedge." He quickly added, "To root them and grow bushes at her place. She's an avid gardener."

This was news to me, but who knew? Maybe it was true.

"When was she doing this?" I asked. "I mean, was it a weekday, weekend? Was the place busy?"

He shook his head. "The place was dead. Okay, bad choice of words. It was around sunup. Sometimes when I'm stressed I like to come in super early and walk the grounds when there's no one else around. Helps to keep me from relapsing."

"Madison must've been surprised to see you."

"I'm afraid I startled her," he said. "She was on the other side of the fence, and when she saw me, she dropped her pruning shears."

"And that's when she started flirting with you?" I asked.

"I wouldn't put it like that."

I wanted to say, *Sorry, Frank, but "a little more than friendly" equals flirting.*

Instead I said, "Let me guess. She asked you not to mention it to anyone—that she was helping herself to a few sprigs."

"She was embarrassed," he said. "'Cause it could look like

she was stealing from the cemetery or something. I assured her it would be our secret."

To some, it might appear that Frank had been given a little extra incentive to make Larry stop breathing, in the form of his gorgeous, and flirtatious, young wife.

"And after Larry died?" I asked. "How long until you two—"

"I left her alone." He raised his palms. "Figured she needed time, you know? To heal and whatever. And then, well, I found out she was seeing your ex. Dom Faso."

"And you thought, dang, I didn't move fast enough."

He grimaced. "Something like that."

"So when did it get more serious between you and Madison?" I asked.

"When she was back home from the hospital, she called and asked if I'd come over and change a light bulb that was too high for her to get to."

Good grief, how fast did this woman's light bulbs burn out? First Dom and then Frank. I pictured her dragging a ladder into the house to replace working bulbs with duds before picking up the phone.

"And naturally, you ran right over there," I said.

"Well, sure, why wouldn't I? I offered to help her in any way I could."

"Frank, we both know what you were offering and that she took you up on it."

"Jeez, Jane…"

It would seem Madison had not been too debilitated by her brush with death to launch into a hot and heavy affair with Frank. By that time everyone in town, including Frank, knew that Larry had been poisoned by a tincture made from the yew plant.

Put yourself in Madison's shoes. Let's say, for the sake of argument, that you're more than a little nervous at having been caught with the pruning shears by the administrator of the cemetery, someone you scarcely know. Your nervousness has less to do with the unauthorized hedge trimming than with the kind of hedge it is, and to what illicit purposes such plant matter might be put.

How to keep the cemetery guy from blabbing about your foray into toxic horticulture? Well, when you're a beautiful, desirable young woman, you have options. You start by softening him up with a little flirting over the yew hedge. Get the poor schlub's hopes up. Elicit a promise to keep his yap shut.

That seems to have done the trick, but *dang!* Now your husband's "natural" death has been proven to be anything but. The cemetery guy just might decide he needs to tell someone about your gardening hobby. That's when you turn yourself into a helpless, sexy, grieving, sexy, emotionally fragile, sexy victim of attempted murder. Throw in a few sessions between the sheets and in no time you have him saying, *Huh? What yew cuttings?*

"I'm telling you," Frank said, "Madison is one hundred percent innocent. I'd stake my life on it."

"BEN, I NEED YOU."

"Hallelujah, my prayers have been answered." Ben Ralston closed his laptop and leaned back in his leather office chair.

"Now it's just a matter of bumping off Martin and we're in business."

"Stevie might have something to say about that."

I was standing in the open doorway of Ralston Investigations, a no-frills one-person office located on the top floor of an old, three-story brick building on Main Street. Ben had started his PI business several years earlier after retiring from the Crystal Harbor Police Department with his twenty-year pension. I'd driven there straight from the cemetery.

Ben was a middle-aged Black man, on the short side but in great shape if you didn't count the small paunch stretching his plum-colored polo shirt. He and Martin's mom, Stevie Borden, had been an item for the past year and a half. They lived together in her modest home in Rocky Bay. She was about thirteen years older than Ben, and if that raises your eyebrows, then consider that Larry could have been Madison's grandpa.

I parked my behind in one of a pair of guest chairs facing his desk. "Rex Noble told me he sometimes hires you to do background checks on women he's dating."

"If he said it, it must be true." A small frown marred his features. "I hope you're not here about Martin." Who happened to be one of Ben's best buddies.

"No, of course not!" I said. "I'm fully up to speed on the padre's background—the good, the bad, and everything in between. Speaking of which, we recently got together with his half sister, Claudia, and her son."

"I know. Stevie told me. Can you believe my foxy woman is a great-grandmother?"

"It's difficult to fathom," I agreed.

"So." Ben thumped his desk, his cue that the chitchat

segment was over and it was time to get down to business. "What's on your mind, Jane? Something about Rex?"

"He shared some information with me," I said. "Stuff you unearthed during one of the background checks. This goes back maybe five years, before Larry Kool started seeing his wife, Madison."

"Right," he said, "Rex was dating her for a short while."

"Apparently, when you looked into her background," I said, "you turned up some boyfriend who took a tumble down a staircase in his house and died."

"Guy's blood alcohol level was up there, as I recall," he said.

"And he was alone, right?" I asked. "No family around? Madison was in Kentucky visiting her grandparents?"

"I'd have to check my records, but that sounds right. I do remember that it was unquestionably an accident." He gave me a no-nonsense stare. "Is this going where I think it's going?"

"I want to hire you to reopen your file on Madison Kool," I said. "Revisit the boyfriend incident and whatever else you can dig up."

"You know the cops are already on that, right?" he said. "It's standard procedure, her being the spouse of a murder victim and all."

"They think they have the killer in custody," I said. "I respect the detectives, but I just can't see Liddy Kool pulling off a sophisticated crime like this. Have you met the woman?"

Ben wagged a finger at me. "What do you know about Madison? I don't like surprises."

I told him about her inheriting virtually all of her wealthy husband's assets. I told him about her sneaking cuttings from the yew hedge, supposedly for rooting. I told him about the new boyfriend who witnessed her taking the cuttings. I told him about the other new boyfriend who just happened to be loaded and my ex-husband. "And don't even start with me, Ben, because it's not about that."

And lastly, I told him I'd already run all this past Martin and that he was prepared to assist in the investigation. Anything to speed things up.

"Cool," he said. "I'll give him a call and we'll get the ball rolling."

"DON'T YOU THINK you're overreacting?"

I hated it when Dom adopted that condescending tone. I realized now that I'd always hated it, starting in Mr. Bender's eighth-grade Spanish class when I'd had a little trouble conjugating verbs. *No me gustamos tu actitud,* Dom.

As soon as I got home, I phoned my ex. "I'm not saying I think she's a murderer, Dom. I'm just giving you a heads-up. This is serious stuff. She was collecting *yew cuttings,* for crying out loud. Shortly before her husband was killed by what? By *yew*! I don't mean, um, *you*. It's one of those… What do they call those words that sound the same—"

"Homonyms. I know what you meant."

"So for the record, no," I said, "I do not think I'm overreacting. I think *you're* willfully ignoring the potential danger you face."

"Janey, I know this woman. She's not capable—"

"Oh, please. You *know* her? You met her a month ago."

"We go back further than that." he said. "Larry introduced us about a year ago when I ran into them at a charity gala to benefit homeless veterans. And we chatted again at the annual street fair in July."

"*Oh.* Well then, I take it back. What *don't* you know about the woman after all that?" Without pausing to let him regroup, I added, "Here's what *I* know about her. She only goes after wealthy men."

"Rex doesn't fall into that category," Dom said.

"I doubt she realized that when they started dating," I said. "He puts on a good show. Aren't you going to ask what she wanted the cuttings for?"

He thought for a moment. "To add to her floral arrangements, I imagine."

"Really? Have you ever seen sprigs of yew in her vases?" I knew the answer to that one, so I just barreled ahead. "I'll tell you what she told Frank Martinez. She told him she's an avid gardener and planned to propagate the cuttings."

"Well, there you go," he said.

"Tell me, Dom. Is Madison into gardening?"

"I don't know," he said.

"You two never discussed your hobbies?" I said. "Pretty odd considering how well you know her."

"It never came up," he said, irritably. "I'll tell you what I think's going on here, Janey. You're jealous."

I couldn't help it, I erupted in giggles. I swear I heard my ex-husband's ego shrivel over the phone line. "Dom, come on, you know that's not true, so can we just—"

"It's no secret you wanted to get back together ever since our divorce."

"Yeah," I said, "and then I got over it about the time that

you wanted to get back together. Oh, except for when you decided to go back on your promise to give me time to think about it and went running back to Bonnie. Does any of this sound familiar?"

He sighed. "How did we get on to this?"

"Quote, 'I'll tell you what I think's going on here, Janey. You're jealous.' End quote."

"All right, all right," he grumbled. "I was out of line."

"Listen, Dom, there's something else you need to know." How to say it? "I don't know if you and Madison are, um, exclusive, but she's been seeing someone else."

He was silent for a couple of beats. "What makes you think that?"

"I found something of Frank's in her bedroom," I said, "and when I asked him about it, he admitted they've been… you know."

Dom's voice was tight as he said, "What was it you found?"

"A pocket square. I recognized it. It must have slipped out of his jacket when he was, um…" *Undressing.*

Silence on the other end.

"I just have one favor to ask," I said. "It's real important that you not mention the yew cuttings to anyone—especially Madison."

"Anything else?" I'd rarely heard his voice so hard.

"No, that's it."

He said a curt good-bye and hung up.

19

It's Time to Turn Up the Heat

"SO MADISON WASN'T LYING," I said, "when she told Larry that she grew up poor."

"I wouldn't call it dirt-poor," Ben said, "but well within the lower middle class. I might even throw another 'lower' in there."

Martin spoke up. "And she was indeed a preschool teacher, at The Daffodil Learning Center. Did that for four years after earning her associate's degree in early childhood education. She quit her job when she got engaged to Larry."

It was Thursday afternoon and I was back in Ben's office, learning the results of his investigation into Madison Kool's background. With Martin's help, he'd managed to unearth a good deal of useful information in the three days since I'd hired him. The padre and I occupied the pair of leather guest chairs facing his desk.

"Was she ever arrested?" I asked. Both men shook their heads.

"Two years ago she got a ticket for rolling through a stop sign," Ben said, "That's the only thing on record."

"And no problems at her place of work, I assume? At this, what was it, Daffodil School?"

"'Learning Center,'" Martin said. "Sounds much more la-dee-dah. And no, no issues there. She was a good employee. Loved by kids, parents, and teachers."

"Madison never knew her dad," Ben said. "She was raised by a single mom who died eight years ago at age forty-three."

"So young," I said. "What was the cause of death?"

"According to the death certificate, heart failure. Apparently she'd been sick for over a year."

"Madison took good care of her," Martin said. "At least that's what her mom's friends and neighbors say. They lived in a small rental house in rural Pennsylvania. Madison kept the place clean, cooked nutritious meals, took her mom to the doctor and to church. All while holding down her job at the preschool."

No one said anything for long moments, and I imagined we were all thinking the same thing. A woman in her early forties succumbing to heart failure. Not common, but not unheard-of either.

"Was an autopsy performed?" I asked.

The padre shook his head. "Wasn't called for under the circumstances. Her mother had a history of illness and died in a hospital."

"And before you ask," Ben said, "she was buried, not cremated."

Which left open the possibility of exhumation and toxicology testing. I didn't even know whether taxine, the poison that killed Larry, would be detectable in a body that had been in the ground for eight years.

"Okay," I said, "what about the boyfriend? When did that happen?"

"Six years ago," Martin said. "His name was Cole

Hutchison. They were living together in his house, engaged to be married. She'd flown out to Kentucky to visit her grandparents. Was there for three days when Cole took his tumble down the stairs."

"With a little help from demon rum, right?" I said.

"His blood alcohol level was high but not off the charts," Ben said. "He'd had the equivalent of maybe three or four stiff drinks. A six-pack if we're talking beer."

"Well, that certainly sounds like enough to compromise someone's balance at the top of a staircase."

"Depends how well he held his liquor," Martin said. "If he was used to drinking that much…" He shrugged.

"Cole's sister lived in North Carolina, and they spoke most days," Ben said. "When she couldn't get ahold of him, she called the cops and asked for a welfare check. The sister called Madison with the news and she caught the next flight home."

"I'm thinking there had to have been an autopsy," I said.

Ben nodded. "Standard in accidental deaths. Nothing suspicious was found."

"I can guess the next part," I said. "They found no reason to do specialized tox screening."

"Just the basic panel. For what it's worth, Cole didn't have any recreational drugs in his system, aside from the booze."

"Which Madison could have poisoned before she left on her trip," I said. "A hands-off murder. Unless he was a beer drinker. You can't reseal a bottle or can."

"But hold on," Martin said. "You'd taste this stuff, right? The poison? Not that I know what it tastes like, but I'd be willing to bet it's an attention-getter."

"Madison mentioned it had a bitter taste," I said, "when she took a few bites of that tainted fruit and ended up in the emergency room."

"So how could it go undetected in a drink?" Martin shook his head, clearly not buying it.

"What did Cole do for a living?" I asked.

"He was an X-ray technician," Ben said.

"Did he own the house?"

"Yes," Martin said, "and it was almost paid off. Madison inherited it, along with almost thirty grand in savings."

"Really?" I said. "They weren't married yet."

"But they were engaged," he said, "so it's not unreasonable for him to have added her to his will."

"Course, there might've been a little persuasion involved," Ben said.

"Or a lot," I agreed. "Sounds like she'd found herself a fiscally responsible middle-class guy. A definite step up from her previous standard of living, though he was nowhere near as stinking rich as her more recent conquests."

"Anticipating your next question," Ben said, "Cole was buried, not burned."

"And an autopsy means they should have retained some bodily tissues, which can be tested if it comes to that."

"All this speculation is intriguing," he said, "but as a practical matter, we don't have any more answers than we did before."

My frustrated exhalation said what I thought about that.

Martin turned to me. "So did you hear about Liddy?"

I groaned. "What now?"

"She's out on bail as of this morning."

"What?" I straightened, searching their faces, waiting for the punch line. Liddy had been cooling her heels in jail for the past week. "Is this a joke? Who'd put up that kind of bread?"

Ben wore a bemused smile. "Her loving sister-in-law."

I shook my head, trying to make sense of it.

"Curiouser and curiouser," Martin said.

THE ROSE BOOKSHOP wasn't just a bookshop. By constantly reinventing itself, it had managed to stay in business, in the same location on Main Street, since 1946— while so many other independent bookstores went the way of the brontosaurus, stegosaurus, and all those other extinct sauruses.

In its current incarnation, The Rose consisted of three separate but connected parts: a regular bookstore at one end, a children's room with books and toys at the other end, and a charming café in between, which hosted regular book-signings and musical performances.

The café was one of my favorite places to grab a bite, especially during slow weekday afternoons like this one when I had the place practically to myself. I settled in with the mystery novel I'd just bought and was halfway through a late lunch of mushroom-and-spinach quiche and store-made raspberry soda when two ladies stopped by my table.

"Well, isn't this a lovely surprise," Madison said, as she set down her herbal tea. It smelled vaguely citrusy. "Don't let us interrupt you if you'd rather sit here all by yourself, reading."

Well, gee, when you put it like that…

I closed my book, slipped it into my purse, and returned her smile. "No, please, I'd love the company," I lied.

As Madison and her companion seated themselves, she said, "Dolly, this is my friend Jane—the one I told you about, who's been so helpful since Larry passed."

Dolly placed a bacon-cheddar scone and cappuccino on the table. "A pleasure, Jane." She was a nondescript middle-aged woman, her pudgy figure encased in a lilac polyester pantsuit and floral blouse, accessorized with a chunky yellow choker necklace and pink-framed cat-eye glasses.

Madison stirred her tea. "Dolly and I used to work together at The Daffodil Learning Center. We reconnected a couple of weeks ago at the memorial service."

"Terrible tragedy," Dolly mumbled, mouth full. "Could you pass me the sugar, dear?"

I slid the container of sweetener packets across the table. "Nice to meet you, Dolly." I didn't recall seeing her at Larry's send-off, which wasn't surprising considering the number of people in attendance.

"Well, I had a little excitement yesterday afternoon," Madison said. "The police knocked on my door. It was those two detectives, the ones who spoke with me last week after they found out Larry was murdered. The tall Black man and the woman with the curly hair."

I nodded. "Howie Werker and Cookie Kaplan. What did they want?" As if I didn't know.

"They'd heard I was cultivating some yew cuttings I'd taken from the cemetery. I told the detectives I'd forgotten all about those cuttings. I gave them to my gardener, and he took care of rooting them."

So much for her horticultural hobby.

"And did Howie and Cookie accept that explanation?" I asked.

"Certainly." She sipped her tea. "Once I showed them the seedlings."

Dolly poked a long, neatly manicured fingernail between two teeth to dislodge a bit of bacon, while Madison failed to conceal her distaste.

"You have seedlings?" I asked.

"Well, of course," she said, "and apparently they're doing quite well. I took the detectives out to the little greenhouse near the south side of the house and showed them the pots. Detective Kaplan actually pulled one of the seedlings out of the dirt to examine its roots, can you imagine?"

"Why would she do that?"

"I suppose she was looking for proof they'd been growing for several weeks, since mid-August," she said, "and that I hadn't just stuck them in the dirt a few days ago, after it became known that Larry died of yew poisoning."

I saw where she was going with this. "Because once the cops knew he'd been murdered, a guilty person would be worried they'd find out about those cuttings. The solution? Shove a few freshly cut sprigs into pots, and if the cops come sniffing around, pretend the 'seedlings' had been there the whole time."

"Precisely." Madison grinned. "See, Dolly? I told you she was smart."

"Well, I'm glad you were able to straighten that out," I said.

"After the detectives left, I called Frank Martinez. You must know Frank, Jane—the cemetery's administrator? He's the one who saw me taking those cuttings."

Dolly was clearly struggling to follow along. "So he's the one that ratted you out to the cops?"

"No, Frank told Jane about the cuttings," Madison said, "and *she* ratted me out to the cops. I've always wanted to use that phrase, 'ratted me out to the cops.' It's so colorful."

I pushed away the remains of my quiche, my appetite gone. "It wasn't me, Madison. This whole thing is none of my bus—"

"Oh, of course it was you," she said. "Don't be silly. I'm not angry, Jane. Your actions were perfectly reasonable."

"They were?"

My suspicions about Madison began to fizzle. Maybe the cops had it right. Maybe Liddy got tired of waiting for the inheritance she assumed would be hers and decided to hurry things along.

"I must admit, though," she said, "I'm disappointed in Frank. First he promises not to tell anyone about my little adventure with the pruning shears, and then what does he do? He turns right around and blabs to *you*. I'm not at all happy that my secret got out."

"Because it made you look like you were stealing from the cemetery?" I asked.

"Well, that," she said, "but mainly because I used those cuttings to kill Larry."

Her words squeezed the air from my lungs. Our table was at the sunlit front of the café, far from the food-service counter in the rear. The young man on duty was occupied with wiping down the glass cases. I turned to look at the one other table that had been occupied when I'd arrived. It was now vacant.

I started to rise.

Dolly said, "You don't wanna do that, dear." She reached into her right jacket pocket and withdrew a handgun—a small, black semiautomatic—made sure I saw it, then slipped it back out of sight.

I fell heavily back onto the chair and sucked in lungfuls of air, trying to clear my head. Trying to think.

"In case you haven't figured it out," Madison said, "I used some of that yew I took to make the tincture, and gave the leftover sprigs to my gardener to propagate. So they've been putting out roots for, what, six weeks or so. Insurance. Yes, Frank promised to keep mum, but could I trust him? Well, we learned the answer to that one, didn't we?"

"That was, um…" I cleared my throat, struggling for composure. "Clever of you. Rooting the extra cuttings."

Madison gave me a patronizing smile. "Don't patronize me, Jane."

"Don't patronize her, Jane," Dolly said.

I was beginning to suspect her name wasn't really Dolly. In fact, I was beginning to suspect—a little late, I know—that she'd never worked at The Daffodil Learning Center with Madison. Her tidy, light-brown coiffure looked a little too perfect. A wig?

"You knew I was here, at The Rose," I said. "Did you follow me?"

Madison said, "Dolly, you have a cappuccino mustache."

"A what?"

Madison tapped her own upper lip. "The milk foam. It's all I can see. Just…" She tossed a couple of paper napkins at the other woman.

"All right, all right." Dolly wiped away the foam. "Good grief."

Madison leaned toward me. "I like you, Jane. You and I have a lot in common. It's important to me that you understand that I am a good person."

"Oh, I… I know you must've had your reasons," I croaked.

She pressed her hands together, as if imparting the wisdom of the ages. "There's a way the world is meant to work, and for that to happen, all the elements need to be in alignment."

"Oh. Okay."

"And when the elements aren't in alignment, they need to be adjusted."

"Right. Um, that's how I've always felt." I kept one eye on Dolly and her trigger finger, which at the moment she was using to scavenge scone crumbs, making sure every last one made it into her mouth.

"Case in point," Madison continued. "I've always known it's my destiny to bring children into the world. Motherhood is my sacred role in life. We're alike in that way, you and I."

"Well, I mean, I don't know about *sacred,* but yeah, I guess you could say we're sort of alike."

Like hell, I thought. *But please, keep talking while I wait for the Crystal Harbor Police SWAT team to storm the place.*

Okay, you got me. Crystal Harbor doesn't have a SWAT team. A girl can dream, can't she?

"Speaking of things that are out of alignment," Madison said, "there's always the issue of our chakras. I hesitate to mention it, Jane, but it would appear your crown chakra is blocked."

"Not so much since I started eating more fiber," I said.

Dolly looked up from her spanking-clean plate. "We gonna do this or what? I've got a five-o'clock in Queens."

What was *this?* Was *this* what I thought it was? In which case, nah, I could sit there and chat all day.

Madison and I must've had our chakras in alignment or something, because she scowled at her companion. "You're being paid plenty, Dolly. It's not my fault if you overbooked your time. We're done here when I say we're done."

Personally, I wouldn't want a professional hit woman—don't tell me you didn't figure that one out—looking at me the way Dolly was looking at Madison at that moment.

Oh wait, she was looking at me that way, too. And I wasn't the one signing her paycheck. Or transferring cryptocurrencies or however individuals in her line of work got paid.

The guy behind the food-service counter, besides being out of earshot, was preoccupied with preparing salad ingredients and dinner specials. An occasional customer hurried through the café, heading for the children's room or the bookstore, but no one even glanced our way. We could've been furniture.

I was thinking the plan was for Dolly to take me somewhere suitably remote where she could dispose of the body. And let's face it, once she got me in her vehicle, I was a dead woman. Meanwhile Madison would take pains to see and be seen around town, in order to establish an airtight alibi.

I knew that if I were to become a liability to Dolly by, say, leaping out of my chair and screaming for help, she wouldn't hesitate to put one between my eyes and disappear before I hit the floor. Oh, someone might recall a plump matron in cat-eye glasses and a lilac pantsuit, for all the good it would do. A quick change of disguise and she'd make her five-o'clock with time to spare.

That scenario would, naturally, leave her employer in a bit of a pickle. Madison was a regular customer at The Rose. She'd had to pass through the bookstore today to enter the café, and all the staff knew her, including the young man who'd sold her that cup of herbal tea. She'd be immediately identified, even if she ran.

As much as I enjoyed picturing Madison Kool in an orange

jumpsuit, the image of Jane Delaney in a body bag held less appeal. That pesky instinct for survival is what kept me compliant while my overtaxed brain tried to figure out a way to survive my predicament.

Madison turned back to me. "Where was I?"

"You were saying how alike we are. Chakra buddies. Practically sisters. Why haven't we done lunch?"

"Six years ago," she said, "I found myself in an unfulfilling relationship, about to make the biggest mistake of my life. I knew then that some drastic changes were in order. That's when I made a solemn vow to myself that I'd be married to a wealthy man and have my first child by the time I turned thirty. Whatever it took. No excuses."

"Well, you still have time, right?" I said.

"My thirtieth birthday is next month." Madison indicated her slim waistline. "Do I look like I'm about to give birth?"

Dolly snorted, then quickly sobered when her employer turned her frigid gaze on her. "Sorry, thought it was a joke."

"I took that vow very seriously, Jane. And now it's too late. Because of *him*." Even flushed with rage, Madison Kool was stunning, which was, let's face it, so unfair. "Do you know what that old bastard did?"

I actually did know what he did, but I meekly shook my head.

"He got a *vasectomy*! Without consulting me! Just two months into our marriage. I was making progress in getting him to agree to a baby. At least I thought I was. Obviously I was being too subtle. And you want to know the kicker?"

"If you, um, feel like sharing."

"He thought I'd be *thrilled*!" she said. "He did it so I could stop using birth control. What a joke. I stopped using birth control the day that man put a ring on my finger."

Dolly cackled. "Only, you 'forgot' to tell him, right?"

"If only I'd managed to get pregnant before he got himself fixed," she said, "I'd have fulfilled my solemn vow."

"So I have to ask," I said. "Why did you stay with him? If you'd divorced him back then and found yourself another wealthy man, you could've, you know, fulfilled your vow."

"You make it sound so easy," she sneered. "Do you have any idea how challenging it is to find, attract, and actually marry a man as rich as Larry? I've spent the past four years trying to get him to have that damn vasectomy surgically reversed. The longer you wait, the smaller the chance of success. At a certain point I knew it was never going to happen. I had to move on."

Dolly said, "You did the right thing, dear. Guys like that are hopeless. You shoulda called me instead of messing around with plants and all that malarkey. Too unpredictable."

"It worked, didn't it?" Madison said. "Anyway, I like doing things the natural way. It helps to keep my ch'i in balance."

"Your what?"

"Ch'i," she said. "The life energy that flows through all of us."

"So why not do the natural thing with this one?" Dolly tossed her hand toward me. It was a slim hand, I noticed, not as plump as I'd have expected based on the way she filled out that pantsuit.

"That way was good while it lasted," Madison said, "but I won't get away with it a fourth time. The cops aren't *that* stupid."

Fourth time? Okay, she definitely wasn't going to let me live after hearing that little revelation, chakra buddies or no.

"I'd just like to point out," I said, "that you're a very wealthy woman now, Madison. So that part of your solemn vow has been fulfilled, right? I mean, you got your wealthy husband, and now you have all his stuff without the… inconvenience of having him around. Now you can concentrate on having that baby."

"I refuse to have a child out of wedlock," she said. "That's not part of my plan."

"Well then, go snag another rich husband—one who's as eager for kids as you are. I have zero interest in getting in your way, trust me."

"You've heard too much," Madison said.

"You've heard too much," Dolly said.

I couldn't help myself. "Well, why the heck did you let me hear too much? I mean, you showed the cops your seedlings. They have Liddy and her fingerprints. You're basically in the clear. *I* was buying it, too, until you flat-out told me you killed Larry." My dumbfounded looked asked why on earth she'd do such a thing.

"Talking about it helps me to feel balanced and at peace," she said. "And you need to be eliminated in any event. Don't you get it? It's not about Larry. It's about Dom."

"Dom?" Had my fears been justified? Was my ex in danger from Madison?

"We met last year at a charity gala," she said. "Dom was so tall, so handsome—and utterly charming, not that that's news to you. Next to him, Larry looked like a geriatric troll stuffed into a tuxedo. We only chatted for a few minutes, but believe me, your ex-husband made quite an impression. I took it upon myself to find out everything I could about him."

"Starting with the fact that he's rich," I said.

"Well, I knew that already from the gala's program. Dom was a platinum-level sponsor. Just as important is the fact that he has three children—not by you, sadly—and according to the feelers I put out, he's eager for more. I also know he wants to remarry you."

My mouth felt too dry to speak. I lifted my glass and swallowed the last of my raspberry soda. "He *used to* want to remarry me," I said. "He's known for some time now that that will never happen."

"Which just… and I don't mean to be rude," Madison said, "but to me that is utterly incomprehensible. I'm not saying there's anything wrong with your Martin. He's a fine-looking man, and I'm sure he tries to make you happy. But, Jane, he's a *bartender.*"

I could've mentioned that the padre was also a private investigator and executive protection specialist, but I'd just be helping to make her point. Martin wasn't a multimillionaire and never would be.

"He lives in a tiny apartment over a *bar,*" she added.

Dolly snickered.

"Dom is still in love with you." Madison raised her palm to forestall my objection. "Don't try to deny it. If you gave him the slightest encouragement, he'd go running back to you in a heartbeat."

I recalled our uncomfortable conversation that day at her house, when Madison pointed out how "devoted" Dom was to me. *He still cares deeply for you.*

I cleared my throat. "So what you're saying is, you intend to eliminate the competition by…"

"Eliminating you," she said. "Now, tell me that doesn't make perfect sense."

Dolly glanced at her wristwatch. "Works for me. Ready whenever you are."

I pressed a hand to my heart. "I absolutely guarantee that Dom and I will never get back together, Madison. Also that your secrets are safe with me. The cops are satisfied they have the culprit, and let's face it, Liddy's probably better off behind bars. She wasn't doing such a great job taking care of herself, am I right?"

"First of all," Madison said, "please stop insulting my intelligence. Of course you'd rat me out to the cops. As for Dom, I have little doubt that when you inevitably get tired of your blue-collar boy toy, you'll let your devoted ex drag you back to the altar. I'm surprised you've waited this long. Those eggs of yours must be stale as week-old bread."

"Week-old bread," Dolly chortled.

Madison sighed. "Unfortunately, I'm having a little trouble with Dom. Yesterday he suddenly stopped answering my texts and phone calls. He's ghosting me. Did you tell him about the yew cuttings?"

Yeah, and also about you doing the wild thing with Frank.

"No!" I said. "I haven't spoken to him in days."

"I don't believe you. In any event, with you out of the way, I'm sure I can undo the damage and renew his interest. Certainly, consummating our relationship would do the trick. So far he's been too gentlemanly to initiate anything. Giving me time to get past my grief. Isn't that sweet?"

"A keeper," Dolly said.

"Yeah," I said, "until you decide he's in the way. Then he'll become expendable, like Larry and your late fiancé, Cole Hutchison."

She gave me a sharp look. "How do you know about Cole?"

"I'll let you guess." I was feeling reckless. After all, what did I have to lose at that point? "And for your information, I'm not the only one who knows you managed to murder Cole while you were halfway across the country in Kentucky."

Dolly turned to her employer, clearly impressed. "You did that? Nice work."

"Thank you," Madison said tightly. "Cole had a taste for bitter drinks. Turkish coffee, highly hopped beers, that sort of thing. His favorite cocktail was something called a black Manhattan. Like a regular Manhattan but made with a bitter liqueur called amaro instead of vermouth. He never stopped at one, either. I used to tell him alcohol would be the death of him, but did he listen?"

Whoa, did she just say that?

"Before flying to Kentucky," she continued, "I added plenty of yew tincture to his bottle of amaro, knowing it would mask the taste. I was a little nervous, to be honest. I mean, a healthy young man like Cole dying of sudden cardiac arrest? I anticipated awkward questions. Fortunately, he was at the top of the stairs when it happened, so it looked like a simple accident—with alcohol a contributing factor."

She did say I'd be her *fourth* murder, right? "And then there's the matter of your mother," I said, "who died of lingering heart trouble in her early forties."

Madison scanned our surroundings, even though we were alone in the café. "Who else knows about Cole and Mom?" she demanded.

"Do you seriously think I'd tell you?" I said. "It's some comfort to know that when I'm gone, if you're stupid enough to add me to your list of victims, there are people who won't stop until you're put away for life. They know all about how you cold-bloodedly murdered your fiancé and your own mother."

"You're bluffing. And as for my mother, she had an empty life. Living in that crummy little rental, working as a waitress, dating a string of losers, eating junk food every day."

"Oh, so you did her a *favor* by killing her slowly and painfully over the course of a year?" I said.

Even Dolly gave her some serious side-eye over that one.

"People can speculate all they like," Madison said, "but neither of those deaths was deemed suspicious. I was a bit nervous, of course, about Cole's autopsy, but the poison was never detected. That's why I didn't object to Larry's autopsy. I wish now that I had."

I didn't think it politic to mention that if not for Louise pressuring the ME, we might never have learned that Larry had been murdered.

"Did you know," I said, "that tissues from autopsies are saved in case they need to be studied at a later date? It'll be a simple matter to determine that Cole died from yew poisoning. Same with your mom, once they exhume her. And then, of course, it'll be obvious you killed Larry the same way. You added it to his kale protein shake, didn't you? The day before the cook-off when he was doing laps in the pool. Did you make sure he drank it all?"

Madison held my gaze for long, intense moments before saying, "Yes. I used plenty of kale, which can be quite bitter. He never questioned the taste." She turned to Dolly. "We're done here."

Dolly started to rise.

"Not yet!" I said, thinking fast. "There's something that's been driving me crazy, Madison. I heard you bailed Liddy out of jail. I'll bet you had some clever reason for doing that, but for the life of me, I can't imagine what it is."

Dolly slid her hand into her pocket. "Get up and act normal, dear. We're going—"

"All right, if you must know." Madison flapped her hand at Dolly, a wordless order to sit. Her ego wouldn't let her ignore my question.

The hit woman leaned in close to her employer, and hissed, "Five minutes. That's all you get, then I'm outta here and you can deal with her on your own." She made a point of looking at her watch.

"Relax. This won't take even that long." She turned to me. "I wanted Liddy on the loose so she can take the rap for your murder, of course. When Dolly's done with you, she'll plant the gun in Liddy's car."

"Ah. I get it now." I'd actually figured that part out, I just wanted to keep Madison talking long enough for Dolly to get fed up and clear out. "She must've been thrilled to walk out of that jail."

"My sister-in-law is pitifully easy to manipulate," she said. "I took her out for an expensive lunch. The poor thing was falling all over herself with gratitude for springing her from that 'yucky' place. I told her I knew she couldn't have poisoned me. Well, that's true, of course. Could you see Liddy concocting a tincture from raw plant material? As far as the police and everyone else is concerned, I bailed her out because I truly believe in my sister-in-law's innocence, despite abundant evidence to the contrary. I'm a little naïve that way, you see."

"Won't the cops wonder about her motive for my murder?" I asked. "I mean, what does she have against me?"

"We had a lively discussion, the two of us. I told her about that terrible Jane Delaney. How duplicitous she is, how she made fun of Liddy behind her back, how she was convinced of her guilt. It helped, by the way," she said, "that you failed to keep the police from searching her apartment."

"As if I could have," I said. "They had a warrant."

"I convinced her it was well within your Death Diva powers to stop them. You simply chose not to. Also that you could've swiped Larry's ashes for her, that you routinely do that and much worse things for your clients."

"She told you about that?" I said. "Wanting to steal his ashes from you?"

"You get enough skinny mojitos into that woman and she's even more of a chatterbox, if that's possible. After she's arrested for your murder, she'll make sure the cops know how much she despised her victim. She won't be able to help herself."

"Obviously it was you," I said, "not Liddy, who added poison to the fruit salad Dom made. And you actually ate some of it?"

"Of course. I knew they'd be looking for yew toxin in my stomach contents."

"Well, damn," Dolly said.

"I mixed the poison into the fruit," Madison said, "took a couple of bites—nowhere near a fatal dose, believe me—and called Dom. The ambulance was there within minutes."

"How did you know Liddy's prints would be on the fruit bowl and the fridge?"

"After you left the house so precipitously," she said, "Liddy visited the bathroom. I heard her sneak into the kitchen and open the refrigerator. Apparently she'd been intrigued by Dom's description of fruit with a pomegranate balsamic dressing and decided to taste it. I didn't think anything of it at the time."

"At that point you didn't know the tox lab had found poison in Larry's system," I said.

"Correct. After Liddy and Dom left, I received a call from Detective Werker, who informed me that my husband had not in fact died of natural causes but had been murdered. You can imagine my shock and horror upon hearing this."

Dolly barked a laugh.

"I knew Liddy had been arrested once, on a DUI," she continued, "so her prints would be in the system. I also knew she was on her way to a party in New Jersey and wouldn't be home until late that night."

"Which gave you time to plant the vial of poison in her apartment," I said.

"I was careful to avoid being seen in her building, but I also took the precaution of wearing a disguise. So many people have those doorbell cameras nowadays."

Automatically I glanced at Dolly, who nodded sagely.

"How did you get into her apartment?" I asked.

"Years ago she gave Larry a key for emergencies. He never had a reason to use it, and I knew she'd probably forgotten all about it. That woman is so scattered. After I let myself in to her horrid little apartment, I noticed that she had a fondness for labeling her possessions. It took some time, but I finally located the label maker under her bed. I made sure to use Liddy's own baggie and tape, too, when hiding the tincture inside her toilet tank."

"Naturally, you wore gloves," I said.

"Naturally. In the end, Liddy will be convicted of murdering you and Larry, and trying to murder me. At least her constant begging for money should stop once she's behind bars for good."

I finally comprehended how and why Madison, and only Madison, had gotten sick from eating the fruit Dom had brought over that day. After I got the phone call from Louise and abruptly left Madison's house, Liddy slipped into the kitchen to satisfy her curiosity about the "yucky" fruit salad. Then, after she and Dom both left, Detective Howie Werker called Madison to inform her that her husband had been poisoned.

How to deflect suspicion from herself? Liddy had no doubt left her fingerprints in Madison's kitchen, turning herself into the perfect fall guy. Madison mixed some of the yew toxin into the fruit, then planted the vial in Liddy's apartment. Back home, she'd eaten a couple of bites of the poisoned fruit before calling her new beau, who'd lost no time rushing her to the emergency room.

I had to admire Madison's ingenuity—up to a point. That point came when Dolly stood and said, "Time's up. Give me your phone, dear." Her gun hand was once more in her pocket. The look in her eyes, behind those cat-eye glasses, warned me I'd better cooperate.

Or what? She'd kill me? When I just sat there, Madison grabbed my purse with an impatient huff, located my phone, and passed it under the table to Dolly, who turned it off and slipped it into her own bag.

"This is where we part ways." Madison stood. "I'm sorry it had to end this way, Jane. I meant what I said. I like you. When Dom and I have our first child, I'm even thinking of naming it after you. Maybe James if it's a boy. Close enough."

What the heck was I supposed to say to that? The idea of a serial murderer naming her child after me was beyond repugnant.

After her employer strolled out of the café, Dolly got to her feet. "Okay, let's go."

When I just folded my arms, she said, "I'm going to start counting, dear. If you are not on your feet and walking by the time I get to three, I will not only drop you where you sit, but I will kill your precious Martin McAuliffe, his daughter Lexie, his son-in-law Dillon, and his new grandson. Cooperate and nothing will happen to them. One. Two—"

I stood. With no other choice, I started moving with her toward the bookstore, where the main entrance was located.

Before we'd gone two steps, Rex Noble entered the café, with his trusty attaché case. "Jane! Great to see you again. And who might this lovely young lady be?"

I had to hand it to Dolly, she didn't skip a beat. "Oh!" she giggled. "Isn't this one a charmer."

As she started to introduce herself, I blurted, "Rex, this is my friend Wanda Schmidt."

Dolly stiffened, no doubt wondering why I used that fake name and not the fake name I already knew her by.

I watched Rex closely, watched the glimmer of name recognition turn into an actual memory. As he opened his mouth to remark on the coincidence, I said, "Wanda, I'm guessing you don't recognize Rex. Do you ever watch that old detective show *Chase & Knabbe*?"

"Not really," she said. "I might've caught a few minutes here and there."

"Well, Rex was one of the costars," I said. "Rex Noble. He played Detective Samson Chase."

"You don't say. Well, isn't that something. I know I've heard your name," she told Rex. "I'll make it a point to catch the show."

"Well, Wanda," he said, "when you do, don't be surprised if you hear—"

"Rex!" I definitely did not want him to finish that sentence. "Are you still doing interviews?"

"I sure am. I was told the café at The Rose is a great place to connect with folks, but it looks like I chose the wrong time."

"Try weekends or any lunchtime," I said.

Dolly made sure I saw her slide her hand into her pocket. Message received.

Rex, however, hadn't a clue. "Let me ask you, Wanda. Did you know Larry Kool, my costar on *Chase & Knabbe*? He lived here in Crystal Harbor. I'm conducting interviews—"

"I'm afraid not." She started edging toward the exit, her fingers on my elbow. "It was a pleasure, Rex."

"Same here."

I said, "We have to go, but don't forget." I gave Rex a perky grin and a thumbs-up. "It's time to turn up the heat!"

Dolly's pleasant expression never faltered, but her grip on my elbow tightened. "What does that mean, dear?"

Rex answered. "That's the show's catchphrase, Wanda. Larry—that is, Detective Eddie Knabbe—used to say it during every episode."

"Rex and I always say it to each other instead of good-bye," I said. "In Larry's honor."

He gave me a snappy salute. "It's time to turn up the heat, Jane!"

Dolly bade a polite farewell to Rex and hustled me into the bookstore and out onto the sidewalk. Her gun hand remained in her pocket as we strolled the half block to her car, a dark-gray Corolla that was as nondescript as she was. Idly I wondered how many different license plates this car had sported, and who it was registered to. Some fictitious owner, no doubt.

With the threat to Martin and his family hanging over my head, I had little choice but to slide into the passenger seat. Dolly got behind the wheel, started the car, and pulled out of the parking space. She kept her right hand in her pocket as she negotiated the traffic on Main Street, which was growing heavier with the approach of rush hour. I could tell the gun was pointed right at me.

As much as I prayed Rex had picked up on my hints, I knew that was just wishful thinking. Yes, he'd recognized the name Wanda Schmidt—the character who turned out to be the murderer in that episode Leonora Romano played a clip of on her show. But obviously he thought it was just coincidence that my good friend had the same name. I'd been watching him closely and saw no indication that he'd gotten my message, that message being *She's a murderer, Rex! Just like Wanda Schmidt and her cranium-crushing ashtray!*

And as I'm sure you know by now, Rex and I are not, in fact, in the habit of repeating the show's catchphrase to each other. But you'd never know that by how readily he went along with it—again, without the slightest sign that he got it.

After a few blocks, Dolly turned right, obviously headed out of town to some secluded spot where she could turn Jane Delaney into the late Jane Delaney.

"Whatever Madison's paying you," I said, "I'll double it. Triple it. Name your price." I had no doubt Dom would cough up any amount to ensure my safety.

"Don't beg, dear." Dolly stopped at a red light. Her hand never left her pocket. "It's beneath you."

I tried a different tack. "People saw Madison with us at the café," I said. "Someone's bound to connect her to my disappearance."

"Not my problem. I told her to let me handle it solo, but oh no, she had to come with. Something about the alignment of her chakras or some such hippy-dippy crap. Talk about micromanaging. Anyway, she already forked over the down payment, so we're good there. My advice?" The light turned green and we entered the intersection. "If you're gonna shell out the big bucks for a pro, then let the pro do her—"

We both screamed as a car blew through the red light and clipped the back of the Corolla. A crunching jolt, a sickening spin, and we were left facing oncoming traffic as drivers slowed and pulled over.

Dolly and I looked at each other. Neither of us was hurt. Fortunately, it had been a low-speed collision. Still, I was a little dazed.

A young woman rapped on Dolly's window, startling her. "Are you all right, ma'am?" The hit woman nodded but didn't move. No doubt weighing her options.

Vaguely I sensed someone yanking on my door handle, yelling my name and telling me to unlock it.

I fumbled with the lock, and the door abruptly swung open. Strong arms hauled me out of the car. "Are you okay, Jane?"

"Rex?" I squinted up at him. "What are you doing here?"

He gave me the megawatt Samson Chase grin. "Turning up the heat, what else?" Only then did I notice the car that had struck us. It was Rex's over-the-hill, light-blue BMW.

The Corolla's driver's-side door opened. He growled, "Oh no you don't," and promptly vaulted over the car's hood, a move I'd seen him do countless times in old *Chase & Knabbe* reruns. But I mean, the guy was in his seventies now.

Maybe I should renew my gym membership. And actually use it this time.

As Dolly attempted to flee, the onetime TV detective seized her and shoved her against the car, manacling her wrists one-handed as bystanders gasped.

"*Help!*" she screeched. "Somebody help! He's attacking me!"

Before anyone could intervene on her behalf, Rex patted her jacket pockets and relieved her of her gun, keeping it safely pointed at the street. "Keep your distance," he ordered the onlookers. "This woman is a dangerous criminal. The police are on their way."

"Oh my God," a woman cried, "*it's Samson Chase!*"

A couple of kids exchanged perplexed frowns, but everyone else responded enthusiastically as they recognized the handsome detective from *Chase & Knabbe*.

Sirens wailed from multiple directions as Crystal Harbor's Finest converged on the scene. Officers poured out of their vehicles and quickly assessed the situation. Dolly kept mum as she was cuffed and placed in the back of a patrol car.

Looked like she wouldn't be making her five-o'clock after all.

For my part, I did the opposite of keeping mum. Soon enough, Detectives Werker and Kaplan showed up, and I found myself repeating my story for them. Not that I minded. It beat whatever Dolly had planned for me.

Rex, meanwhile, was happily signing autographs and posing for selfies with his adoring public, whose numbers rapidly swelled as word of his heroics spread.

I persuaded the detectives to retrieve my phone from

Dolly's purse. Turning it back on, I called a certain local bartender, who answered with, "Hey, beautiful."

"I'm guessing you don't have your police scanner on."

A tense pause, then, "Where are you, Jane? Tell me you're all right."

"I'm fine, Padre. But I could use a ride if you're not too busy."

20

She Can Take Him and/or Leave Him

"I WAS CONVINCED my hints went right over your head," I told Rex. "You seemed oblivious."

"I'm an actor, remember?"

It wasn't the first time I'd heard him say that, but I was beginning to realize it was more than an idle boast.

"So, Rex," Louise said, "when did you realize Jane was in trouble?"

Ten days had passed since Madison had sicced a professional hit woman on me. Rex, Louise, and I sat on cushioned rattan chairs on the long redwood deck behind my house, sipping hot chocolate and nibbling cheese and crackers. The early-October afternoon had turned blustery, but we were all dressed for the chill, and this way we could keep an eye on the dogs as they chased each other around my five-acre property.

Well, two of the dogs were running around. Rex's geriatric pug, Piglet, lay snoring under a small fleece blanket on his master's lap, rousing himself every few minutes to scarf down a bit of cheese.

"To be honest, I'm embarrassed by how slow on the uptake I was." Rex cut a slice of extra-sharp cheddar and slapped it onto a poppy-seed cracker. "I was fixated on the interviews I was trying to do, so when you introduced me to Wanda Schmidt—"

"Real name Katherine Krupa, as it turned out," I said. "Called herself Dolly. Apparently she's turned into quite the snitch, trying to cut a deal with the prosecutor."

"Well, when you introduced us, I wasn't thinking about anything beyond the fact that her name sounded familiar," he admitted. "Even after I made the connection, I thought it was just coincidence."

"I was just praying you wouldn't say something like, 'Did you know you have the same name as the murderer in an episode of *Chase & Knabbe?*'"

Louise set down her mug. "Well, something must've given it away, because you called nine-one-one the instant Jane and this Wanda left The Rose, right?"

He nodded. "It was that business with the catchphrase. 'It's time to turn up the heat.' That's when the sledgehammer finally whacked me on the noggin and I realized 'Wanda Schmidt' was a message. And something else had been bothering me. I'd just been too distracted to pay attention."

"Well, don't keep us in suspense." She plucked a breadstick from the platter.

"Wanda's—or Katherine, whatever her name is," he said, "her disguise was serviceable, but I have a good deal of experience with theatrical costumes, and I had to ask myself, why would a slim woman willingly make herself appear thirty, forty pounds heavier?"

Excited barking drew my attention to the rear of the

property where the scattered shade trees gave way to thicker woods. I couldn't see the dogs, but obviously they'd chased something up a tree. I pictured an impudent squirrel sitting high in the branches, thumbing its nose at them.

"But you didn't just call nine-one-one," Louise said. "You went after them."

"Well, of course I did."

I had to laugh. "Might I remind you, Rex, you aren't a police detective. You just played one on TV."

"My intention at first," he said, "was simply to keep Wanda's car in my sights so I could give the cops the license-plate number and location."

"But you weren't behind us when you clipped her car," I reminded him. "You ran the red light on the street we were crossing."

"When you turned right off Main Street," he said, "I was about a block behind you, in heavy traffic. I learned a surprising amount about tailing suspects while working on the show, not to mention all the police ride-alongs I went on. I still do those once in a while. The cops love me."

Louise said, "Get to the good part."

"When you made that turn, I was at the previous intersection, so I made a quick right, then a left. I saw your car waiting at the red light up ahead. I knew that once you got on the parkway, I'd lose you for good. And still no sign of the cops."

I said, "So you thought, what the heck, I'll just slam into their car?"

"Do you remember the episode with the ancient Egyptian mummy, only it turned out not to be a mummy at all under the wrappings, but a fresh murder victim?"

"Oh yeah," I said. "That's one of my favorites."

"Chase and Knabbe tailed the perp in that one, if you'll recall," he said.

"Yes!" I jabbed my finger toward him. "And you guys did the same move. Going around the block to cut him off and ram his car."

"I saw an opportunity," Rex said, "and I went for it."

"Life imitating art," Louise said.

"In that moment…" He hesitated. "This will sound kind of silly."

"Hey, we're down with silly," I said.

"Whatever it is," Louise said, "it goes no further. Doctor-patient privilege. Or something."

"Well, in that moment I became Samson Chase again. The past four decades fell away, just like that." He snapped his fingers. His voice was husky as he added, "And let me tell you, it felt damn good."

I reached across the table and squeezed his hand. I looked him in the eye. "Well, whoever you were right then, I owe you my life. Thank you, Rex."

He winked, giving his words the full Samson Chase treatment. "Anything for a gorgeous doll like you, miss."

"What about your car?" Louise asked. "Will insurance pay for the repair, considering you deliberately caused the accident?"

"That old heap owes me nothing at this point. I have a brand-new BMW convertible, all tricked out. Electric blue. It's parked out front. I'll show it to you later."

"Wow. Nice," I said, while inwardly wondering how Rex was able to afford a pricey ride like that.

My expression must have given me away, because he

smiled, and said, "You might've noticed one of those bystanders videoing the whole thing, Jane. When I apprehended Wanda."

Louise said, "That footage was all over the news. You springing over that car hood like a teenager. Going all Samson Chase on her."

"The news shows kept replaying the clip," I said. "It went viral on social media. The whole world saw it."

"Including Taralee Winter," he said, naming one of Hollywood's hottest young stars. Well, young*ish*, probably in her late thirties. "She wants to do a TV series with me."

"Really?" Louise said. "What kind of series?"

"*Chase & Knabbe*, forty years later. I'd wanted to do that with Larry at one time, but he wasn't interested. But now with Taralee on board, it's a whole different ball game. The streaming services have started a bidding war."

"How exciting!" I said. "Who's going to play Eddie Knabbe?"

"No one could fill Larry's shoes," he said. "In the first episode, Eddie's been murdered. Taralee will play his daughter, Eden Knabbe."

"Don't tell me," Louise said. "Eden also happens to be a police detective."

He wore a lopsided grin. "How'd you guess? She'll bring Samson Chase out of retirement to help solve his old pal's murder, and after that, they'll collaborate on more investigations during season one."

"Art imitating life," Louise said.

"So you bought yourself a brand-new BMW to celebrate?" I asked.

"Actually, Taralee bought that for me, to replace the

vehicle I sacrificed through my selfless act of heroism." He had the grace to appear embarrassed. "She considers it a fitting way to cement our new partnership. And I ask you, how could I argue with such impeccable logic?"

"Still charming the ladies," Louise said. "Some things never change."

"So Chase and Knabbe will be partners once more," I said. "I'm so happy for you, Rex."

"I like to think Larry's happy, too," he said, "wherever he is. I've done a bit of soul-searching lately. I know I blamed some of my troubles on him. I guess it was easier than taking responsibility for my own lousy decisions. I hope all that's in the past."

"I'd say you made it up to him," I said, "by helping to bring his murderer to justice."

Louise said, "I heard Madison's been remanded without bond."

"That's right," I said. "She'll remain in jail until her trial."

"Conviction must be pretty much guaranteed," Rex said, "considering the overwhelming evidence against her. Which means she'll be spending the rest of her life in prison."

I nodded. "For three murders and an attempted fourth? I'd say there's almost no chance she'll ever walk free."

"A lot of good her fortune will do her behind bars," he said.

"Oh, she'll be disqualified from inheriting. It's called the slayer statute. You can't inherit from someone you've murdered."

"Makes sense," Louise said.

"For purposes of inheritance," I said, "it'll be as if Madison predeceased Larry."

"So then, what happens to everything that would've gone to her?" Rex asked.

"It'll now go to the contingent beneficiary—the next in line to inherit under the terms of his will. Which happens to be Liddy."

"Hmm," he said. "I'm thinking of all that money, and how fast she'll blow through it."

"I'm thinking of that beautiful old house," Louise said.

"So was Larry," I said. "He knew his sister, which is why Liddy's bequest is by testamentary trust."

"Which means what exactly?" Rex said.

"Liddy will own everything," I said, "but Larry's lawyer, Sten Jakobsen, will act as trustee. He'll manage it all, properties and investments, and ensure it's well cared for and not squandered."

"Well, that's a relief," Louise said.

"I've known Sten a long time," I said. "He's smart, savvy, and endlessly patient with those who are, to put it kindly, endlessly trying."

"I know we all expect Madison to be convicted," Rex said, "but what if, by some miracle, she's acquitted? Then she'll still be able to inherit, right?"

"I asked Sten that same question," I said. "The way he explained it is, the slayer rule applies to civil, not criminal, law. The burden of proof is much higher in criminal cases—you know, twelve jurors finding her guilty beyond a reasonable doubt and all that. Civil cases have lower standards and are easier to prove. So in the unlikely event Madison escapes conviction in the criminal case—"

"And what are the chances of that?" Louise said.

"—then she's still not off the hook. In a civil proceeding,

as long as Liddy's lawyers can prove that Madison was responsible for Larry's wrongful death by a preponderance of evidence—and they certainly have that—the slayer statute will keep her from inheriting one dime or receiving Larry's life-insurance payout."

"I like the sound of that." It was Martin, rounding the stone path from the side of the house and joining us on the deck. He gave me a kiss, greeted my guests, and settled in the chair next to mine. "Where's SB?"

I waved toward the tree-shrouded rear of the property. "The dogs are out there somewhere."

"Protecting us from all those terrifying chipmunks and field mice," Louise said.

"Well, I've got to be going." Rex stood, swaddling Piglet in the fleece throw. "Thanks for the invitation, Jane. It was good catching up."

"It's time I headed out, too." Louise snugged her red cashmere scarf around her throat. "And I want to see that fancy ride of yours, Rex."

"That's your BMW out front?" Martin asked him. "Nice wheels, man."

I said, "It was a gift from Taralee Winter."

The padre's eyes widened. "Even nicer! I just know there's a juicy story behind that."

"If only," Rex said. "Jane will fill you in. It's time I got this old boy home. He's not the party animal he once was."

Piglet gave him a look that said, *Speak for yourself, old man.*

As the two visitors turned to go, Martin said, "Aren't you forgetting something, Louise?"

The look she gave him said, *Such as…?*

"Luci?" He nodded toward the backyard. "Your dog?"

"Oh, Luci's home with Ray," she said, and waved good-bye.

After they left, Martin turned to me. "I could've sworn you said 'the *dogs* are out there.' As in more than one."

I cupped my hands around my mouth and called, *"Who wants treats?"*

I watched Martin's face as they came into view, the big, black one galloping with long-legged strides, the little, apricot one bringing up the rear, both of them barking happily.

His gobsmacked expression brought a huge grin to my face. It wasn't often I was able to render my man speechless, and I savored the moment.

Layla bounded up the steps and threw herself on Martin. The two of them tumbled to the deck, the padre laughing, the big dog licking, barking, positively euphoric to be play-wrestling with her favorite human.

I didn't blame her one bit. After all, when it comes to the padre, what's not to love?

Sexy Beast, meanwhile, ran in circles yipping like the high-strung little maniac he is.

I distracted Layla with the promised treat, a chunk of Havarti. SB, being a fraction of her size, happily settled for a smaller piece.

Martin hauled himself back into his chair, breathless, grinning, his hair a matted mess from Layla's loving ministrations. She lay down on his feet, lest her beloved alpha male threaten to go somewhere without her.

"How long do you have her for?" he asked.

"What do you mean?"

"You're fostering her, I assume." Absentmindedly he scratched behind the big dog's floppy ears. "Until they can find a home for her."

"I hope this doesn't come as too much of a shock, Padre," I said, "but Layla is home. I adopted her this morning."

He went still, studying my expression as if waiting for me to say, *Just kidding!* When I simply smiled, he said, "I thought you told me you weren't in the market for another dog."

"I wasn't. Then I was. Funny how that happens."

"You never cease to surprise me," he said.

"I hope that's a compliment."

"Oh, it's definitely a compliment." Sexy Beast curled up next to Layla, and Martin gave him a few pats. "She and SB certainly seem to get along."

"Now, of course," I said, "you'll have to move in with us."

He gaped at me, speechless.

"Well, dang, looks like I've gone and done it again," I said. "Me and my goofy surprises."

"Do you mean it?"

"Do it for poor Layla," I said. "She'll be bereft if you're not around for regular wrestling and hair-grooming sessions."

A slow smile spread on his face. "Do it for 'poor Layla,' huh? The lady of the house can take me or leave me?"

I reached over and trailed my fingers up his jeans-clad thigh. "The lady of the house knows just where she wants to take you right now, and in what condition she intends to leave you. Does that answer your question?"

"Well, in that case, the new gentleman of the house gladly accepts." He leaned over and treated me to a long, slow, bone-melting kiss full of promise.

"I don't have a lot of stuff," he said. "A few carloads. I can bring it over today."

"I'll give you a hand." Something about his expression

made me add, "Okay, let's have it."

"I just want to make sure..." He looked into my eyes. "Victor."

It was a legitimate concern. I'd met Victor Dewatre a year earlier when he'd traveled here from his home in Paris following the murder of his brother, Pierre, a local chef. Victor stayed with me for a month during the investigation, purely as a houseguest. There was no hanky-panky, although we became quite close during that time. So close, in fact, that Victor asked me to move with him to Paris, an impossibility since, as SB's guardian, I was required to live with the little poodle in "his house" during his lifetime. I hadn't seen Victor since he'd left, though we'd kept in touch.

"He's entirely out of the picture," I said. "Back in June I told him about you and me, that we're in a committed relationship. I won't say he was thrilled, but he likes you. He claimed to be happy for us."

"Well, the guy's French," Martin said. "They're civilized about these things. Not like us barbaric Americans. Still, if I were him, I might be saying the right things and waiting for an opportunity to pick up where I left off."

He said nothing about Dom, which I took as a good sign. It meant he'd internalized the fact that although my ex-husband and I would always be friends, he'd never again be anything more.

"Come on." He gave my thigh a brisk pat and stood. The dogs leapt to their feet, tails wagging, ready for the next adventure. "The sooner we get me moved in, the sooner you can take me and leave me."

About the Author

Pamela Burford comes from a funny family. You may take that any way you want. She was raised in a household that valued laughter above all, so of course the first thing she looked for in a husband was a sense of humor. Is it any wonder their grown kids are into stand-up comedy and improv? Oh, and here's another fun fact: Pamela's identical twin sister, Patricia Ryan, aka P.B. Ryan, is also a published novelist. Patricia is the Good Twin, and yeah, Pamela knows what that makes her. But hey, Evil Twins have more fun!

It should come as no surprise that everything Pamela writes is infused with her own quirky brand of humor, from her feel-good contemporary romance and romantic suspense novels to her popular Jane Delaney mystery series, featuring snarky "Death Diva" Jane, her canine sidekick Sexy Beast, and a fun love-triangle subplot. Pamela's own beloved poodle, Murray, wants you to know that any similarities between himself and neurotic, high-strung Sexy Beast are purely coincidental.

Pamela is the proud founder and past president of Long Island Romance Writers. Her books have won awards and sold millions of copies, but what excites her most is hearing from readers. Swing by and say hi at pamelaburford.com.